A Murder in Eight Cocktails

Also by Kelly Mullen

This Is Not a Game

A Murder in Eight Cocktails

KELLY MULLEN

CENTURY

UK | USA | Canada | Ireland | Australia
India | New Zealand | South Africa

Century is part of the Penguin Random House group of companies
whose addresses can be found at global.penguinrandomhouse.com

Penguin Random House UK,
One Embassy Gardens, 8 Viaduct Gardens, London SW11 7BW

penguin.co.uk
global.penguinrandomhouse.com

First published 2026
001

Copyright © Kelly Mullen, 2026

The moral right of the author has been asserted

Penguin Random House values and supports copyright. Copyright fuels creativity, encourages diverse voices, promotes freedom of expression and supports a vibrant culture. Thank you for purchasing an authorised edition of this book and for respecting intellectual property laws by not reproducing, scanning or distributing any part of it by any means without permission. You are supporting authors and enabling Penguin Random House to continue to publish books for everyone. No part of this book may be used or reproduced in any manner for the purpose of training artificial intelligence technologies or systems. In accordance with Article 4(3) of the DSM Directive 2019/790, Penguin Random House expressly reserves this work from the text and data mining exception.

Set in in 13.75/17.25 pt Fournier MT Std
Typeset by Six Red Marbles UK, Thetford, Norfolk

Printed and bound in Great Britain by Clays Ltd, Elcograf S.p.A.

The authorised representative in the EEA is Penguin Random House Ireland,
Morrison Chambers, 32 Nassau Street, Dublin D02 YH68

A CIP catalogue record for this book is available from the British Library

ISBN: 978–1–529–94518–8 (hardback)
ISBN: 978–1–529–94519–5 (trade paperback)

 Penguin Random House is committed to a sustainable future for our business, our readers and our planet. This book is made from Forest Stewardship Council® certified paper.

Dear Reader,

Throughout this book, there are cocktail recipes that are meant to provide a taste-along "soundtrack" to the story. Some are simple to make, others are more complicated endeavors. Try one or try them all! If you don't have a particular ingredient handy, I encourage you to experiment with substitutes, which can make for pleasant surprises.

I'd love to hear what you think of the story and the drinks on social media @KellyMullenAuthor.

Cheers!

Kelly

In memory of Diane Keaton

> I'll be your mirror
> Reflect what you are
> In case you don't know
>
> — The Velvet Underground and Nico

> At every party, there are two kinds of people, those who want to go home and those who don't. The trouble is, they are usually married to each other.
>
> — Ann Landers

Prologue

When I was eleven years old, Alison Aldrich, the girl seated next to me in science class, took out a case of highlighters. As she began to use them in her notebook, pausing occasionally to switch colors and uncap another one, a warm tingling sensation came over me. It started at my scalp, lifting my hairs and traveling the length of my body down to my toes. *Click* went the cap. *Swish* went the highlighter's tip on the paper. The subtleties of the sounds melted together and relaxed me. I was practically drooling as I glanced around the room at my classmates, expecting to find them in a similar state of bliss. But no, they were oblivious to this little "trip" I was taking all by myself.

This was my first experience with ASMR, which stands for autonomous sensory meridian response. ASMR is part emotional state, part physical sensation. Have you ever experienced this feeling? You know, when someone gives you a scalp massage while washing your hair at the salon, and you feel so deeply soothed that you want to purr like a kitten? Or when someone treats you to a back scratch and the unpredictable tracing of their fingers on your skin gives you buzzy vibrations? Only some people experience it, about ten to twenty percent of the population, and those who do show much higher levels of sensory sensitivity and more active neural pathways than those who do not.

Millions of people around the world watch ASMR videos, from a woman softly explaining how pencils are made, to a corgi crunching on kibble, to a guy folding warm towels from the dryer. It's the third most popular search term on YouTube, but it has yet to be fully understood by science. ASMR is a tingly mystery, and like all mysteries, it's magnetic. Once you experience it, it draws you in and you want more of it.

I am an ASMRtist. When someone watches my YouTube channel, *Sips and Whispers*, they're treated to a coordinated symphony of visuals and sounds about cocktail-making. I tell the story of a drink or a particular ingredient while gently layering my voice over a calming mix of stirring, shaking, and pouring.

My subscribers see my smile, the art on my walls, the sumptuous décor of my home. They squint to read the spines of the books on my shelf. They admire the antique crystal glasses of different shapes and sizes, the carefully prepped ingredients and garnishes, and the polished bottles of spirits arranged around me. They listen to the soothing sound of my voice and think I have a perfect life in peaceful Carmel-by-the-Sea, and that nothing bad ever happens here. Certainly not murder.

And they are wrong.

Friday

1

"I need your eyes, Marty," I say to my husband of twenty-four years, from the passenger seat of our silver Audi A5.

He's gripping the steering wheel, deep in thought, as we drive along the undulating curves of the Pacific Coast Highway. The early evening sky is softening into a velvety rose dusk. Sweeping views stretch out in front of us. Towering cliffs that drop dramatically to the sea, shaped and layered by the effects of time. We round a bend, and a glittering expanse of ocean comes into view.

I look over at Marty's face. A face I know so well. In some ways, he resembles an owl. His wide-set, brown eyes observe the world from behind round tortoiseshell glasses, and a generous torso sits atop two spindly legs. He often scowls as though his feathers are ruffled, but it usually only means that he's deep in thought. I can tell he's in one of his contemplative moods now, where all my words seem to bounce off his impenetrable wall of introspection.

The vertical frown line between his brows deepens as he turns to me. "Huh?"

"I said I need you to clock everything tonight because I've got to focus on the cocktails. Just pretend you're in birding mode. There is no one who can more accurately absorb minutiae right down to a gnat's ass than you, darling."

My ASMR channel, *Sips and Whispers*, has just hit 50,000 subscribers. As a "micro cocktail influencer," I usually only receive shipments of free espresso beans or cases of flavored tonic water. But this is different. I have been hired to make three promotional videos about a new cocktail bar, Mysa, that's opening tonight. It's my first real, paid engagement as a professional influencer, and I'm a spinning pinwheel of armpit sweat and nerves.

I pull down the visor and check myself in the mirror. I hope I don't look as antsy as I feel. Ever since Marty and I retired a few years ago, *Sips and Whispers* has been the only thing that brings any excitement into my life. I want this gig to go well so they'll hire me again.

I turn back to Marty, awaiting some kind of verbal response. "Marty? Hello?" I know that he doesn't intend to seem cold whenever he gets like this. His brain just runs on a different operating system than mine.

He grips the wheel tighter. "Sorry. I didn't know I was required to respond. You want me to make a mental note of everything tonight. Because being a stickler for details is one of the characteristics about me that you most admire."

A MURDER IN EIGHT COCKTAILS

I smile and give him a pat on the arm. "Thank you."

Reaching into the backseat, I grab my purse. It's the big, slouchy one I carry whenever I'm filming something. I check to make sure everything I need is in there: my phone, a camera stabilizer, the notebook I use for jotting down ideas, and a small lighting kit.

"Who is this guy again?" asks Marty. "'Max Magnussen' sounds like a Marvel villain."

I take out my phone and pull up an article, reading it aloud:

Ultra-private Swedish billionaire Max Magnussen's liquor business has gotten too big to avoid the limelight. In less than a decade, he's turned it into the second-largest spirits group in Europe, with a huge portfolio of international brands. Among them are Italy's top-selling liqueur and his very own aquavit brand, *Tempus Fugit,* which has come to dominate the Scandinavian market. The private company, Hyperion, which Magnussen wholly owns, has 17 production sites throughout the world and sells product in more than 100 countries.

His next conquest? Becoming a nightlife impresario. His first cocktail concept, Mysa, opens on California's Monterey Peninsula this summer. Why the bar business? Sources close to Magnussen explain that his goal is to make aquavit as popular as gin or vodka in the States, and in order to do that, he's launching an elegant destination bar that will give aquavit the starring role in its imaginative cocktails.

I set my phone down. "And to think, he's hired *me* to promote this place! I'm counting on you to help me complete my deliverables."

"Deliverables? Sounds like a drug deal."

I give him a playful elbow. "You know, the contractual stuff I have to do to get paid. He wants me to feature one of their cocktails, the *Carmel Sunset*, in the first video. Then I can talk about why *the* Max Magnussen has chosen Carmel as the location for his first aquavit bar."

"Remind me again, what exactly is aquavit?"

"It's a Scandinavian liquor that's made with caraway or dill."

He grimaces. "I don't want a drink that tastes like an 'everything' bagel. I wish we were home enjoying a nice bottle of Caymus after an evening walk. But for you, I'll try to survive the night."

"You're a real profile in courage, babe."

I open my window, and the briny, seaweed smell of the ocean wafts into the car. Marty is all about routine. He likes giving a sense of structure to our endless days of retirement. Every day around 8:00 p.m., we go for an hour-long walk after dinner. Then we come home and have a glass of wine. Our walks together used to be filled with animated conversation and laughter. But recently, I've noticed that we've both become quieter, and I've become a fast walker. Sometimes, Marty can barely keep up with me.

I check the time: 5:56. "The invitation said to be punctual

and arrive no later than 6 p.m. We're going to be late." I swallow hard. Nerves are tightening my throat, so I sift through my purse for a cough drop.

"We're running late because you kept fussing with your hair."

"Which is exactly why I want to cut it short," I respond, realizing there's a grumpy edge to my voice. "I'm getting too old to have hair past my shoulders." I catch a glimpse of myself in the side-view mirror. I'm wearing my go-to LBD, a sleeveless number with a stretchy fabric that forgives my midriff bulge, and my favorite cashmere pashmina. I play with a wisp of my hair. It feels thin and lifeless between my fingers.

"Please don't cut it. I love your long hair." Marty gives me a flirtatious look. "And that shawl is very fetching on you."

"It's a pashmina. 'Shawl' makes me feel like Grandma Moses."

As we pull off the highway into Mysa's parking lot, Marty predictably chooses a spot that's far away from the other cars to minimize the risk of dents. He shuts off the engine and turns toward me, staring intently. From the look on his face, I think he's going to say something profound, or perhaps even frisky. Then I realize he's looking past me. As he points beyond the parking lot, I turn to see two magpies perched on a wooden fence behind us. They're bickering back and forth in loud, staccato squawks.

"That's us," says Marty, "arguing about your hair." He

pulls out his birding notebook. "As a matter of fact, it's a magpie that you don't usually see this close to the ocean."

I give him a weak smile and wait patiently as he writes down the bird's name, along with the time, place, and weather conditions. Over the years, I've learned that birding is more about recording than anything else. Before retirement, Marty was a climatologist, which explains his interest in patterns and systems of all kinds, along with his hyper-organized and methodical disposition. Once he retired, this sensibility was swiftly channeled into birding. Every kind of bird he's ever seen has been documented, sketched, or photographed.

As Marty continues to write in his notebook, my mind drifts. Something is happening between us. My husband was once a passionate man. About me. Now he's only passionate about birds. Marty is sixty-one and I'm fifty-five. We've been lucky. His strategic investment in a sustainable vineyard allowed us to retire early a few years ago. It enabled me to quit working as an interior designer and spend more time at home with our son Zack before he left for college. It's no coincidence that around that same time, I launched *Sips and Whispers*. I needed something new to fill my days after my sense of identity had been so wrapped up in motherhood for all those years.

But now that Zack has been away at college for almost a year, I worry that Marty and I are drifting onto separate paths. The thought of our son brings a smile to my face. When he was living with us, we were a compatible family unit. No matter how busy we were, Zack's activities were always top priority, as evidenced by the large monthly calendar thumbtacked to the bulletin board in the laundry room. Whether it was a soccer game, a chess tournament or taking in a new action movie, Marty and I always made sure we were there, like groupies hanging around a rock star. Then, in a matter of minutes, or so it seemed, he was off to college. "Mom and Dad, you're always headed off in different directions," he said to us as he climbed into his SUV. "Don't lose track of each other, okay?" The comment confused me at the time. But in those first lonely days after he was gone, I began to understand what he meant.

As I step out of the car, I breathe in the evening air, freshened by a light rain earlier in the day. I take in the panoramic view. Nestled on the cliffside above, Mysa is an imposing, dark-wood-and-glass structure with an expansive outdoor terrace. Floor-to-ceiling windows provide what look to be unparalleled views of the Pacific. Even though we are only a few minutes from our home in Carmel, the whole place casts an aura of seclusion and unfamiliarity.

The building's history is well known to locals. Designed by an acolyte of Frank Lloyd Wright, it was once a popular Italian restaurant and a favorite haunt of Henry Miller, as well as Anjelica Huston and Jack Nicholson. But its heyday has long passed. For years it stood vacant. I remember reading somewhere that it was due to structural issues, which had led to leaks and mold. Apparently, it took an outsider, an enterprising Scandinavian like Max Magnussen, to restore an eyesore into a local gem oozing with California cool. The transformation is incredible – tastefully refreshed, yet honoring the original intention of the designer. Appreciating its beauty, I feel an ache for my previous interior design career.

I shift my purse to my other shoulder and scan the parking lot. Only about twenty cars are here. I'm surprised by the small number. It's a soft opening, but this seems particularly soft. Must be quite an exclusive guest list. I continue to wait as Marty fumbles around in the car. It's part of his usual "make sure I have everything with me" routine. He has a series of acronyms and mnemonics to keep our lives on track. This one is CHIRPS:

> C – credit cards/cash
> H – house keys
> I – iPhone
> R – Ray-Bans
> P – Pepto Bismol tablets
> S – Swiss Army Knife

Finally, he exits the car and offers his arm. "Shall we?"

I accept it, and together we cross the lot and climb the wide steps leading up to the entrance, an immense set of burnished wood doors. Beneath my pashmina, little prickles of anticipation are sparking on my skin. Tonight, I'm not Marty's wife or Zack's mom. I'm Willa Keane, the host of *Sips and Whispers*. Somehow, with every fiber of my being, I sense that something exciting is about to happen. That an unknowable adventure waits on the other side of those magnificent doors.

Carmel Sunset

Ingredients:

1.5 parts aquavit or gin, dyed blue*
1.5 parts grapefruit juice, dyed blue*
1 part elderflower liqueur, dyed blue*
Rosé champagne or sparkling rosé wine

Method:

Fill a mixing glass with ice, add first 3 ingredients and stir
Strain into a rocks glass over one large ice cube
Top with rosé (for maximum ombre effect, pour gently, and directly onto ice cube)

These ingredients can be dyed easily and naturally with butterfly pea flowers, which are inexpensive to buy online. Steep in a handful of butterfly pea flowers overnight in the fridge, then strain.

Carmel-By-The-Sea is one of the most unique places in the world. We don't have home addresses or traffic lights. Both Ansel Adams and Doris Day once called this tiny town of around 3,000 people home, and Clint Eastwood was our mayor for twenty years. Geographically speaking, we are part of the Central Coast of California, a quaint, foggy region which is very different from the rest of the state. Rolling hills, majestic redwood forests, beautiful vineyards and stunning beaches abound, and we have the most enchanting afternoon light. Everyone in Carmel knows that, as the sun goes down, you are entering The Golden Hour. Whether you're dining at a favorite oceanside restaurant, taking in our fairytale architecture, or even sitting on a chaise right in your own back yard, you can always find a front-row seat to enjoy our spectacular sunsets. This drink captures the magical ombre color of our skies at dusk.

2

A tall, angular woman speaks to us without looking up from her hostess podium. "Welcome to Mysa," she says brusquely. She's mid-thirties, with blonde hair pulled back in a prim bun and the austere disposition of a no-nonsense schoolmarm.

I look down at my phone. We're late. I'm *never* late. This is not the first impression I was aiming for. "I'm so sorry. We're—"

"You're the last to arrive," she interrupts. "Do you see the clocks back there?" She points to the wall behind us. I note the chic Verdura pineapple watch on her wrist, an expensive antique. As her arm moves, the pineapple-shaped charm clicks against the watch's delicate bracelet.

Marty and I obediently turn our heads toward the wall of clocks. They're antiques from different eras, beautifully arranged. Some Victorian, others whimsical, one is encased in ornate ironwork. All keeping accurate time, with their hands and pendulums moving together in syncopated harmony.

"They're synched with the atomic clock," she says. "You're Willa and Marty, I presume?"

"We are."

She makes two bold tick marks by our names in the guest book.

"Max invited me," I explain. "I'm here to capture some promotional content for my channel, *Sips and Whispers*."

She raises a microbladed eyebrow. "You're thirteen minutes late and you've therefore missed the first of our eight featured cocktails." She gestures to a board beside her that reads:

> Malmo Fizz
> Primeval Forest
> Aquavit Negroni
> Tempus Fugit
> Carmel Sunset
> The Haunted Lingonberry
> Bananavit
> Fikatini

She snaps the guest book shut. "The *Primeval Forest* will be served in precisely two minutes. Enjoy your evening." She marches away.

Aghast, I turn to Marty. "My first paid gig and I've already committed a soft-opening faux pas."

"*Eight* cocktails?" Marty snorts. "Now I understand why there are so few cars in the parking lot. I'm only going to try a sip of each one, so we don't have to take a cab home."

We head into the main room, lined with enormous windows

that capture the ocean view. Bathed in evening glow, the place is humming with the sounds of conversation and rattling cocktail shakers. Soft yellow light flickers from carefully placed candles around the room, and a variety of elegant table lamps give it a cozy warmth. Fifty or so guests stand in clusters, sipping the first featured cocktail, the *Malmo Fizz*, which is served in an elegant crystal glass and garnished with a sprig of fresh rosemary.

I look around. The crowd is mostly younger — thirty- and fortysomethings. Attractive, cultured, monied. Even though it's a cocktail bar, there is an almost meditative quality to it.

"Our bickering magpie act ends now," I whisper to Marty. "I'm an influencer. You're a sophisticated oenophile. Got it?"

Marty nods. I hold up my phone and do a quick pan of the room, capturing some of the guests and the elegant décor. I zoom in on a pair of well-dressed bartenders pouring drinks from great heights.

"Won't all this background noise affect your acoustics?" asks Marty.

"No. I'm filming Mysa content 'in the wild' and then I'll dub my voice over it later."

"Zack really did teach you a thing or two, didn't he?"

I give him a wink. Once a technophobe, I now do all my own editing and posting. Zack taught me basic editing techniques and how to organize various media files on my desktop. After *Sips and Whispers* took off, he helped me convert the studio above our garage into the Drinks Cabinet, an acoustically perfect haven with a calming set design where I shoot all my content.

I scan the room, and a couple looking blissfully in love catches my eye. A large diamond engagement ring glitters on the woman's perfectly manicured hand as she touches the man's chest and whispers in his ear. He's gazing at her with a look of perma-lust. I feel a flash of jealousy. They're probably planning their next vacation together, where they'll lie in each other's arms all day. The thought stings. Sometimes it feels as though every other woman in the world knows the secret of how to maintain a passionate relationship except for me.

A quartet of servers appears and begins distributing the second cocktail as all the clocks chime at once. It's a jewel-green drink glimmering in a chilled coupe. One of the servers takes out an elegant perfume bottle. I smile at the soothing wispy sounds of the sprayer as she disperses a fine mist over each cocktail.

"This is the *Primeval Forest*," she announces.

Marty and I each take one. I note that the ice cube is stamped with an elegant insignia that reads *Mysa*. We clink our glasses together.

I take a sip, and the vegetal notes of Chartreuse flood my tastebuds. I hold it in my mouth and let the crisp freshness of the aquavit wash over my tongue, imagining the dewy grass of a Swedish forest in early spring. This unusual, verdant drink is a masterpiece. It evokes the simple pleasure of a woodland walk, the rustle of leaves and snapping branches underfoot.

I turn to Marty. "What do you think?"

"Well, it's certainly . . . herbaceous," he says.

I roll my eyes. Marty has always been finicky, but lately he's become even more so. He has a whole list of foods he won't eat, such as capers ("briny little dinosaur eggs"), coconut ("tastes how it looks, like dandruff"), and cucumber ("why would I want to eat watermelon rind?"). The list seems to be growing every year. Although now it's not just food. It's as if he has an aversion to new experiences in general.

Looking around, I spot Max Magnussen standing in a back corner, talking to a small circle of guests. He's late forties, wearing a sleek black suit, and handsome. Sharp cheekbones and a cleft chin emphasize his strong jawline. A thin, gold hoop earring embellishes his right ear and the hint of a neck tattoo peeks above his collar. Even from across the room, I can sense there's an intensity to him.

Marty gives me a gentle nudge. "Look at that colossal stack of hair," he says, directing my attention to a woman wearing a mauve cocktail dress with big shoulder pads and matching mauve patent-leather pumps. A fluffy blonde bouffant erupts from her head. Her full, glossed lips look medically enhanced, and not in a good way.

I gasp in recognition. "I know her!" I say, leaning over to Marty. "Well, I mean I don't *know* her, but we've met in passing a few times. That's Rosetta Rawling, also known as 'The Bitter Woman.' She revamped her family's local brand of bitters and now it's famous all over the world." I catch her eye. She nods at me and begins heading in our direction.

The heavy scent of Shalimar perfume and cigarettes wafts toward us as she approaches. "You're the decorator lady, aren't you? Lila, I think?"

"Willa," I say warmly, "and this is my husband, Marty."

"You do those *Whips and Scissors* videos, right?"

I nod, but decide not to correct her, feeling my cheeks turn pink. I'm not often "recognized," so this is truly a boost to my ego. Zack once warned me about social media as my channel began to grow: *Mom, you have to be careful. People are going to talk to you like they know you. Parasocial relationships can be dangerous. Make sure to always have your guard up.*

"Your voice is lovely," she says. As she smiles, I watch the thick makeup around her eyes crack like a dry lakebed.

I notice a distinctive brooch pinned to her dress. It's a little brown lizard, tied to a leash and anchored to an ornately bejeweled green leaf. Suddenly, the creature scurries across her blouse, above the rise of her left breast.

A small shriek flies out of my throat. "It's real?!" Instinctively, I grab onto Marty's arm. He startles and jumps back with me.

The tiny reptile reaches the end of its leash and looks up at me with a pair of dark, beady eyes.

Rosetta gives a loud, sharp laugh like the honk of an airhorn. "Don't be scared. This is Orson. He's my chameleon. He goes everywhere with me."

Resisting a shudder, I stare at him in disbelief.

She honks again. "They change colors, like mood rings." She pats his little warty head. "Here, baby," she says, picking up a leafy garnish from her *Primeval Forest* cocktail and feeding it to him. A long tongue pops out of his head and snaps it into his mouth. "Do you ever do interior decorating work anymore? My place needs a makeover."

"Oh, I retired a while back. Those days are behind me." As the words pass my lips, I feel a pang as I recall the pleasant chaos of paint chips and upholstery samples strewn all over my studio. "Although I sometimes miss it," I add.

There's an awkward silence as we both struggle to find a new topic of conversation. I look around anxiously. I should be capturing more Mysa footage, not making polite chit-chat with this strange woman.

Marty chimes in. "So, how do you know Max?"

She snorts. "Ha. Max. He's a human cold sore. Let's not ruin our lovely evening by talking about him."

I raise an eyebrow, unsure how to respond.

Rosetta sets her half-finished *Primeval Forest* down on a passing tray. "Well, Orson and I need to go mingle. Although he's not much of a party animal. He prefers to fade into the background. Loved talking to you, Mila. Nice meeting you, Marvin."

"*Marvin?*" Marty sputters as she saunters away. "What a wingnut."

We negotiate our way through the crowd toward a set of open sliding doors and step out onto a sweeping flagstone terrace. A stunning view surrounds us. Waves lap against the rocks below in a comforting rhythm, and I can taste the salt in the cool evening air. We walk to the edge of the terrace and gaze out toward the pinkish-purple horizon.

"That view is worth every krone Max paid for this place," Marty says.

A server presents a tray of hors d'oeuvres that look irresistible.

"Burnt Basque chili cheese bites," he offers.

I smile and take one, popping it into my mouth.

He offers one to Marty, who waves it away. "No thanks. I had burnt cheese for lunch." He sets his cocktail down on a table. "I'll be right back. I'm going to ask for a glass of cab."

I wander back over to the server with the cheese bites and take one more, savoring the crumbly sensation on my tongue. I stare out at the water as a cool breeze wafts across the nape of my neck. The visual of the moonlight sparkling on the ocean, creating a long path of light up to the moon, gives me chills. The place is so peaceful. I close my eyes.

"Willa."

I freeze. For a moment, I think I've imagined it. I know that voice. With my mouth still half full of spicy cheese, I turn around.

A MURDER IN EIGHT COCKTAILS

Standing in front of me is my ex-husband, Paul. We were only married two years, and I haven't seen him since we divorced thirty years ago. His eyes are exactly how I remember them—soft brown and filled with optimism. They crinkle as he smiles at me. He looks the same but also different. His eyebrows have grown in a bit bushier, and his sandy hair has flecks of gray. He was always handsome, but somehow, annoyingly, he's gotten better looking with age.

I feel a swell of clashing emotions all at once. Our marriage was brief and passionate, but ultimately ill-fated. We didn't have any children together. Thank goodness for that because he was flaky, and terrible with money. But we did have an electric, fizzing chemistry that temporarily corroded the sensible parts of my brain. I finally ended it after realizing how completely self-centered he was, and that I only played a small role in the *Paul Hammond Show*. After the divorce, it took a lot of healing for me to get to a place where I felt ready to love again. In fact, Paul's devil-may-care qualities were exactly what drew me to reliable, dependable Marty in the first place.

Stunned, I take a step backward and fumble my drink, sloshing the *Primeval Forest*'s green liquid onto the flagstone.

"Paul? What the hell are you doing here?"

3

Paul laughs gently. "It's good to see you, too."

While I flounder and struggle to find my words, he seems unaffected. He gives me a hug, and I'm suddenly aware of his hands around my waist. I feel self-conscious. The only thing I can come up with is a dull question that I already know the answer to. "How long has it been?"

"Only about thirty years." He points to the corner of his mouth and nods at mine, "Crumb check," he whispers.

"Oh!" I reach up and brush away the offending flecks of Basque bite from my lips.

"You look great, Wil."

His eyes are bright with interest, but I still can't find the right words. The space has suddenly become claustrophobic. I glance around. Marty is at the bar with his back turned, oblivious to the fact that his wife is talking to the man who, at one point, ruined the very idea of marriage for her.

"Sorry, I'm still . . . I'm just a bit surprised that you're here." Ugh. Where are my usual witty rejoinders?

Paul laughs. He's only a few years younger than me, but

even now, he seems almost boyish. "Well, I have a confession to make. I'm the person who invited you. I'm the beverage director here, and a minority owner."

I force a smile. How has he finagled his way into this much-anticipated event? Tonight was supposed to be my big night. Receiving an invitation to Max Magnussen's coveted party had sent a welcome charge of excitement through me. Now, after all these years, I have my ex-husband to thank for bringing me here? I feel the familiar, dispiriting haze of being an insignificant, bit player in the *Paul Hammond Show*.

"Max loves Carmel," he continues, "so when he told me he wanted to locate his first bar here, I told him about your videos."

"Oh, that's lovely," I respond politely.

I have to admit it's a pleasant feeling, knowing that he's looked me up and watched my videos. Of course, I've occasionally thought about him over the years too. But he wasn't on social media whenever I checked, so my curiosity was never very piqued. I glance over at Marty again, feeling mounting trepidation at the thought of having to introduce the two of them. Two worlds, two different lives, colliding.

Marty returns to the terrace and approaches us. "I opted for champagne," he says to me, nodding to the flute in his hand.

I barely register his presence and turn back to Paul. "So, you're a co-owner?"

He nods. "I met Max a few years ago when I was bartending at one of his places in San Diego."

"I didn't know you were a bartender."

"Yeah. I kind of fell into it. Max came in one day with a bottle of aquavit and asked me to make him a cocktail. He liked the one I made so much that we started developing some ideas together."

I nod along, still disoriented. Paul had once embodied all the romantic ideals of the husband I'd dreamed of marrying. Quoting poetry and making me laugh with ease, he was sexy and incredibly well-read. He was always reading, in fact. Reading more than helping around the house or earning a living, that's for sure. He was also impulsive. From those first weeks after the wedding, when he quit his PhD program and bought a car we couldn't afford, I knew the marriage was in trouble. Two years later, I was the one who asked for a divorce after winding myself up into a frenzy over his perpetual money problems and emotional immaturity. He agreed to separate without much protest, and that was that.

He smiles at me sheepishly. "You're probably wondering how I became a co-owner. I had just sold my mom's house for a tidy profit after she passed away. So, I used some of that money to invest in this place with Max."

"Oh no, Marie's gone? I'm so sorry to hear that."

"Thanks. Yes. Gone six years now." He sighs. "Anyway, Max sent me all over Europe and South America for research. As much as he cares about the quality of the drinks, his real focus is on creating the perfect setting. So, I became a bit of an expert in bar design. You would have loved visiting all those spaces. Max believes that people will forgive a bad drink in a beautiful place, but not the other way around."

As we make eye contact, I wonder if Paul has possibly had a fully mature brain transplanted into his formerly thick skull.

"If this place does well," he continues, "we have plans to expand the concept into other markets." He pauses. "It's really good to see you."

Marty gives a small cough. "Hello," he says, nodding to Paul. "I'm Marty, Willa's husband, nice to meet you."

"Oh! Marty, sorry. This is . . . well, this is my ex-husband, Paul."

I see Marty's eyebrows twitch as he turns to Paul and shakes his hand.

"Pleasure," says Paul.

I can't help but notice the stark contrast between them as they stand across from one another. It isn't just the age difference between fifty-two-year-old Paul and sixty-one-year-old Marty. They're opposites in every way. Short and tall. Sensible and whimsical. Fastidious and breezy.

"Did you ever remarry?" I ask Paul.

"Nope. It's just me and Noodles." He takes out his phone and shows me a photo of a fuzzy, two-toned mutt with a patch of black fur that looks like a skier's mask has been pulled down around his eyes. The rest of his face and body are a dingy white, including a little beard on his chin. His eyes are milky gray.

I smile. "What a sweetie. Is he blind?"

Paul nods. "Found him at a shelter. Last owner gave up on him. I've been adopting the 'lost causes' just like you used to."

I look down.

"Tell me you still take in the blind ones and the diabetic ones?"

I shake my head. "We haven't had a pet in years. There was a stray cat we took in when our son, Zack, was young. But she passed away, so . . ." I make brief eye contact with Marty, "we decided we needed a break from the commitment after that."

"Well, Noodles reminds me to appreciate the simple things in life. Eating good food. Running around in the sand," Paul says, smiling. "*Dreams and beasts are two keys by which we are to find out the secrets of our own nature.*"

"Thoreau?" I guess, amused that he still quotes poetry every chance he gets.

"Emerson."

"So, you're living down south?"

"Yep. Still in San Diego, most of the time. Although, technically, I'm mobile because I went tiny."

"Tiny?"

"A tiny house. Living at my mother's reminded me how

lonely I was. All that space to myself. Realized that four hundred square feet is all I need. I drive a pickup, and I use it to tow my house around whenever I need a change of scenery. You'd be surprised how nice it is. There's a skylight and a loft."

Marty frowns. "So is it sort of like an RV?"

"No, no. An RV is a vehicle first and a home second. Tiny houses are more of an off-grid lifestyle."

I smile at the thought. Paul was always a bit bohemian. Somehow all of this seems perfectly fitting.

The clocks on the wall chime, and right on cue a server appears, handing each of us the next cocktail. This one is a deep red-orange.

Paul gestures to the glass. "This is a negroni made with aquavit. I wanted to serve something classic that celebrates the spirit itself."

Marty takes a sip and makes a few noncommittal eye blinks.

Paul continues. "Honestly, it was a shock to me when Max first proposed that we focus on aquavit. It's mostly considered an old man's drink in Scandinavia. But he has a vision. He wants to popularize it here and make it a cool drinker's drink, like Fernet-Branca."

Out of the corner of my eye, I note Marty's grimace as he takes another sip. I tense, hoping Paul doesn't mind that my "old man" isn't enjoying himself very much.

I lift the glass to my lips and take a sip. The citrus scent of the orange laced with caraway and a subtle thread of anise enhances the flavor of the Campari. It's a beautiful drink. I might have become an official aquavit convert with this one.

"Max initially intended for the cocktails here to be more complex and made with all these rarefied, funky ingredients," Paul continues. "He wanted the *Primeval Forest* to be made with actual tree sap. But I convinced him that people might want something uncomplicated, so they can appreciate the different flavors that the aquavit brings."

I nod along. "I couldn't agree more. My *Sips and Whispers* cocktails are all relatively easy to make. Max probably wouldn't be very impressed with them."

"Speak of the Nordic devil," says Paul.

I turn to see that Max has joined us.

"Willa and Marty, meet the man responsible for bringing this forgotten old place back to life." He places a hand on Max's shoulder.

"Thank you for inviting me," I say warmly. "I'm Willa, from *Sips and Whispers*."

The blankness in his eyes signals cool indifference. Clearly, Max Magnussen has no clue who I am.

Paul steps in to explain. "We've invited Willa, a local influencer, to help us generate some word-of-mouth buzz."

I know it's not intentional, but Paul has made me feel even smaller with this introduction. It's like he's done me a favor by bringing me here. I'm annoyed, but I keep my feelings to myself. I am a professional, after all, and this is part of the job.

Max eyes me skeptically. "You're not the type of influencer we usually work with. Do many people your age do this?"

Startled by the abruptness of the question, I ponder an answer as I take another sip of my drink. I've encountered this kind of stinging comment before. That I'm "too old" to be an influencer. The baseline assumption being that because I have gray hair, I have no clue about technology in general, let alone social media. At first, these kinds of comments bothered me, but as my subscriber numbers grew, my confidence did too. Now, whenever I encounter ageism like this, I'm just irritated more than anything else.

"You better be careful what you say," I respond dryly, "I can make or break you in this town, Max."

He throws his head back and gives a throaty laugh. Even though my assertion isn't entirely true, I can tell he appreciates that I'm fiery. Leveling his gaze at me again, his eyes soften and register interest. "So, tell me. Why cocktails?"

I tilt my head. "Because ASMR is about relaxation, and making a cocktail can help shift your mindset. Choosing the right glass. Going through the steps. Learning the story behind a drink. It's a soothing ritual that signals it's time to unwind after a long day."

He nods in silent appreciation, then turns to Marty and frowns, noting his champagne glass. "Not a cocktail drinker?"

"No," says Marty. "Makes my 'check liver light' come on. I prefer wine."

I watch Max's lip curl with disapproval.

Heads turn, and a strikingly beautiful woman comes toward us. She's tall and lean, wearing a satin bias-cut evening dress and looking like she's stepped out of a black-and-white film. Upon her arrival, I notice Max's eyes light up and a smile crawls across his face.

"Max, I need to talk to you," she says tightly.

"Of course," he says, placing his hand on the small of her back. "Everyone, this is my fiancée, Tess Hitcham. We're looking to settle down here in Carmel and make it our primary residence, aren't we, darling?"

She gives a faint nod, and I watch her lips press the glass as she raises it high to gulp down the rest of her negroni. It's as if drinking it is the only thing preventing her from saying what she really wants to say.

"We have some of the best restaurants in the world here. Chains are banned," I chime in, attempting to fill the silence. "Sometime I'll take you to Chez Noir. They've got a crème brûlée that will make you forget your name."

Max shakes his head. "No desserts for me. I'm watching my cholesterol these days."

A couple step forward and introduce themselves to Max and Tess, who turn away from us to talk to them. I purse my lips.

A MURDER IN EIGHT COCKTAILS

All in all, meeting him went well, but it wasn't exactly what I'd hoped it would be. I feel rusty. As an interior designer, I had been quite good at schmoozing potential clients. But Max's iciness is throwing off my usual social rhythms.

Paul leans toward me. "Listen, I should probably get back to work. But hey," he reaches into his pocket and retrieves a business card, handing it to me, "I want you to have my number. Maybe we could catch up before I go back to San Diego?"

"Sure," I say. Although I'm not really sure if I mean it.

As he turns to leave, he hesitates for a moment. Perhaps I'm imagining it, but it seems as if he wants to say something more.

Once he's out of earshot, Marty looks over at me. "So, that's your ex-husband? The guy who couldn't hold down a decent job and borrowed a bunch of money from you that he never paid back?"

I nod. "It appears he's evolved into something resembling a grown man."

A ringing sound pierces the air and Max walks to the center of the room. He holds up an old-fashioned alarm clock. The jangling sound lowers the room's chatter to whispers, which eventually fade into complete silence. After a few seconds, he hits the button and the ringing stops.

"I have a surprise for you all," he says. His voice is crisp and rigid, made even more severe by the blunt Scandinavian accent.

My gaze travels around the room's perimeter. The lightheartedness of the party has suddenly shifted. Everyone seems to be watching Max with a mixture of nervousness and intensity. No one is making direct eye contact. I clutch my negroni and sip it slowly, feeling the alcohol's warmth rush through my body. There's a buzz of suspense and expectation in the air.

"Now," he says, scanning the crowd. "Follow me."

Aquavit Negroni

Ingredients:
- 1 part aquavit
- 1 part Campari
- 1 part sweet vermouth
- Orange, grapefruit, or clementine, for garnish

Method:
Add the ingredients to a mixing glass filled with ice and stir until well chilled

Strain into a rocks glass over a large ice cube

Garnish with a slice of your preferred citrus fruit

Aquavit was created in the fifteenth century and was once believed to have healing powers. Each Scandinavian country brings its own nuances to aquavit, and some styles have geographic protections. Sweden's aquavit tends to be crisp and clear, while Norway's is often barrel-aged and darker in color. Iceland's national spirit is Brennivín, or "Black Death," an aquavit made from fermented potatoes and caraway. Aquavit's savory flavor profile means it pairs well with food. Serve it with smoked salmon, cheese, or marinated olives for a complementary mingling of flavors.

4

Marty and I share a look of nervous anticipation as we follow the group down a long hallway, which ends at an elevator with steel doors. From its sleek look, I expect there to be a bank-vault-style requirement to open it, perhaps a retinal scan or a touchscreen. Instead, Max reaches into his pocket and pulls out an old-fashioned, cast-iron key that looks like it might open a pirate's treasure chest. He turns to the group and gives us a roguish smile, then inserts the key into a keyhole in the wall and turns the lock.

The doors whoosh open. Marty and I are part of the first group inside the elevator, which is large and accommodates about twenty people. As we ascend the shaft, the glass walls reveal a magnificent rooftop. We file out into a wide expanse — a spectacular outdoor living room with a cliffside view of the Pacific. On one side of the space there's a long bar with glass shelves showcasing some of Max's aquavit bottles along with a variety of rare whiskies and other liquors. Throughout the center area, sleek furniture is arranged around a group of large firepits, their orange blazes flickering against the twilight sky. I can feel their heat reddening my cheeks.

A waist-high, plexiglass-and-steel railing creates a nearly invisible border around the perimeter. The effect is vertigo-inducing. Marty has never been good with heights, so I worry this will send him into a panic.

He grasps my arm and points. That's when I see it — a dramatic, six-foot-wide opening in the railing, allowing guests to walk out onto a ledge that spans the length of the rooftop. It's both the most terrifying and beautiful thing I have ever seen.

"Uncorralled rooftops, steep cliffsides, and alcohol do not mix," says Marty.

The second elevator full of guests arrives. Everyone is milling around, admiring the stunning views. I take out my phone and film a panoramic shot. Then I stick my hand in the frame to show that I'm holding the next cocktail they've served, the *Tempus Fugit*. It's a golden yellow color, slightly bitter, and delicious.

Max looks to the group and speaks in the authoritative tone of someone accustomed to people listening to him. "Welcome, everyone. It's been my dream to make Mysa unique and unforgettable." He presses a remote control in his hand, illuminating a glass-bottomed floor. I look down at the dizzying view underneath our feet: an elaborate storage cellar lined with bottles of aquavit.

Marty shakes his head. "No way the city engineer deemed this place 'up to code.'"

I shush him.

"Come closer," says Max, gesturing for all of us to gather around.

Concerned that I might lose my equilibrium, I grasp Marty's arm and we take tentative steps away from the glass floor toward the firepits, where Max is standing. The night breeze gently tickles the back of my neck. I wrap my pashmina tighter around me.

A group of servers emerge from the elevator, carrying trays of small glasses and handing them out to guests.

Max takes one and raises it high in the air. "Aquavit means *water for life*. It is meant to be sipped slowly, like wine. And, as with life, we should take time to savor it." He pauses. "Many bartenders in America dismiss aquavit. They say it's not appreciated, that it's too strong, to the point of being off-putting." He smiles, "I've heard a few comments like that made about myself, as well."

Some knowing laughs and nods ripple through the group.

"But I would suggest to you that both aquavit and I are misunderstood." A smile spreads across his chiseled face. "Aquavit, for me, means memories with my grandfather. On cold winter nights in Malmo, we'd gather around and listen to his stories. I wanted to create a place where people could go to enjoy aquavit's exemplary qualities while sharing their own stories, ideas and dreams with friends."

I set down the *Tempus Fugit* and take two glasses from a passing tray, handing one to Marty.

"I don't want any more of that stuff," he grunts. "Tastes like rye bread."

I give him an elbow, insisting that he take it.

Max holds his glass of aquavit high. "To my grandfather, Maximilian Magnussen. A good man. *Skol*!"

We all reply "*Skol*" in unison. With the toast complete, I notice everyone seems to relax a bit. I catch Marty dumping his aquavit in a nearby potted plant.

Max continues. "My aquavit brand, and the cocktail you're having now, is called *Tempus Fugit*. It's a bit of a motto for me. Many of you know I'm obsessed with time. In fact, I attribute most of my success to getting up early. I like to be punctual and precise. Right, friends?"

More soft laughter rises into the night air.

"Because what is time, really? A construct. A series of artificial markers that divides our lives into years, weeks, minutes. But for me, time isn't arbitrary. Time is what separates order from chaos."

I look over at Paul, standing at the front and listening intently to Max's speech. I can't help but be amused at the irony that Max hired Paul, a man who's flakier than all-butter puff pastry, to run his bar. He couldn't be punctual if he tried, much less keep track of his house keys or find a matching pair of socks in his heaping laundry pile. We'd only dated four months before he proposed. I was twenty-three and too naïve to realize that I barely knew him at all. "Fairytale" and "whirlwind" were the words thrown around by my friends at the time. "Foolish" was more accurate. I return my attention to Max as he continues his speech.

He gestures to the blonde hostess, who's standing nearby, holding a black lacquer box. She steps forward and opens the lid, revealing a red velvet lining displaying four keys. They look exactly like the one Max used to activate the elevator. "As many of you know, I lost my dear wife Bronwen seven years ago today. Four wonderful people in my life helped get me through that difficult period with small gestures of kindness. Cards. Text messages. A knowing look. A hug. An inside joke. Those four people, who are here tonight, have shown me that time is not the only thing that matters. Love is what endures."

Marty leans over to me. "C-SPAN is more interesting than this."

I keep my gaze on Max. "Do you know how many speeches on sustainable viticulture I've had to sit through?"

"You don't think this is all a bit ridiculous? He's pretentious."

"He's not pretentious. He's European."

Max turns to a man with thick, dark hair that comes to a sharp widow's peak, and hands him a key. "My brother, Claes."

Claes looks a bit younger and has the same cleft chin and well-defined jawline as Max. He looks like a more artistic, laid-back version of his older brother. The cut of his shirt and trousers is impeccable. But the linen is rumpled and the shirt is partially unbuttoned, revealing a tanned chest underneath.

He's stylishly disheveled, in the way that only wealthy European men seem to be able to pull off. I'd learned a word for this look once: *sprezzatura*, in Italian. The art of looking intentionally unintentional.

Max turns to Tess. "My love, you know how much you mean to me."

As he holds out the key to her, there's a moment of silence. She appears tense, uncomfortable. As if she can't stand him and she's barely making an effort to mask it. The awkward tension creates an absolute stillness. Even the ocean breeze seems to ebb for a moment. Finally, she steps forward to accept the key, and the crowd claps in relief.

"My financial adviser and friend of twenty years, Daniel," he says, nodding to a man wearing an expensive-looking suit. An aura of calm intelligence surrounds him. He shakes Max's hand, takes his key, and stands next to Claes.

"And finally, my *oldest* and dearest friend, Rosetta," Max says, gesturing to The Bitter Woman without looking at her. I note the way she flinches when he says "oldest." He hands her a key, and she gives him a half-hearted hug.

As the polite applause dies down, Max looks around at the group. "Each of these keys provides elevator access to the rooftop. At all Mysa locations, there will be four keys given out annually to locals who have helped preserve and renew aging buildings in their own communities. We want to reward them by offering a special key to any Mysa in the world where they and their guests can enjoy aquavit, on the house, on the exclusive rooftop bar reserved only for keyholders."

"Marketing gimmick," I hear someone murmur behind me.

Reaching for my phone, I snap a quick photo of Max standing next to his friends. The setting sun is providing soft lighting and the distant ocean is a gorgeous backdrop. I'll use the visual in one of my videos as I whisper about the key ceremony and describe the sweeping rooftop views. It will all make for lovely ASMR fodder.

A hush settles over everyone as Max's voice cracks with emotion. "This first key I wear around my neck was made for me by Claes, in memory of Bronwen. It's made from her ashes."

Everyone falls silent as the servers emerge from the elevator once again, carrying more trays of drinks. This time, the liquor is slightly golden in color. I take a glass and wait for Max to continue as the energy seems to change around us.

"As a further memorial to Bronwen," he says, "this special aquavit was made from her wedding bouquet of flowers. A bit of liquid history for you to internalize."

The collective discomfort at this revelation is palpable. A server offers a glass to Marty, who waves it away. I join with the rest of the group in raising our glasses in acknowledgment of Max's words. I notice how Tess doesn't raise her glass. She stands motionless, her eyes looking vacant.

"To Bronwen," Max declares.

"To Bronwen," we all reply in unison, like monks chanting a mantra for the dead.

5

We file back into the elevator and find ourselves jostled into a corner next to Claes. I notice the fusty, unpleasant smell of cigarette smoke permeating his clothes.

I introduce myself to him and we shake hands. "So, is it really true that Max's key is made from Bronwen's ashes?"

He looks at me, eyes sparkling. "Yes. My company, *Deathsmith*, made it. We have an incredible team of artisans who can transform any object into a person's final resting place. A necklace, a sculpture . . . even a vinyl record that plays their favorite song. With the digital world being so ephemeral, I've discovered there's a huge demand for physical memory tokens."

Ooookay. This guy is a weirdo, but he's interesting, and I want to know more. "How did Bronwen pass away?"

He shakes his head. "It was a skiing accident in the Alps. Tragic."

The elevator dings and we exit, making our way over to a cluster of chairs. A server appears and hands each of us a heavy crystal tumbler. "Please enjoy our *Carmel Sunset*," he says.

"So, do you live in Sweden?" I ask Claes.

"No, not for a long time. I live here now," he says. "In fact, I'm the person who introduced Max to Carmel."

I give him a warm smile. It never surprises me that people from all corners of the world are drawn to our town's storybook charm. Although over the years, I've noticed it has changed. From a characterful place where everyone knows everyone to something commercialized and global, attracting more tourists than ever before. I have to acknowledge the irony that social media has contributed to this, and I am playing my own part in Carmel's shift from a village filled with familiar faces to something more impersonal. Thankfully, for the most part, it still retains its uniqueness.

"Well, I can understand why you must like it here. We take great pride in the creative legacy of our community. Have you been to the Carmel Art Association yet?"

He nods. "Oh yes, many times. In fact, *Deathsmith*'s artisans are all local to the area."

I look at Marty, who is almost twitching with boredom and shifting his weight from one foot to the other. The owl wants to take flight. I note in my peripheral vision that several guests are leaving early. They're saying polite goodbyes to Max. Claes and I exchange a few more pleasantries before he wanders off to talk to someone else.

For the next few minutes, Marty and I are an island unto

ourselves as we sip the next cocktail, *The Haunted Lingonberry*. I scan the room for someone worth talking to and use my phone to take more video and photos. I zoom in on the pretty red drinks around the room, then take a few candid snaps of some of the party guests.

A pleasant sound – someone tapping long fingernails on glass – makes me turn my head. Behind me, I see that Tess is holding a glass bottle of seltzer water and drumming her nails on it. She's clutching a wet napkin. I can see a large stain smudged on the front of her elegant satin dress. It's the same color as *The Haunted Lingonberry*. She's definitely ruined the dress. I feel bad for her. We make eye contact and she looks away.

Drink seven, the *Bananavit*, comes next. I take a sip. Yikes. It tastes like something a college kid would drink on spring break. The aquavit clashes with the other flavors, and it's not balanced at all. Paul has been spot-on with all the drinks thus far, but this one is a major fumble. Kind of like us. I hold it up and study the silly-shaped glass and tacky cocktail umbrella. Yep. My marriage to Paul was one big *Bananavit*.

A sharp sound jars me from my thoughts.

I look around, but the party appears to be humming along as normal. I look at Marty. From his flaring nostrils, I know he has lost patience with this place, especially now that a brusque host wearing a cremains key and my ex-husband are part of the equation. "Did you hear that?"

He shakes his head. "Hear what?"

"It was like a scream," I say. "A little, hoarse scream."

"Nope, I didn't hear anything." Marty nods in Claes' direction. "Look at this bizarre crew. We've got the bereavement entrepreneur over there." He turns toward The Bitter Woman at the far end of the room, "and Miss Havisham and her gecko over there." He looks around, nodding in Paul's direction, "and your seven-foot-tall ex-husband who lives in a hut built for Lilliputians. I think we've journeyed far enough inside the circus tent tonight. Can we go home now?"

"Okay. I'm going to capture a little more footage, and I want to say goodbye to Max and Paul, and then we can go."

The whirring and grinding sounds of a large espresso machine pierce the air. As the rich scent of brewing coffee fills the room, I note Paul talking to someone. I look around for Max, but I don't see him anywhere.

"This is the *Fikatini*, our eighth and final cocktail," announces a server. I take a photo of the drinks, which are arranged neatly on the counter. The *Fikatini* resembles a mini espresso martini, with a rich brown base and a foamy textured top. "It's a drink that honors the Scandinavian tradition of 'fika,' or taking a coffee break during the day to relax." She gestures to the counter. "This one is self-serve."

I note the crowd has dwindled to about half the size, around twenty people, maybe twenty-five. Marty hands me a *Fikatini*. As the froth hits my lips, I inhale the deep scent of the espresso beans. It's the perfect final drink. Another hit for Paul. Simple sweetness that feels like dessert, but with the refreshing zing of caffeine. I remind myself that I should compliment him on the drinks before we leave. As much as I still feel some vestigial resentment, I am proud of him. It also seemed as if he was trying to tell me something earlier, so I want to give him a chance to say whatever it is.

I offer my glass to Marty, who takes a small sip. "Wow. That'll bend your hair."

Suddenly, I sense a stirring around me. A low, confused hum ripples through the group, and a few people are frowning down at their phone screens. Someone gasps. I whip my head around to see Rosetta with her hand covering her mouth. She looks horrified.

The room quiets and people seem frozen in various states of panic and confusion, glasses held in mid-air. My heart begins to race.

"Is this some kind of twisted joke? It's not funny!" says Rosetta.

"What the hell is going on?" says Claes, holding up his phone. "Who did this?"

"You got it too?" she shrieks.

Paul steps toward Claes. "What is it?"

His voice trembling, Claes reads from his phone: "*You should now be receiving your eighth and final cocktail. By this time, I am dead. My heart tells me that time is no longer my friend. The constant ticking of the clocks has become unbearable. I only wish to be with my beloved Bronwen. As you will see, I am with her now."*

Before anyone can react, a guttural cry from somewhere above us cuts through the chatter. The room goes silent. It's coming from above, on the rooftop.

A woman is screaming.

"Stairs! Where are the stairs?" someone shouts.

"This way!" Paul calls out.

We all run to the stairwell door, but it's locked. As we turn and scramble toward the elevator, I look at Paul. Fear is flickering in his eyes. I feel my stomach drop.

The blonde hostess darts forward and yanks a lanyard from around her neck. It has a key on it, just like the four Max handed out, and she uses it to open the elevator. Marty and I hustle inside, the crowd bottlenecking behind us. Paul jabs at the "Close Door" button, and a group of us ride up to the roof. As the ding sounds, we all charge toward the screaming woman.

It's Tess, Max's girlfriend. She's out on the ledge. Collectively, we slow down and gingerly inch our way closer to her.

"I . . . I was coming up here to tell him something," she sobs. "I couldn't find him . . . until I looked down."

As we get to the ledge, panic bubbles up in my chest, pressing against my lungs and preventing me from making a sound. Below, on the rocks, the building's floodlights illuminate a crumpled form. It's Max Magnussen. A broken, lifeless shape.

A MURDER IN EIGHT COCKTAILS

His left leg is so badly mangled that it splays out at a gruesome angle. For a moment, I can't move or breathe or even think. Blood is seeping from his skull, sluicing down onto the jagged rocks. My stomach curdles and my throat tightens. I want to look away, but I can't.

6

The car ride home is silent. Images of the events following Max's death flash through my mind and blur together like a fever dream. Wailing ambulance sirens. A cluster of police officers speaking in low, hushed tones. The black body bag on a stretcher. Snippets of conversation between police and party guests. *What brought you here tonight? Did you know the deceased?*

I can't imagine anything worse than wanting to kill yourself. And doing it in such a public way, for your loved ones and colleagues to find you like that. I think about that terrifying ledge and the dizzying drop to the rocks. Max falling suddenly, vertically, noiselessly onto the sharp jagged edges below. I feel nauseous.

My mind drifts to the conversation we'd had earlier that evening. *No desserts for me. I'm watching my cholesterol.* Why would Max care about his diet if he was planning to commit suicide? *We're looking to settle down here in Carmel and make it our primary residence.* His future plans had seemed so concrete, so genuine.

A MURDER IN EIGHT COCKTAILS

As we approach the city limits, we pass the familiar rustic roadside sign: *You are now entering Carmel-By-The-Sea*. Relief washes over me as we zig-zag through the streets of orderly cottages and manicured lawns. We pass by houses whose interiors I've redone or refreshed. Remembering the satisfaction I gave my clients with their renewed home environments helps to calm my anxious mind. As we turn onto our street, I remind myself how lucky we are to live in such a safe corner of the world. Things like this just don't happen in Carmel.

We pull into our brick driveway, and the bougainvillea-covered walls of our home greet us. I never tire of the gently pitched terracotta roof and cream-colored stucco exterior. Black-steel-framed windows add a clean, contemporary touch, while the massive, arched front door and Marty's huge clay pots bursting with red flowers give it a quaint, Mediterranean feel.

"Are you okay?" Marty asks me as we get out of the car.

I try to form the words to express what's going on in my head, but my brain won't connect to my mouth. I can only give a silent nod as we trudge into the house. He kicks off his shoes and heads up the stairs. I trail along behind him and go into the bathroom to wash my face. Marty zonks out quickly, but I lay awake for hours, thinking in the darkness.

After a while, I roll over on my side and check my phone: 4:22 a.m. Swinging my legs off the bed, I get up and wrap a robe around myself. After making a cup of tea in the kitchen, I grab my purse and tiptoe outside. I climb the steps up to the Drinks Cabinet, my ASMR studio above the garage. This is my private creative domain where I always do my best thinking.

I walk in and flip on the lights. The walls are an inviting, creamy biscuit color and the furniture, imported from Puglia, is elegant and simple. It's open plan with a vaulted ceiling and a large gabled window. A marble work surface anchors the center. The acoustics are excellent, thanks to thick carpeting, and I shoot most of my videos in front of the sumptuous bookcase-bar area decorated with cocktail bibles, vintage decanters, and crystal bitters bottles.

I sit down on one of the barstools and clasp the warm ceramic mug of tea in my fingers. The unease I've been feeling since Max's death is still gnawing at my guts. Something is off. Yes, I often let my imagination run away with me. But this is not that. Deep in my core, I know that the confident man I met last night would not have put all that effort and expense into his dream cocktail establishment just to throw himself off the roof.

I wonder if Paul is awake too. Drawing in a breath, I reach for my purse and take out the notebook I use to write down all of my video ideas for *Sips and Whispers*. I'd slipped the business card Paul gave me at the party inside its pages:

A MURDER IN EIGHT COCKTAILS

Paul Hammond
Beverage Director and Co-Owner, Mysa
Bar Consultant at Booker Hospitality

I smile at his company name, feeling an instant heart squeeze. When we were first married, Paul and I took in an elderly golden retriever named Booker from the local pound. Our shared love of animals was a perennial source of connection. Neither of us had owned a dog before, so Booker won a special place in our hearts. We only had him for a year, but we cherished that time. If only Marty would be open to rescuing another animal, so we could experience that special, rewarding love once again.

I fiddle with the card, staring at Paul's name as dusty memories slip out from hidden spaces in my head. Not all of them are unpleasant. Is it okay to call him? *Should* I call him? It's so late. He's probably asleep. I reach for my phone and dial his number. My finger hovers over the green "call" button. Is calling him even the right thing to do at a time like this? And if I do, might he interpret my call as more than just concern? Given the extenuating circumstances, I decide it's okay to try him. Besides, if he doesn't answer, I can leave a voicemail and let him know I'm here if he needs me. I hit "call."

He picks up after a single ring. "Hey."

My hand tightens around the phone. "Um, hey. Hi. Are you doing okay?" I ask, swallowing nervously.

Paul makes a sound on the other end. I know that sound. It's the low hum he makes whenever he's deep in thought. "I don't know. I guess I'm alright." There's a fragility in his voice. It's the strained, whispered way that he speaks whenever he's trying to hold it together. I remember when we took poor Booker to the vet for the last time, I had to do all the talking. Paul's voice was so thin and quavering that Dr. Whitney couldn't understand what he was saying. I'd held Paul's hand in a vice grip the entire time, trying to give him strength as we said our final goodbyes to Booker.

I shake off my thoughts. "I tried to find you before we left Mysa, but it was all so chaotic."

"It's okay. We were all in shock."

"I'm so sorry about Max."

I hear papers rustling on the other end. "It doesn't make any sense. I'm sitting here staring at his planner. It's filled with future commitments. Trips, galas, openings, business meetings, anniversaries . . ."

"Where did you find his planner?"

"On his desk. In the back office. We'd had a meeting in there before the party. So, I went to get it for the police and offered it to them, but they told me to hold onto it. They said it was late and I should go home, that they'd reach out later this week if they needed to talk to me."

I sit there, blinking. "So, you mean they didn't ask you any questions?"

"Not really. It all felt very perfunctory."

I touch my forehead in disbelief. I'm truly stunned that the police aren't doing more to look into this. A layer of nerves and goosebumps rises all over my body. "You know, I keep replaying last night over and over in my head. Max wasn't talking like someone who was planning to kill himself."

There's a long silence.

"Unless . . ." I clear my throat. "What if it wasn't suicide. What if it was murder, carefully orchestrated to look like suicide?" I tense, realizing what I've just said might sound completely ridiculous. My creative imagination at work, as usual. I wait for Paul to laugh.

He doesn't laugh. "It's possible."

Brimming with nervous energy, I stand up, clutching the phone to my ear as I start pacing around the room. "I mean, you're the business partner. The police should have questioned you," I say, pausing to choose my next words carefully. "Wouldn't they want to probe a bit further, just to be on the safe side?" As the words leave my mouth, I realize the implication of what I'm saying. Paul isn't capable of such an act, I know that much. Despite his many faults, he's a tenderheart. But hopefully the point I'm making – that the police don't know that – is clear.

I hear him sigh through the phone. "You're right. They should be considering every possibility."

"Do you have the guest list? Maybe we could look at it and see if anyone suspicious was there?"

"I can get it from Edith."

"Who's Edith?"

"Edith Stonewall. The blonde hostess."

"Ah yes, the gonzo timekeeper." I bite my lip as I pause to think. "You must feel so overwhelmed. What are you going to do now?"

"Well, my original plan was to go back down to San Diego this weekend, but I think I need to stick around and make sure the staff are doing okay."

My eyes wander over to my copy of *The Quiet American*, lying on the countertop. "Listen, we're hosting book club tonight with some couple friends. Why don't you join us? There'll be plenty of food. I don't want you to be alone. You can bring Noodles."

I hear him smile through the phone. "Tough for me to turn down the chance to enjoy your cooking again."

"Great. I'll text you the details. We'll talk more then."

I put the phone down and run a hand over my face. I sit for a moment and finish my tea, drumming my fingers on the mug. Being in touch with Paul again is surreal. Wired from all the thoughts running through my mind, I open my laptop. A yellow sticky note I placed on the screen yesterday greets me: *Don't forget to buy Marty anniversary gift!!* Our twenty-fifth wedding anniversary is coming up in June, and I still have no clue what to get him.

I move the note over to the side and go back to my phone. Selecting all the footage I took at Mysa, I upload it from my phone to my laptop. There must be something in here. A clue or a photo of someone doing something suspicious. I scroll through it and stop at the photo I took on the rooftop of Rosetta, Claes, Daniel, and Tess standing next to Max. Edith, positioned off to the side, is holding the lacquer box which displayed the keys he gave to each of them. I flip through the other photos and videos, but nothing stands out. I yawn, distracted, and stare at a couple of the selfies I took. My hair is definitely too long. It looks dull and limp.

Opening my web browser, I Google Rosetta Rawling. The first result takes me to her company's landing page, BitterWomanBitters.com:

Originally founded by Ebenezer Rawling in 1831, *Strange Tinctures* gained popularity around the world as the premier American bitters maker during the era known as the Golden Age of Cocktails. Rawling is often credited as the creator of the Manhattan, although it is possible this is apocryphal since there are several myths surrounding the drink's invention. After nearly a century of success, the company shut down in the 1920s due to Prohibition.

It was revived and brought back to market in the 1990s by Rawling's descendent, his fourth-great-granddaughter Rosetta, after she unearthed a treasure trove of old family recipes. The intensely fragrant bitters she has refined over the years are unmistakably original and favored by bartenders all over the world. Our logo, the pine cone, signifies the company's location in Carmel and our values – harmony and renewal – which guide us every day.

I look up Rosetta on various social media sites but find nothing. Next, I click on an article from *California Dream* magazine:

The Most Bitter Woman in California?

When Rosetta Rawling sold her bitters brand, *Strange Tinctures*, to Max Magnussen's alcohol conglomerate, Hyperion, in 2017, it was a jubilant moment for the woman who had revamped her family's nearly 200-year-old brand. Rawling reportedly secured a $40 million exit.

Four years later, her product was recalled and taken off store shelves in the United States. Rawling believes her decision to sell *Strange Tinctures* to Magnussen's group was "a devastating mistake."

"*Strange Tinctures* had been defunct for decades. All I had was my family name and recipes. I took out a loan and $60,000 of credit card debt to bootstrap the relaunch and built it into a highly profitable business. We went from obscurity to prominence as the preferred bitters brand of bartenders in only a few years. Now all of that brand equity has dissipated, thanks to the carelessness of Hyperion."

Their nondisparagement agreement recently expired, so Rawling is free to discuss her feelings on the matter for the first time. Speaking exclusively with *California Dream* magazine, she explains, "Magnussen's team mismanaged the brand from day one. They fired the agency that created our iconic,

A MURDER IN EIGHT COCKTAILS

award-winning marketing campaigns, and they changed our formulations and packaging to bring down costs. Consumers began reporting a bad aftertaste and allergic reactions shortly after that."

Hyperion recalled *Strange Tinctures* products from store shelves in 2021. They returned to distribution two years later, but Rawling insists the new products are not what they once were and feels the brand has been in decline ever since. "Many things can go wrong after an acquisition," Rawling warns, "but for me, the worst-case scenario happened: ruining my family name."

I lean back and fold my arms across my chest. Some of this information I remembered hearing about over the years. Rosetta had been a fixture in the Carmel community for so long that it all felt familiar, like I was checking up on an old friend. But if she felt so betrayed by Max, how did they ever come to reconcile? He gave her one of the elevator keys, so they must have been on good terms before he died. Although, she did call him a "human cold sore." Strange.

I read through some other articles with headlines like *Rawling Tells the Bitters Truth* and *Local Businesswoman Caught in Bitters Battle Infused with Conflict*, but they all tell a version of the same story.

Next, I look up Claes Magnussen. An array of newspaper articles appears. I click on one dated nine years ago:

KELLY MULLEN

Serial Art Thief Sentenced to Prison

Claes Magnussen, who stole five works from several Stockholm museums over a three-year period, was found guilty on Thursday of art theft and burglary. Magnussen was sentenced to five years in prison.

Earlier this year, his accomplice and getaway driver, Nicholas Coates, was convicted of a lesser charge and sentenced to one year in prison.

"Art is a drug for me, and I am an addict," admitted Magnussen in a statement.

I arch an eyebrow. Weirdo, death-obsessed Claes used to be an art thief? He did have a look about him that was mysterious, and yes, borderline sexy. If international art thieves were your thing. I surf through a few more articles, but there isn't a lot of additional information.

Rubbing my temples, I go to my browser history and review some of the links I visited while researching Max before the party. I click on an article about him from a bar industry trade publication. It features a photo of Max, seated at a table next to a bottle of his *Tempus Fugit* aquavit. He's got the kind of intense, steel-blue gaze that penetrates right through the camera lens. *What happened to you?* I ask the photo.

He stares back at me.

Resolve surges through my blood. This isn't the kind of

adventure I was expecting from my evening at Mysa. It's something entirely different, but I feel a sense of purpose. I take a deep breath and set my jaw in a firm line. I'm going to find out what really happened.

Saturday

7

Crack. Plop. Crack. Plop. Two eggs hiss and sizzle in the pan as I stand at the stove. I watch the translucent egg whites solidify as I think about Max. He must be lying in one of those refrigerated drawers at the morgue by now. Soon they'll be cutting him open to do the autopsy. A shiver runs through me.

The toaster dings. I jump.

"Morning. Smells delicious in here," says Marty, shuffling into the kitchen, wearing his plaid robe and matching slippers. "Did you manage to get any sleep last night?"

I shake my head and don't turn around. "No. I can't stop thinking about what happened." I flip open the waffle-maker and scoop the golden square onto a plate, nestling the two eggs next to it. I set the plate in front of Marty. "How about you?"

"I slept okay. Mmm . . . your waffles are the best," he sighs, inhaling the scent appreciatively. "They ruin all other waffles for me."

"You seem awfully relaxed. None of this is bothering you?"

"Of course it is. But you heard that speech Max gave. The

man clearly had some issues. It's sad, but we didn't know him. Suicide is complicated. What more is there to say?"

"He was talking about watching his cholesterol and his plans to settle down with Tess. Why would he say those things if he was going to kill himself?"

Marty shakes his head. "This has messed with your sleep. You're upset. Tonight, let's go to bed early. Get back to our routine."

"Everything is routine with you."

"I like our routine. Why are you so obsessed with change these days, anyway?"

"I don't know. Don't you ever worry that we've stopped . . . you know, evolving? As a couple? Change is important."

"I think our lives are pretty great as is." Marty goes back to his waffles.

"Well, I've decided that I'm still going to make those promotional videos for Mysa. I don't want the money. I just want to honor Max's vision. The place is truly magnificent. I only hope there's some way for it to survive without him."

I butter a slice of toast and listen to the small television on the counter. It's playing an episode of *48 Hours*. The man onscreen, a grizzled-looking cop, is speaking intently to the journalist off-camera. *As a detective, you must think about every scenario and possibility. Each clue is a seed, and you have to nurture those seeds. You need to be creative, but most importantly, you need passion. The best detectives I know are also the most relentless.*

I consider his words. If there's one thing I am, it's passionate and relentless. The importance of creativity in detective work has never occurred to me before, but it's certainly a quality that I possess. I also know that ASMR gives me an instinctive awareness and highly attuned senses. Combined with my project management skills, an art I honed in my interior design career, why can't I give this investigation thing a whirl?

"Do you think Max could have been murdered?" I ask, turning to face Marty.

A crease forms between his eyebrows. "Murdered? How? Just as he simultaneously texts several people his perfectly composed suicide note, a murderer appears out of nowhere and pushes him off the roof?"

I press my lips together in concentration. "Paul doesn't think Max killed himself either."

Marty sets his fork down. "Paul? When did you talk to him?"

"Last night," I say, hoping I sound breezy and not defensive. "I couldn't sleep, so I called him."

He gives me a look that says *How would you feel if I called my ex in the middle of the night?*

I sigh. "I just wanted to check on him, okay? This whole thing has been so traumatic." I take a bite of toast. "Do you think you could talk to Tim about this?"

Tim Kluver is a Monterey County medical examiner who has been a birding friend of Marty's for years. Their group,

Cluster Flock, or The Flock, as they informally refer to themselves, gathers once a week at their usual spot, Monterey County's Elkhorn Slough Estuary. Tim is held in high esteem by The Flock because he has already ticked over 400 species on his birding "life list."

"You must be kidding. No, I am not speaking to a county official about your murder theories."

"Come on, Marty, talk to Tim for me? He might be able to tell us about the autopsy results."

"Tim compartmentalizes all the horrible stuff he sees. When he's with The Flock he doesn't want to talk about his job." He stands up from his chair. "I'm gonna make some OJ, you want?"

"Sure." I sit down and take a sip of coffee, realizing I've left out another crucial bit of information from my call last night. "Oh, Paul's joining book club tonight. I invited him."

"What?" he calls out to me over the loud whirring of the juicer.

"Paul!" I shout. "He's coming to book club tonight."

Marty places more oranges into the machine as it continues to whine. "Don't you think that's a little intrusive?" He releases the handle and places a glass of foamy, fresh juice in front of me.

"He's all alone here, and his business partner just died. He can come over for a couple of hours to talk about Graham Greene with us." A twinge of guilt stabs at me. Although I realize it's not because I feel bad for inviting Paul to book club without consulting Marty; it's because I *don't* feel bad about inviting Paul without consulting Marty.

He rubs his forehead with his thumb and forefinger. "Well, if you're so concerned about Max's death, shouldn't you start by considering that your ex-husband might have had something to do with it? Maybe he wanted his business partner dead."

I throw my head back and give a laugh. "Paul saves blind dogs and writes poetry. Don't be ridiculous. Besides, he isn't organized enough to commit murder."

"You haven't seen him in decades. How can you be so sure?"

I let out an exasperated sigh. "In the twisty thriller version of this movie, sure, Paul ends up being the baddie in the big reveal. But I'm telling you, that is not the twist here. I was married to him, Marty."

He takes a drink of orange juice. "We spend our whole lives with some people – parents, children, spouses – and sometimes we find out we never really knew them."

"That's a weird thing to say in the middle of a fight."

"Are we fighting?" Marty cleans the juicer and puts it away in silence.

I head upstairs to our bedroom and try to analyze what's happening to me. Do I really think someone murdered Max, or am I just frustrated with my life and trying to stir up a little drama because I'm bored? Both scenarios feel equally plausible.

I fling open the closet door and stand in front of the

full-length mirror, taking in my reflection. I look tired and drawn. A silk blouse tucked into high-waisted trousers flatters my recently slimmed-down waistline. I've lost ten pounds over the last six months, and after watching instructional YouTube videos from a few effortlessly elegant French women, I have carefully curated a new capsule wardrobe. But Marty hasn't noticed.

My eyes stop on the soft, salt-and-pepper gray hair currently imprisoned in a tight ponytail that I hurriedly pulled together this morning. I grit my teeth and reach for a pair of scissors. With one firm snip, I chop off the end of the ponytail. I pull my remaining hair forward and shake my head, revealing a bouncy, chin-length bob.

A thrill runs down my spine. I've always wanted short hair. Something easy and simple to wash and dry. I trim the edges until it falls perfectly smooth at my jawline. Gliding my favorite deep burgundy lipstick over my mouth, I smile at myself and note the satisfying *click* of the cap snapping back into place. I might have to use that sound in one of my ASMR videos.

I march back into the kitchen to face Marty. "I'm going to the farmers' market. I need tomatoes for book club tonight. And lemons. I'm making your favorite lemon cake."

Marty takes a step back. "What happened to your hair?!"

"Embrace change, Marty!" I say, as I turn around and walk out the door.

8

Carmel's farmers' market blossoms every Saturday along Sixth Avenue, which is blocked off for pedestrians. There's a beautiful symmetry in the market stalls, laid out with colorful displays of fresh flowers, fruits and vegetables, fragrant bunches of herbs, and artisanal baked goods arranged in neat rows. It's a permanent entry on my weekly "to do" list because there's always something new to try, and it never fails to inspire cocktail ideas for *Sips and Whispers*.

It's a cool spring morning and gauzy clouds streak the sky. I shuffle and sidestep my way through the crowd, past the warm, sweet scent of crepes and the hissing of the espresso machine at the coffee stall, toward one of the vegetable stands. A bright mound of fresh tomatoes stops me in my tracks. I reach for a plump one and lift it to my nose. The familiar, ripe scent permeates the skin. I imagine biting into it and the acidic juice spilling down my chin. These are definitely the right ones for my signature tomato salad that I'll be serving at couples' book club tonight. Well, couples, plus one Paul.

"I'll take six of these, please." As I pay the merchant and take the bag, I hear a male voice speaking in a thick accent.

I turn around. Claes Magnussen is behind me, a few feet away. I instantly recognize his tall frame, cleft chin, and sharp widow's peak. Momentarily stunned, I watch as he speaks animatedly with a pretty redhead working at the flower stall. He throws his head back and laughs, his white teeth shining in the warm morning sun. I note his outfit: crisp shirt, linen trousers, and boat shoes.

I frown. He's certainly well put together considering it's only been a few hours since his brother's untimely death. Why is he out for a leisurely stroll, dressed like he's heading to a yacht party and flirting with a woman half his age? I lower the bag of tomatoes into my canvas tote bag as I keep an eye on him.

Suddenly, he turns around. I duck behind a pile of avocados and pull my large sunglasses down from the top of my head to cover my eyes. As I crouch low, I bump into the leg of a woman test-squeezing an avocado. She gasps and looks down at me in surprise.

"Excuse me," I say. "I'm sorry. I can't find my sunglasses."

Her eyes narrow. "They're on your face."

"Oh! So they are!" I exclaim, reaching up to touch them. "I think I'll just stay down here a bit longer. Large crowds frighten me. I have reclusive tendencies."

The woman sets down the avocado and hurries away to another stall.

I stand up slowly. I'm unsure whether Claes will recognize me since we only met briefly at Mysa. My new, shorter 'do probably helps. I keep my sunglasses perched on my nose to be safe.

Hustling over to a bakery stall closer to where he's standing, I pretend to examine an elegant arrangement of glazed donuts. As I watch Claes survey the profusion of flowers, I realize my heart is racing. This is exciting. I'm trailing a suspect! Although I'm sweating at an alarming rate and probably resemble a glazed donut myself.

He points to a dazzling cluster of orange poppies. The flower stall redhead pulls a bunch from a large bucket of water.

"More please," I hear him say firmly. The woman selects several more. "Yes. That's just the right amount." He pays, then turns and strides down the street in the direction of the ocean.

Quickly, I place a baguette and a couple of plump croissants in a brown paper bag and hand some cash to the vendor before rushing off after Claes.

I apologize to several people as I jostle my way through the crowd. The market is especially busy today, which is hampering my reconnaissance mission. I adjust the canvas tote bag on my shoulder as I pick up the pace, the paper bags of produce and bread rustling around inside it.

Claes is moving at a brisk speed, his shirt billowing in the ocean breeze. Occasionally, he turns to take in the sights along the way, the bouquet in his hand swinging back and forth at his side. Where is this guy going? Those orange poppies are way too cheerful for a day of mourning. Why isn't he holed up somewhere, grieving his dead brother?

I keep pace behind him, doing my best to act natural. Not like a neurotic woman with an overactive imagination trailing a Swedish art thief. When he reaches Monte Verde Street, he pauses. I hide behind a cypress tree and watch as a woman approaches him. I squint to see better. She's attractive. Average height, with dark hair and high cheekbones.

As they embrace, I note how his lips linger on her cheek. That was more than an air-kiss hello. He hands her the bouquet, and she smiles back at him. I look on as he reaches for a pack of cigarettes and offers one to her. They stand together and smoke for a few minutes, talking and flirting. Then he reaches into his pocket and gives her an envelope. The woman takes it and slips it into her backpack. They hug again, then turn and head in opposite directions.

Decision time. Should I follow Claes or this mysterious woman? I already know who Claes is, so I can track him down later. But if I let the woman walk away, any clues or leads she could offer will be lost, and she will remain anonymous forever.

I decide to follow the woman.

My determination powers up. Think like a detective, Willa! Quickly, I grab my phone to take a photo but she's walking too damn fast! I pour on the steam to keep my legs moving.

A MURDER IN EIGHT COCKTAILS

Abruptly, the woman turns and heads down a side street. Finally, she slows down, so I raise my phone and quickly snap some photos of her in profile.

I drop back a little. If I follow her too closely, she might notice me now that we're farther away from the tourist hub and there aren't as many people around. I lift my eyebrows higher and compose a casual smile on my lips. *Try to look carefree!* The few people I pass don't seem to notice anything strange. I must be looking quite breezy with this bouncy new hairdo.

She reaches The Monterey, a quaint boutique hotel popular with tourists, and I watch as she goes inside. How can I follow her into that tiny place and not look like some interloper?

The croissants! I rustle around in my shopping bag and fish one out. The first buttery bite melts in my mouth as I stride coolly into the lobby, closing my eyes in consummate appreciation of the art of French baking. I nod to the bellman and the man at the front desk as I chew another flaky bite into oblivion. Neither of them seem fazed.

I look on as the woman walks to the elevator. With a gentle ding, the doors open and she steps inside. After the doors slide closed, I head over to a striped ottoman and sit down. I make brief eye contact with the front desk clerk who has a strange, shiny mustache that curls up at the ends.

Nothing to see here, Weird Mustache Guy, I'm just an ordinary tourist, sitting on her tuffet, checking out your lobby. I place the remaining half of the croissant back in the bag and take out a wet wipe, conspicuously dabbing at my lips and fingers so Weird Mustache Guy can be assured that I won't soil his lovely furnishings.

I move over to a more comfortable chair and reach for the latest edition of *The Carmel Pine Cone*. I unfold it and hold it in front of my face, trying to appear as though I'm reading an in-depth article about the alarming decrease in books being returned to the Carmel Public Library. Occasionally, I risk glances in the direction of the elevator and Weird Mustache Guy, then I go back to the article. It turns out that a "Book Retrieval Posse" has been deputized by the library's board of directors and the offenders are to be summoned for a fine assessment and a firm dressing-down at a later date.

I check my watch. It's kind of lonely handling this situation alone. I need a partner in crime. Someone to share ideas and theories with. I consider texting Marty, but I know how that will go. Before I can talk myself out of it, I take in a breath and send Paul a text:

Hey. I'm at The Monterey, it's a hotel in downtown Carmel. Can you meet me here? It's urgent.

I watch as typing bubbles churn and his reply appears:

You make a tempting offer, milady, but I don't think we should. What about Marty?

Flustered, I write back:

Very funny. Listen, I ran into Claes when I was out shopping. He's not acting like someone whose brother just died. He met up

A MURDER IN EIGHT COCKTAILS

with a woman, and I followed her here. Can you please come meet me here? I need backup, okay?

Paul's response comes immediately:

Be there ASAP.

9

"Your hair! I love it," says Paul, strolling into the lobby with Noodles in tow.

Dressed casually in a simple black T-shirt and jeans, he has a bit of unshaven stubble on his face. As he approaches, I notice there are bags under his eyes, and he looks wan. I can tell the loss of his business partner is hitting him hard.

"Oh, thank you," I say, popping up from the seat where I've been annihilating the other half of the croissant for the last few minutes.

Noodles squeezes his milky eyes shut with joy and wags his tail "hello" as I pet him.

"Bow down," Paul commands.

"Huh?" I stammer, stepping back.

Noodles obediently lowers his front legs and fuzzy head toward me.

"Oh!" I say, realizing the command was for Noodles. "You're such a smart boy!" I smile as he bumps against my leg, tail whirring.

"Now, give her a paw," instructs Paul.

A MURDER IN EIGHT COCKTAILS

Noodles presents his paw to me, and I give it a gentle squeeze. "Good boy!" I scratch his ears as I look up at Paul. "So, here's the plan. I say we hang out in the lobby and wait for the girl to reappear. Act natural, like we have a reason to be here. It's lunchtime, so she'll probably come out again soon."

He nods in agreement and we sit down. I catch our reflection in a mirror. The sight of us side by side together, after all these years, startles me. A passing stranger might assume we're a couple.

I blink and turn to Paul. "So, did you talk to Edith?"

He nods, pulls out a piece of paper from his pocket and unfolds it, handing it to me. "She gave me the guest list. I checked the names. Most of them are local to Northern California. Business people. Influencers. A couple of local politicians and city council members. No one with a suspicious past, from what I can tell."

I scan the printed-out email from Edith to Paul. Most of the names I don't recognize. "There are forty-two guests here, plus seven staff," I say, after counting them. "That's a lot of suspects to look at."

"Well, minus you and Marty, it's only forty-seven. But if you add me, then it's forty-eight, I guess."

I laugh. "Don't be ridiculous."

He shakes his head. "Well, I *should* be a suspect. If the police would take this crime seriously."

"They don't think a crime took place." I reach out and

squeeze his hand. "I want you to know I'm truly sorry. Whatever it was . . . suicide, murder, accident . . . it's awful."

"Thank you," he sighs. "I still can't believe this happened."

"Listen," I say. "I don't know anything about murder investigations. My knowledge is limited to golden age detective fiction and watching true crime. But usually the killer is someone who was close to the victim."

Paul nods. "Agreed. So where do we start, then?"

I think for a moment, then take out my phone and scroll to the group photo I took on Mysa's rooftop. Showing it to Paul, I point to Claes, Tess, Daniel, and Rosetta. "Those four people had keys to the elevator. And access to the rooftop was restricted, right? We tried to get into the stairwell when we heard Tess screaming, but the door was locked."

Paul nods. "And when I spoke to the police, they told me those were the four people who received Max's suicide text. They knew him well, but so did Edith. She worked for Max prior to Mysa, at another bar. I think they had a fling once, too."

I point to Edith in the photo. "She was wearing a key on a lanyard around her neck. That's how we got up to the rooftop and found Max."

"Yes. Edith's a real control freak. Given all the safety issues, she kept the staff key on her during business hours because she didn't want anyone to access the roof without her permission. Any time a member of staff needed to go up there, they had to ask her."

A MURDER IN EIGHT COCKTAILS

I take my cocktail notebook out of my bag and jot down the five names, referencing the guest list to ensure I spell each one correctly:

> Claes Magnussen, Max's brother
> Tess Hitcham, Max's girlfriend
> The Bitter Woman/Rosetta Rawling
> Daniel Williams, Max's financial adviser
> Edith Stonewall, Mysa hostess

"So, do we agree that these five people are our main suspects?" I ask.

"I think so," Paul nods. "We should talk to them. And soon, while things are still fresh in their minds."

"Okay. But wait a minute. Since Edith is a suspect, are we sure we can trust the guest list she sent you?"

"Definitely," he says, pointing to the email. "She cc'd our operations manager, Alex. Trust me, he's very precise and detail-oriented. That's why Max loved him. She couldn't get any false information past that guy."

I check the "cc" line and see he's right. "Okay. What about the staff?"

He shakes his head. "Tough to say. I know most of them pretty well. Although a bartender we hired recently, Nick, is a friend of Claes', and I don't really know him. I'll get the staff list from Alex directly and send it to you." He pulls out a small spiral-bound book from his pocket and opens it to a specific page. "I brought Max's planner. See all the plans he had for the week?" he says, pointing to several entries in the schedule. "Monday: 'Meet with city attorney re: rooftop bar, 10:00 a.m.' Tuesday: 'Meet Daniel and realtor to tour beach house, 1:00 p.m.' Wednesday: 'Flight to Singapore, 8:20 a.m.' He very clearly had future plans."

I look down at the planner. "Handwritten? Didn't he have an assistant to keep track of things?"

Paul gives a small laugh and hands it to me. "Nope. Max was so particular about time that he always ran his own schedule. And he always did it old school, with pen and paper."

"That is indeed eccentric," I say, as I leaf through it. "Definitely doesn't look like he was considering his last days on earth." I hand it back to him.

The elevator dings and we both look up. It's the mystery woman, and she's changed into a chic cream-colored suit. The skirt ends several inches above her knees, revealing her long, slim legs. Her stiletto heels, handbag, and floppy hat announce to everyone that she has places to go.

We watch intently as she approaches the front desk, carrying a padded envelope.

"What do we do now?" I whisper.

Paul offers his arm. "Project confidence." Together, we stride up to the front desk and stand in line behind her.

We inch closer so that we can overhear the conversation she's having with Weird Mustache Guy. The heavy funk of cigarette smoke hovers around her in an invisible cloud.

"Can you FedEx this for me?" she asks.

Her voice is creaky and low. A "vocal fry," as it's called. Some people find this sort of voice annoying, but it always provides a relaxing mind-massage for me. I close my eyes briefly as euphoric tingles travel up my spine.

"We don't do FedEx here, but I can mail something for you."

"Fine. May I have a pen, please?"

Paul gives me a nudge and makes a discreet "take a picture" pantomime, so I pull out my phone. He waits for just the right moment, when the girl finishes writing the address, then winks at me and kneels down to whisper something to Noodles.

"Owoooooooooooooo!"

I look down, and Noodle's little dog lips are forming an "O" shape as he belts out a series of long, piercing howls.

The girl and the desk clerk both jump back and stare down at Noodles.

"What's wrong with him?" she asks.

Paul feigns concern as Noodles continues to howl and starts running around in circles. "Wooowowowoo!"

"Are you stepping on his paw?" demands Weird Mustache Guy, leaning over the desk to get a look.

I quickly snap a photo of the address on the envelope.

"I'm sorry, sir, but Noodles is hypoglycemic," Paul explains. "When his blood sugar gets too low, he howls like a wolf baying at the moon. Do you happen to have a can of Coke around?"

The man reaches down and brings up an opened can of Diet Pepsi. "Here."

"No, that won't work! It has to contain sugar!"

Noodles gives a sharp bark, as if in agreement, then continues to howl.

The girl reaches into her purse. "How about a peppermint candy?"

"Yes! Thank you!"

She holds it out to Noodles, who gives it a convincing lick and abruptly stops howling, as if Paul has flipped an "off" switch.

"You saved his life!" I say to her. "Thank you so much. I think we better take him outside for some fresh air."

Paul waves to them and takes my arm. We hurry out of the hotel and walk around to the side of the building, where there are a few park benches. Our eyes meet and we erupt into laughter.

"I feel like a Cold War spy," I say.

"Let's wait for her to come out."

We sit down for a few minutes, pretending to check on Noodles.

"Have your camera ready, Wil."

Hearing Paul call me by his old pet name for me stirs something. I'm unsure if it's butterflies, nostalgia, or both.

"There she is! She's getting into a Mini Cooper. Take a photo of the license plate."

I snap the picture. "Got it!" The car drives off and I show

him the photo. It's blurry, but the plate is readable. I scroll to the previous photo and show him the envelope from the front desk. It reads:

> Millie Hagerty
> 52 Huntington Road
> Madison, Wisconsin 53500

I Google *Millie Hagerty* and scan various articles to confirm I've found the right person. "It appears she's a well-known art collector in Madison."

"Hm. No return address, though," says Paul. "We still don't know who the other woman is."

My mind is going a thousand miles an hour from all the excitement. "Maybe I can get someone to run the license plate."

The corner of his mouth turns up in a wry smile as he looks over at me. "You think this is kind of fun, don't you? It's okay. You don't have to hide it."

I look down, feeling slightly ashamed. Paul could always see right inside my head. "Well, I mean . . . it is kind of exciting. But I hope you don't think I take any of this lightly. Listen, why don't I talk to Rosetta? I can go 'undercover' as a superfan of her bitters brand and suggest we collaborate on some product placement videos. You could come with me?"

"I think she'll probably open up to you more if it's one on one."

"Okay. What are you going to do?"

"I'm going to get the key to Max's rental house. He kept a duplicate in his office. There was always construction going on at Mysa, so we used the house for meetings. I want to check it out and see if he left any clues behind."

I meet Paul's gaze. His eyes glint with a familiar hint of mischief. I feel a twinge of fear mixed with excitement. Like we're opening a forbidden door. Investigating a murder is bonkers, and I know it, but something is percolating in me. I realize now that the doubts I'm having about Max's death aren't simply a case of me being bored, looking for some harebrained, post-menopausal adventure. Well, maybe that's part of it, but something else is driving me. It's the deep, instinctual feeling that something isn't right. I want to pursue this, whatever *this* is.

But there's also a sadness tugging at me. That I'm sharing this wild experience with my ex, and not Marty.

I swing my bag over my shoulder. "I'll let you know how it goes with Rosetta at book club. See you tonight? Eight p.m.?"

"Yes. See you tonight."

10

It's lightly misting as I pull out onto the Pacific Coast Highway toward the home of Rosetta Rawling, The Bitter Woman. She lives in Big Sur, a thirty-mile stretch of scenic coast just south of Carmel. With its chirping birds, unspoiled hiking trails, and massive redwoods, it's a magical place that has a way of immersing you in its natural splendor.

The sunny May morning of the farmers' market has now grayed into the fog clouds of a heavy marine layer, a common occurrence on the Monterey Peninsula. I turn on the windshield wipers and reach for a snack-sized candy bar from the emergency reserve in my purse. I unwrap it and pop it into my mouth, the relaxing ASMR crunching sounds reverberating inside my skull. A caloric recharge is essential before embarking on my first suspect interview with Rosetta Rawling, bitters-maker extraordinaire.

I need to get into character as *Willa, Strange Tinctures Superfan*. I decide my imaginary assistant's name is Leah. She's going to be ordering several cases of Rosetta's bitters, and I want to talk to her about doing a potential collaboration.

I'll essentially be playing a version of myself – only this rendition of me is far more enthusiastic about bitters than I really am. After I build a rapport with her, I'll find a way to casually transition to a chat about Max while I distract her with the promise of further brand promotion.

I focus on the road ahead as I try to organize my disparate thoughts. Before long, my mind locks onto Paul. Was I imagining things or was he . . . flirting with me earlier? My common sense reminds me that we were never a good match. But I have to admit it's refreshing to have Paul's positive energy in the mix. That sense of spontaneity and adventure. I only wish Marty had some of those qualities.

He didn't used to be so closed off to new experiences. When Zack was in elementary school, we'd put a dab of ink on his finger, then blindfold him and spin him around and he'd point to a random spot on a map of the US. Wherever his fingerprint landed, that's where we'd go for a week in the summertime. Marty would spend hours studying the area and report back with all the interesting things we should do and what items we should pack.

I shake off my reverie and check the time: 12:15 p.m. Book club starts at 8:00, so I need to handle this interrogation quickly. Otherwise, I won't have time to do my prep work.

My phone buzzes with a text from Marty:

I checked all the wine glasses for streaks and set out the hors d'oeuvres plates and napkins. Going to take a nap now. Do we need forks? Will you be home soon?

I feel a sting of guilt. Here I am, gallivanting around town with my ex-husband and flitting off to Big Sur, and meanwhile Marty is at home getting things ready for book club. Conscientious, dependable Marty. I text back that I'll be home by 3:00 p.m. and put my phone away.

When I reach Rosetta's private drive, I pull off the road and arrive at a wrought-iron gate flanked by high walls. I roll down the window and press the button. There's no response. I wait a minute or so, then press the button again for another few seconds.

A tinny voice crackles from the speaker. "Yes?"

"Hello. I'm here to see Ms. Rawling. I'm her neighbor, Willa." I realize there's a tremulous edge to my voice, so I clear my throat to regain control. "From Carmel. I want to speak with her about featuring her bitters on my YouTube channel."

"Come on through." There's a loud buzz and the gate slowly opens.

I pull into the driveway of a rosy pink Spanish Colonial mansion. It looks inviting. Given her reputation as a recluse, I was expecting something more gothic, a bit *What Ever Happened to Baby Jane?*, but this seems lovely. A vintage Mercedes convertible is parked out front. A bumper sticker reads *Bitter Is Better*. I get out of my car and walk by it slowly, admiring its sleek, low-slung body and pristine leather seats.

As I get closer to the house, I notice that the paint is peeling from the stucco and the curtains are a bit faded. Cobwebs hang from the gutters. The place is definitely in need of a facelift. I ascend the flagstone steps to the massive front door and knock. I still can't believe that I'm actually doing this. It feels a little dangerous . . . and I like it. I draw in a deep, steadying breath.

Rosetta opens the door. Framed in the doorway, she's wearing a floaty, mauve chiffon caftan and a thick layer of foundation and blush high on her cheekbones. Her wrists are covered in a jumble of gold bangles and bracelets. She looks like a frothy strawberry milkshake that's been left out on the counter overnight.

She gives me a quick once-over, "Hello, Sugarloaf," she purrs, her filler-enhanced lips emphatically forming a round o-shape to make the vowel sounds. "What brings you here? How do you know where I live?"

Suddenly, my mind goes blank. I've forgotten everything I planned to say. All that work to mentally cast myself as the star of some true crime thriller has evaporated. My hands are shaking. "Well," I stammer, "I got your address from the guest list at Mysa. My ex-husband, Paul, I think you know him a little . . . he's devastated by Max's death. I just thought maybe I could talk to you for a moment since you knew Max so well." I pause to take a breath. I have no idea if any of this feels convincing. I watch her face as she evaluates me, deciding whether or not to let me into her home. "I also have to tell you that I love your Orange Blossom Bloom bitters. I want to feature them in one of my videos, for a cocktail I created called *The Orangery*."

"Come on inside then," she says, as she makes a sweeping hand gesture for me to enter. She turns and swirls past me in a diaphanous cloud of mauve, leading me into a foyer with an elaborate cupola ceiling that offers a clear view of the slate-gray sky above. The rain is beginning to pick up, drumming loudly on the glass. It's so cold in the house that my hands are becoming stiff. I shiver.

The house is spacious but cluttered. Peering into some of the rooms, I can see mauve everywhere. A bureau inlaid with mauve mother-of-pearl. Gauzy mauve curtains. Velvet mauve upholstered furniture with tasseled pillows. Mauve picture frames and antiques. This place is like walking into a 1980s photo album.

We make our way into a large, high-ceilinged living room with oil portraits hanging on the walls. Three pairs of French doors flecked with raindrops lead out onto a veranda. Her flouncy caftan puffs out behind her like a cloud scudding in the breeze as she leads us into the center of the room.

Other than the light switch backplates, crown molding, and baseboards, the room is soaked in mauve of every shade and material — linen, velvet, ceramic, wood, and silk. It's clear that she has piles of money, but despite the expensive paintings and antique furniture, most of it is in disrepair. Plaster cracks meander through the ceiling. Stuffing peeks out of a sofa.

"What a gorgeous rug," I say, trying to think of a compliment. "I like how your visual signature is strong. The mauve is so personal. It's really . . . singular."

"Mauve never lets me down," she responds, fiddling with one of her earrings absentmindedly. "Tea?"

"Sure."

She walks over to a sideboard and lifts a silver tea service tray. "Have a seat over there on the mauve sofa."

"Sorry, which one?" I ask, casting my eye around the room, trying to determine, of the three mauve sofa options, which one she means.

"The one right there by Orson," she explains, with another dramatic arm gesture to a Louis XV sofa.

I make my way toward it and sit down, turning to the creature perched on the seat next to me. I can see Orson is living like a tiny little king inside this run-down hacienda. Laid out on the ottoman is his miniature living room, where he sits on a tiny Eames chair. There's a turquoise leather sofa and a bar cart with tiny whisky bottles, and even an itty bitty bottle of bitters. On an end table is a minuscule centerpiece of what appears to be dried crickets in a silver bowl. He wears a miniature beret on his scaly green head, and his beady eyes return my gaze in a way that seems to say, *Is there a problem?* This is one hip chameleon.

Rosetta sits down across from me and places the tray in front of us on the coffee table. While she prepares the tea,

Orson adjusts himself to a more comfortable position on his chair.

"So, does Orson just hang out in his little living room all day?"

"Oh no. He has a few spots around the house. When he's not with me, he spends most of his time in a vivarium with UVB light, a heat lamp, plants, a misting system, substrate tray, hygrometer ... you know, the standard chameleon habitat."

"Oh wow, I had no idea they're such high-maintenance pets."

She beams at him and gives him a tickle under the chin. "Only people who truly appreciate chameleons and have the means to invest in the necessary food and equipment should ever adopt them. They really are wonderful creatures."

"How long have you lived here?" I ask, adjusting the pillow behind me.

She lifts a delicate bone-china cup from the tray, places it on a mauve crocheted coaster in front of me and pours. "This home has been in my family for many generations. I'm paid to look after it. My father's will declared that I would be the caretaker, with the stipulation that I must always live here and keep the place up. I guess he thought as long as I lived here and maintained it, I had some value to him."

She passes me the tray, and I stir some milk and sugar into my tea.

"I had everything redone to suit my taste. Even so, I still feel my father's presence here." She leans over and adjusts the little lampshade on Orson's end table. "Do you think a house can keep the souls of the people who lived in it? Not like ghosts or anything . . . just their presence?"

I consider the thought. "Yes, maybe you're right. Not spirits exactly. But perhaps some sort of essence of who they were."

We sip our teas together in silence.

I shift in my seat, noticing that her hand is resting on the tray next to a small butter knife for the little sandwiches. I watch her fingers. They're trembling. In fact, her entire demeanor has darkened. My heart rate picks up as a wave of clarity hits me. I am alone in an obviously mentally unbalanced woman's home.

Suddenly, she grasps hold of the knife.

I jump.

"Why don't you tell me what's really going on?"

I stare at her, blinking. "What do you mean?" My whole body tenses as I look down at her shaking hand, clutching the knife. Then again, how much damage could a butter knife do, really? Well, it could probably take out an eye.

She glares at me, full of suspicion. "Stop lying to me and tell me why you're really here."

11

"Lying? What do you mean?" I ask, caught somewhere between outrage and assessing what my undercover character of *Willa, Strange Tinctures Superfan* would do. If only I had taken that method acting class at UCLA instead of *The Phallus: from Antiquity to Present*.

There's a challenging tilt to her head as she speaks to me. Her voice is cold. "You're not here about my bitters. When I spoke to you last night, you didn't say a word about my products. Why the sudden interest? You're obviously faking it."

I freeze. It seems Rosetta is a chameleon, too. Capable of adapting and taking on the colors and emotions of whatever suits her in the moment. I look at Orson. He's changed from light green to a dark, dull brown and seems to be quivering with anger. My heart begins to thump in my chest.

She narrows her eyes. "I think you're here because you're looking for some entertainment. Bored housewife, perhaps? Sorry to tell you this, but I don't exist to entertain you."

I decide to change tack and try a little sincerity. "Rosetta, I'm only here as a concerned member of the Monterey community. Paul doesn't think Max killed himself, and I don't either. I just want to talk to the people who knew him best and try to understand what might have been going on in his life before he died."

Her expression changes and she lets go of the knife. "See? That wasn't so hard, was it? More tea?" she asks, with a plastered-on smile that isn't entirely friendly.

I nod yes.

She pours me another cup as I contemplate my next move. "Did Max ever mention he was having personal troubles? Anything that would lead you to believe he wanted to kill himself?"

"Not really. He was a private person. I would even call him secretive. He was lonely, too. I could tell." She pauses. "Lonely recognizes lonely."

I settle back onto the cushions. "You didn't seem to be a fan of his at the party. You called him . . . *a human cold sore*, was it?"

She takes in a sharp breath. "I was just mad at him. We'd had a tiff about something. But we always had our ups and downs."

"What was your 'tiff' about?" I ask.

"That's none of your business," she replies curtly.

"Okay. Well, can you tell me if you noticed anything strange at the party?"

"Well, yes, I did, actually. I was having that green drink. *Ingmar's Garden* or whatever."

"The *Primeval Forest*?"

She takes a sip of her tea. "Yes. The one that tasted like crushed foliage. It was right after I'd been talking to you and Marvin. Anyway, I had left you two to wander around and mingle, and that's when I saw Max having an argument."

"Who was he arguing with?"

"Tess."

I notice she can barely bring herself to say the name. Like the word doesn't belong in her mouth. She spits it out of her plump lips like a discarded olive pit.

"Really?" Alarms go off in my mind as I process this information. If Max and Tess were having an argument at the party *and* she was the person who discovered his body, then Tess is definitely high on the suspect list. Perhaps even more so than Claes. "Did you hear what they were saying?"

"It looked pretty heated. I heard her say, *I can't believe you gave it to her. How could you?* and she stormed away from him." I watch as Rosetta places her hands in her lap, twisting the fabric of her mauve caftan between her fingers.

"Does anything else stick out in your memory?"

She pauses to think. "Later on, I'd gone into the bathroom to get rid of that drink that tasted like suntan lotion."

"The *Bananavit*?"

"Yes. My palate doesn't do sweet drinks. I wanted to get rid of it without anyone seeing, so I snuck into the bathroom and dumped it down the sink. I noticed my mascara was smudged, so I redid my makeup in there for a little bit. That's when I heard someone crying in one of the stalls."

"Really?" I say. "Do you know who it was?"

She shakes her head. "I don't. But they were sobbing. I felt a little awkward being in there alone with them, so I left and picked up one of those lovely espresso drinks from the bar. That one tasted pretty good."

"Yes, the *Fikatini*."

"That's when . . ." She pauses to catch her breath, stifling a wave of emotion. "That's when I got that awful text."

I pause for a moment while she collects herself. "How did you originally meet Max?"

"I'll show you." She stands up and leans over, placing her open palm on the ottoman. Orson looks up at her, and they seem to exchange a moment of telepathic communication, then he scrambles onto her hand. She gently raises him up, and he promptly steps off his personal elevator and settles onto her shoulder.

I drain my tea and follow her down a long hallway to a pair of doors.

"I keep this part of the house locked up." She reaches for the handle and gives the door a gentle shove with her shoulder. Orson is obviously used to this routine. I note how his little clawed feet sink into Rosetta's caftan as he braces for the shove.

We enter a room filled with *Strange Tinctures* paraphernalia.

A shrine to the family business. Old advertising campaigns, stained original recipes, and photos of bartenders using the product in its heyday are artfully arranged on the walls. I study some of the photos. Most of them are of Rosetta over the years, always with her signature bouffant hairstyle. In some pictures, it appears a bit more natural and soft-looking, but as she progresses in age, it seems to get fluffier, taller. I have to wonder if it's a wig. I linger in front of one of the photos. Rosetta is standing in front of the Monterey County Hospital, holding some kind of community service award.

She comes over to stand next to me. "I've volunteered at that hospital for years. I had a brother who died very young. He needed a blood transfusion and couldn't get one. So ever since, I've devoted my life to supporting blood drives." She points to a photo of Max, much younger, standing next to a woman who resembles Rosetta but with subtle differences. "Max was a foreign exchange student at Monterey High School and he was dating my younger sister, Lola. That's her. I was just starting nursing school at the time."

"How long was he over here from Sweden?"

"Only a year. But he stayed in touch with Lola after he moved back. I'd nearly forgotten about him, but years later, when I was revamping the family business, I bumped into him at IBWSS."

I cock my head to the side. "What's that?"

"International Bulk Wine and Spirits Show. It's an alcohol industry trade convention. Of course, the first thing he said to me was 'How's Lola doing?'" She huffs. "He only ever cared about her, not me."

Rosetta's nickname starts to crystallize as I listen to her speak. The resentment and, yes, namesake bitterness, is so present in every word she says that it almost begins to feel like a physical presence hovering in the air. "Where does Lola live now?"

"She married a wealthy real estate developer and moved to Connecticut. But they got divorced and she frittered away whatever money she had. She's still part of the *Strange Tinctures* board, but that's about it."

I walk over to the photo to get a closer look. You can tell they're sisters, same build and face shape, although there is something bolder and stronger in Lola. Rosetta is softer somehow, and the sadness in her eyes is a contrast to the clear brightness in Lola's. I scan the other photos. Her dad in overalls and a T-shirt, a cigarette hanging from his lips, standing outside an old building. A photo of Tony Bennett holding up a *Strange Tinctures* bottle for the camera. Another of the governor of California shaking hands with her dad for some business award. A bartender at the Beverly Hills Hotel, showing the bitters bottles lined up on the backbar.

Rosetta gestures to another photo, of herself and Max toasting flutes of champagne. "Max approached me about buying *Strange Tinctures* ten years ago. His offer was enticing. 'An infusion of cash,' he called it. I was thrilled because I thought this was the universe telling me that Max was supposed to be in my life again. I turned down a higher offer from an American company and sold it to Hyperion instead. They let me retain a leadership role and also gave me a fancy 'entrepreneur-in-residence' title. Max and I worked together for a year or so. It was wonderful." She looks wistful. "Until I realized *Strange Tinctures* was just a tiny, insignificant part of his wider portfolio. He treated my business like a toy. Something that could be dropped on the floor when he lost interest. He started giving more of the decision-making power to his team, and by the time my contract was up, he pushed me out and, well . . ."

"I read some of the articles about what happened," I admit.

The rain begins to let up outside, and an orangey afternoon light slants through the window, throwing a soft glow on everything.

"After the brand fell apart, he brought me back in again to help him revamp it. It was doing really well when he passed away . . ." Her voice cracks. She looks down and pauses. I notice she seems to be speaking more to herself than to me. "There was a time when I was in love with him, you know," she says, her voice sounding weary.

"Max?"

She nods. "I fought it for years. But I finally surrendered to my feelings. That was a mistake. My love for him went unrequited." She looks down, then her eyes flick up and meet mine. "Do you know what that feels like?"

Her question takes me by surprise. I swallow hard. "Well,

not exactly," I reply, realizing if I offer some vulnerability she might open up to me in return. "But I do know what it feels like when loving someone isn't enough, and the relationship fails."

She gestures to a seating area in the center of the room. "Come, let's sit down." She takes a seat. Orson nuzzles up to her and puts his head on her shoulder. "Tell me more."

The Orson

Ingredients:
1 part melon liqueur
1 part vodka
1 part lime juice
0.25–0.5 parts simple syrup, to taste
Lime wedge, for garnish
Optional: Atomized lime bitters*

Method:
Chill a cocktail glass
Add the first four ingredients to a shaker filled with ice and shake vigorously for 15 seconds
Strain into the chilled glass and garnish with lime wedge on rim
Optional: Give *The Orson* a misting with lime bitters

*Pour lime bitters into a small spray bottle

Pygmy chameleons are entertaining and unique pets. They grow to be about four inches long at full size and are extremely delicate, so they must spend most of their time in a well-maintained vivarium. Misting is a critical component of their care, providing the hydration and humidity they require to survive. What they lack in size they make up for in personality. Unfortunately, a number of chameleon species around the globe are endangered or close to extinction, including some types of pygmy chameleon. To learn more and donate to their protection, visit the World Wildlife Fund's website.

12

"It was Paul, actually. My ex-husband, the co-owner and beverage director at Mysa," I explain to Rosetta. I'm sitting in a wing chair across from her, taking in my surroundings, this Rhapsody in Mauve. If I wasn't retired, what a job I could do for her. "We were only married for two years. When I reached my breaking point, I told him I needed him to change, or it was over. I was naïve. I thought he was going to tell me that he would do the work so I'd stay with him. But he didn't put up a fight at all. He just accepted it without hesitation."

"You wanted him to be devastated, didn't you?"

I give a small laugh and nod. "Yes. Childish, I know. He was so cool and calm about the whole thing. I figure it's because he had the confidence that he was going to move on and meet someone else rather easily. At the time, I wasn't so sure that I would." I pause and make eye contact with her. I can see that I've finally made a connection. Seizing the opportunity, I lean forward. "How did you ever reconcile with Max after all the problems he caused for *Strange Tinctures*?"

Her forehead seems to want to crease in concentration, but years of Botox make that expression a challenge. "He reached out to me. Said he wanted to make amends and apologize. I declined. But he sent some flowers and lovely cards. I saved them. This one," she says, showing it to me, "explains how he was diagnosed with alexithymia. Do you know what that is?"

I shake my head 'no' as I scan the letters and cards. It appears to be the same penmanship that was in Max's planner. I pick up a stack. The pages crinkle as I read his neat, crisp handwriting: *I know things with Lola have always made our relationship complicated, but the truth is I never considered your feelings because I didn't understand my own.*

"Alexithymia is a condition where you don't feel your feelings. He said his whole life he worried that maybe he was a sociopath, or a narcissist, but it turned out he was neither. Some expensive therapist helped him understand he didn't experience feelings in the way most people do. That's how he was able to do so well in business."

"And you said he sought therapy?"

"Oh yes. He was regularly going to retreats and seeing specialists of all kinds. Anyway, I eventually agreed to see him. He apologized to me, and we've been friendly ever since." She points to an antique jewelry box on a table nearby. "He gave me that as a gift once because he knows I love to collect old things. We often exchanged thoughtful gifts. It was never about money or luxury."

I study Rosetta. She appears lost in her thoughts.

"So, after he made nice with me and gave me back some equity in the company, I finally shut up in the press. That made him happy. Looking back now, I realize he was just doing a 'keep your friends close and your enemies closer' sort of thing. It was all a manipulative business strategy." She crosses her arms. "Listen, I need to get on with my day. I have a hot stone massage and a seaweed body scrub at the Redwood Ranch in a half-hour."

"I've heard that place is nice."

"Edith gives me a discount."

I frown. "Edith, the Mysa hostess?"

"Yes. She works at Redwood Ranch. Best massage therapist in Monterey. Hands like a Huguenot milkmaid."

"I have one last question for you, and then I'll go." I take out my phone and hold up the blurry photo of the woman getting into the car earlier outside the hotel. "Do you know who this is?"

She frowns down at the photo for a moment, then almost recoils in shock. "I . . . I don't understand this."

"What?" I say. "Who is it?"

"That looks like Bronwen."

"What? You mean . . . Max's dead wife?"

"Yes."

"Was she a twin?"

"No, I don't think so. I mean, I don't know for sure. I only met her a few times." She pauses. "That doesn't make any sense. Bizarre. Are you sure you took *that photo* today?"

"Yes," I say. "She was sending a letter to a woman named Millie Hagerty. Does that ring a bell?"

Rosetta shakes her head. "No, it doesn't." She makes a point of rearranging her overplump lips into a polite smile. "I gotta go now, Sparkleface."

"Okay, thank you for taking the time to speak with me, Rosetta."

Orson opens a wary eye and keeps it trained on me as I turn and leave.

I get back into my car and Google *Bronwen Magnussen*. I spend the next several minutes scanning the various search results but there aren't many, other than a short obituary that gives very little information and no photos. No social media accounts, either. I guess being married to someone so wealthy, it's understandable that Bronwen would have been a private person who left little-to-no digital trace behind.

On the drive back home, I mull over everything I've observed in the last twenty-four hours. I heave a deep sigh. After all that's happened, I can't believe that I now have to go back home to the mundanity of book club. How can I return to normalcy when I've just uncovered a potentially huge clue? *Max's dead wife isn't dead?!*

13

Couples' book club gathers once every three months. Marty and I, our friends Kathleen and Larry Harris, and Gemma and Gavin O'Hara, comprise the group. Kathleen is one of my closest friends. When Zack left for Cal Poly last year, it felt like he was moving to the other side of the world, even though Pomona is only a day's drive away. It was Kathleen who came over with a pizza and let me cry all night. She and Larry were never able to have children, so she "adopted" Zack when he was born and assumed the role of favorite aunt. It pleased Marty and me to share him, since our family was so small. Kathleen owns a mobile pet-grooming service, *Fast and Furriest*, which services the Monterey area.

Marty comes into the kitchen while I'm whisking dressing for the tomato salad. He peers over my shoulder and into the bowl. "Can't wait for your first tomato salad of the season," he says admiringly. "I put on Chet Baker to start, and I've got John Coltrane and Sidney Bechet ready to go after that."

I always appreciate how seriously Marty takes the duties of

hosting, and specifically party music curation. His passion for his record collection is almost as intense as his love for birding. Every record in his vinyl library is assigned its own place on the shelf, sorted by lettered and numbered subsections.

"Babe, I need to ask you a favor." I look over at Marty, but I can see he's distracted.

He's walking over to a pedestal displaying my signature lemon cake, freshly frosted. "Mmm. My favorite. Can't wait for dessert tonight!"

I realize it's an opportune moment while he's giddy from the lemon cake, so I press on. "Marty, I need you to ask Tim if he can run a plate for me."

His brow furrows. "Run a plate?"

I increase my whisking speed, and my words come out in a rush. "Yes. See, I saw this woman today with Max's brother Claes after I ran into him at the farmers' market. It was strange. He wasn't acting like someone in mourning. So, I followed them around town and I got a picture of her car's license plate. Paul met up with me, and we found out she was mailing a package to a well-known art collector in Wisconsin named Millie Hagerty. I'm thinking maybe Claes has gone back to his old art-thieving ways, and he killed Max so he could steal some expensive artwork from him. So then I went to Rosetta Rawling's house to interview her, and she told me that the woman in the photos may be Bronwen. As in Max's dead wife! But I don't understand how that's possible. Even if she was somehow able to fake her death and go into hiding all these years, Claes said she died in a skiing accident. That's not exactly the kind of death that's easy to stage." I pause my whisking and look up at Marty's stunned expression, hoping that this reaction means he will finally take my "murder theories" seriously.

He takes in a sharp breath. "Back up. You've been out with Paul today?"

I squeeze my eyes shut. After hearing all that, his biggest concern is Paul?! I sigh. "Yes, I was with Paul. But there's no reason to be concerned. I know it probably sounds weird that I was spending time with my ex-husband, but we're only investigating a man's murder together."

He rubs his cheeks with his hands. "How reassuring."

I take out my phone and show him the photo. "Here's the license plate."

He waves it away. "No. I'm not asking Tim Kluver, a public official, to 'run a plate' for you. He's not a cop, anyway."

"He'll know someone who can help, though. It's a good lead, Marty. I could blow this case wide open!"

"I think you've been reading too many Raymond Chandler novels. Pretty soon you're going to start talking about 'dames' and 'crooks.' Don't you think it's possible you're getting a bit carried away? This is Carmel, California. Population three thousand."

I pour the dressing over the tomatoes and mix it all together, my nervous energy helping me with the task. "Please, babe. Do it for me?"

Marty leans against the kitchen island and studies me for a moment. "Do you think you should go back to that holistic therapist you were seeing?"

"Ha! No way. She was a flake. Those vibrating gongs gave me migraines."

"Well, I think you need to talk to someone. You've become obsessed with an incident that has nothing to do with you. Are you depressed? It's like you're in a funk or something."

"Read my lips, Martin Keane. This is not mid-life ennui. There is no funk. I'm practically funkless! In fact, this is the most exhilarated I've felt in a very long time!" I walk over to the oven and pull down the door, removing a tray of crab puffs baked to a crisp golden brown. "Look, you know I've always been passionate. Whether it was my interior design career, or ASMR, or helping Zack with his art class homework. Right now, I just happen to be interested in a real-life murder mystery. Okay?" I place the tray on a trivet and reach for the spatula. "Crab puff?"

He looks at me like I'm deranged.

"Oh. And I forgot to tell you that Gavin and Gemma canceled a couple of hours ago. Gavin's come down with something."

"Please tell me you're joking. We have enough food to supply an NFL training table!"

"All the more reason Paul will be a welcome addition, right? I told him to bring an appetite. Otherwise, it would just be Kathleen, Larry and the two of us. And that would be weird." I scoop a crab puff onto a plate for Marty and hand it to him.

He blows on it before popping it into his mouth. "Mmm," he says, pausing to savor the bite. "Little pillows of heaven." He gives my shoulders a squeeze. "Listen, we've got a great book, delicious food, and good wine. Let's try to enjoy our evening."

I give him a kiss on the cheek in agreement and carry the tomato salad out to the living room. Informality is key to book club night, but I always like to overdo it with an elaborate spread of food, a combination of textures and flavors that are bite-sized and self-serve. I arrange the salad next to my display of roasted Cajun shrimp, mushroom croustades, creamy brie cheese, and crusty slices of baguette from the farmers' market.

I'm a veteran entertainer. I learned everything from my mother, who taught me that making food for others is a privilege. "Every morsel, whether simple or fancy, should be presented in a way that says, 'You are worth my time and effort,'" she'd say to me. Those moments in her kitchen were probably the genesis of my love for everything sensorial. Even when I was in another room listening to her work in the kitchen — spoons stirring, beaters beating, knives chopping, timers dinging — those exquisite sounds tingled my synapses and brought my nerve endings to attention. Watching her arrange culinary masterpieces on our table was like visual ASMR. I remember dreaming of the day when I would create that same sense of ease, warmth, and deliciousness for my own family and friends.

The doorbell chimes.

"I'll get it," I say, wiping my hands on my apron as I hurry into the foyer and open the door.

Kathleen is standing on the front porch, alone, smiling brightly. Dressed youthfully in a boxy blazer and slim jeans, she's wearing very little makeup. Kathleen has an effortless, natural beauty untouched by Botox or plastic surgery, and her long, dark hair is always slightly tousled.

I give her a hug as she steps inside. "Where's Larry?"

She hands me a bottle of wine. "We're getting divorced."

I set the bottle down on the console table, fearing I might drop it. "You're what?" For a moment, I'm completely tongue-tied.

"I'm okay. Really."

In disbelief, I wait for her to react further. To fall into my arms, devastated. Or laugh, even. But she is the picture of calm. Utterly unmoved.

Finally, I manage to stammer out a follow-up question. "How . . . how is this possible? We just saw you two a few weeks ago and things were fine."

"They haven't been fine for a while," she says, shrugging off her blazer and draping it over her forearm. "I can honestly tell you, I'm happy. Relieved, actually."

"How did I not see this?" I say, touching my forehead.

Kathleen places a comforting hand on my shoulder. "Hon, I'm doing fine. Are *you* okay?"

I don't answer. Before I can follow my own train of thought, a soft knock at the door derails it. I open the door again to find Paul standing there. As he steps inside, I note his Ferragamo drivers, khaki chinos, and white linen shirt left open at the neck, exposing the tanned skin underneath. His cheeks and chin show a bit of stubble, speckled with gray. How has he managed to change so much since our divorce? Somehow transforming from a dopey man-child who only wore T-shirts into an effortlessly sophisticated gentleman straight out of the pages of *GQ*? Probably a woman sorted him out at some point. Couldn't have been an easy job.

He leans down and kisses me on the cheek as he says hello and hands me a bouquet of peonies and a bottle of champagne. Noodles gives a woof behind him.

"My favorite, thank you," I say, admiring the flowers. "This is my friend, Kathleen. Kathleen, this is my ex-husband, Paul, and his adorable blind rescue pooch, Noodles."

"Nice to meet you both," says Kathleen. She crouches down to pet Noodles and takes out her phone. "I'll show you my two rescues. This is Benedict Cummerbund," she says to Paul, pointing to an elderly tuxedo cat, "and this," she continues, scrolling to a photo of a black cat with yellow eyes, "is Nosfuratu."

Paul laughs. "What dashing fellows!"

As they exchange pleasantries, I think I notice a spark between them. A twinge of discomfort hits me. He is my ex-husband, after all. Not that I have any right to feel possessive of him. It's been three frickin' decades. The statute of limitations for "dibs" on Paul has long expired.

We make our way into the living room. I trail behind, continuing to process Kathleen's divorce news. The last time I saw her and Larry, everything seemed fine. Sure, Larry has a few idiosyncrasies that get on Kathleen's nerves, but what couple doesn't have little things that bug them? Is the divorce Kathleen's idea? She's such a strong, independent person. Perhaps she decided she really would be happier being alone. But why hadn't I ever detected that something was awry between them? Perhaps because I've been too wrapped up in my own issues. Oh my God, could I ever do something that drastic? Oh, right. I already did once.

As we enter the living room, Paul pulls me aside. "So I went back to Mysa," he whispers, "and the key to Max's rental wasn't there."

I frown. "You mean . . . it's missing?"

"Yes. It always stayed in a little tray on Max's desk because he used it as a second office. I asked Edith about it too, and she said it should definitely be there."

"Maybe the killer took it," I say. "We should monitor the house. See if someone goes there. You know, like a stakeout."

Paul nods.

"Okay," I say, processing this. "By the way, I realized I have a ton of footage from the party that I took for *Sips and Whispers*. We should go through it on my laptop together."

"Great."

"Hello, everyone!" says Marty, carrying a bottle of chilled champagne. He kisses Kathleen on the cheek and nods stiffly to Paul. "Please, help yourselves to the spread over there. We don't want to see any leftovers. Where's Larry?"

"Marty, can you help me with something?" I say, looking back to Kathleen with a face that says *Don't worry, I'll tell Marty* as I hustle him into the kitchen.

"What's going on?" Marty says. He stops at the center island and whips around so we're standing face-to-face. "I don't understand. Where's Larry?"

"They're getting a divorce!" I whisper-shout.

"What? Oh." He pauses for a moment to let the information soak in. "Well," he sighs, "I can't say I'm surprised to hear that."

I take a step back. "You mean, you knew about this already? Larry mentioned something to you, didn't he? Why didn't Kathleen say something to me sooner?"

"I swear I didn't know. He didn't tell me anything. I just kind of had this feeling that things weren't right with them."

I can't believe it. How did Marty figure this out before me? Am I the only person who didn't see this coming? I walk over to my laptop on the counter, unplug it, and scoop it up under my arm.

"What's that for?" he asks, nodding to the laptop.

"We're going to examine the footage I shot at Mysa."

"No way. This is supposed to be book club night, not 'let's play detective' night."

"Marty, I just want to look through some of this stuff while Paul is here and all of our memories are still fresh. Please?"

He gives a low, rumbling sigh. "I don't know how much patience I'm going to have for your pretentious, long-winded ex-husband tonight."

I frown. "How do you know he's pretentious and long-winded? You've barely spoken a word to him."

"Not true, I made an effort to chat with him at Mysa when you were mingling. I tried to make polite conversation, but the pianist started playing Bach so he started bloviating about the 'precision and logical structure' of the *Goldberg Variations*. Then I tried to change the subject, and somehow he got us onto Hellenistic pottery."

"Paul is a polymath. Many people find him charismatic. Sorry that he's so tedious for you."

"If I recall, many years ago, he was tedious for you, too."

His comment takes me by surprise. I didn't think Marty remembered anything I'd ever mentioned regarding my first marriage. But apparently, it had stayed with him. And now he is using it as ammunition against me.

I roll my eyes and march back into the living room. Spring

nights get chilly in Monterey, so Marty has a fire going in the fireplace. Paul and Kathleen have already poured themselves some wine, and I note that they are seated together on the fireside sofa, looking cozy.

"Well, I'm sorry that our group is missing three of our regulars this evening," says Marty warmly, rubbing his hands together. "But that doesn't mean we can't have some fun, right?"

We all nod in agreement and clink our wine glasses. I set the laptop on the coffee table and flip open the lid.

"So, *The Quiet American*." Marty holds up his copy. It's well-worn and thumbed-through, with sticky notes fanned out at the edges where he has marked key passages.

Kathleen leans forward. "Hold on a minute. Let's chat a little first. You guys were at Mysa last night, right? It's all over the news. Tell me everything!"

"Yes. Graham Greene can wait," I say firmly, opening my laptop and turning it on.

Marty rolls his eyes. "Please. We don't need to dredge up that nightmare. Paul is probably still reeling from all this." He turns to Paul. "Max was your business partner, I can't imagine how upset you must be."

Paul shrugs. "To be honest, I might feel better if we talk about it."

In my peripheral vision, I can see Marty tense up. I look to Paul, who gives me a subtle nod to "go ahead." I turn to Kathleen and proceed to recap how the previous night's events unfolded. Keeping it succinct, I mention Max's toast and presentation of the keys, the suicide text message and the horror of everyone finding his dead body on the rocks below. She listens, riveted.

I open the file of Mysa photos and videos that I've uploaded from my phone. First, I toggle to the photo I took of Max on the rooftop after the key ceremony, and then I point to each of the five people standing next to him: Rosetta, Daniel, Tess, Claes, and Edith. I explain how Paul and I agreed that this was our group of primary suspects. We then scan through the rest of the album together, studying the kaleidoscope of images. Max, surrounded by fawning guests. Edith, clutching a cocktail and talking to Claes. A female guest I don't recognize, staring out at the ocean view. Max's financial adviser, Daniel, sitting at the bar talking to a woman in a sequined dress.

"Wait, go back!" orders Kathleen.

I toggle through the previous images.

"There!" she says, tapping on the photo of Edith. "Look! Her drink is lighter than the others," she says, pointing to a few guests holding glasses that appear to be a darker color.

"It could just be the lighting," says Marty.

Paul looks at Kathleen appreciatively and smiles. "That's the *Carmel Sunset*," he says, leaning forward and looking closer at the screen. I can smell his cologne, a masculine, woodsy vetiver, the same one he always wore when we were together. "It's made with blue aquavit and topped with sparkling rosé. The rosé creates the ombre 'sunset' effect because it floats on top while the darker-colored, higher pH ingredients stay at the bottom of the glass. We offered mocktail versions of the drinks. This one was made with Seedlip and watermelon juice, so the colors didn't quite match. That does look like the nonalcoholic version."

"Maybe she's a teetotaler," I offer. "Or maybe she didn't want to drink while she was working?"

Paul shakes his head. "Max encouraged all of us to try the cocktails that night. The party was a celebration for the staff, too."

"Maybe she's pregnant," says Kathleen.

Paul turns to her and then to me, eyes shining. "Where did you find this woman?"

Kathleen smiles and gives a subtle nod, pleased with her deduction. She sits back on the sofa, reaching for her hair and pushing it back behind her ears. The firelight glints on Paul's wine glass as he extends it for a refill. Marty's knuckles whiten as he grasps the bottle tightly, pouring another one for him.

"I have an idea," I say. "Why don't we relocate to my ASMR studio above the garage? I have a big whiteboard in there that I use for planning my videos. Maybe we can chart out some of our theories?"

"Sounds great to me," says Kathleen.

Paul nods and stands up to follow her, taking the bottle of wine with him.

Marty grunts. "I'll get the lemon cake."

Lemon Caketini

Ingredients:

1.5 parts limoncello
0.75 parts lemon juice
0.75 parts vodka or gin
0.75 parts vanilla simple syrup*

Method:

Chill a martini glass
Add the ingredients to a shaker filled with ice and shake vigorously for 15 seconds
Strain into the chilled glass

*You can buy this or make it yourself. To make: mix equal parts granulated white sugar and room temperature water. Whisk together, then add vanilla bean paste, a teaspoon at a time, until well integrated. Repeat until the desired vanilla intensity is reached.

Moist, sweet lemon cake is best made with fresh lemons, not artificial flavoring. California is known for its lemons, and in particular the Meyer and Eureka varieties. My lemon cake is Marty's favorite sweet treat. Back when we first started dating, I came down with the flu and had to cancel our plans last minute. It was only our third date, so I was worried that Marty would think I wasn't interested and things might fizzle out. But to my surprise, he had soup and flowers delivered to my door every day until I got better. It was the most romantic thing anyone has ever done for me. On our first post-flu date, I made a lemon cake for him, and it remains his favorite to this day.

14

Two hours later, we're on our third bottle of wine, seated around the bar area in the Drinks Cabinet. It's become a murder mystery war room. The whiteboard I normally use to plan my weekly content calendar is now filled with theories and suspects. Looking at it, I feel a pang of guilt that I haven't posted anything to *Sips and Whispers* in two days. Normally, I keep to a strict posting schedule. Zack warned me about taking long breaks. *You'll lose engagement, Mom. Post regularly if you want to keep growing your audience. In the attention economy, it's more about quantity, not quality.*

We've spent the last few minutes discussing the suicide text. Paul got a screenshot of it from Daniel, hoping that there might be a clue in Max's final words. We've been examining it closely, but so far we've come up with nothing.

Marty sets his book down on the counter. Drumming his fingers on the cover, he stares off into that unknown place he retreats to whenever he's deep in thought or upset about something. I'm guessing it's the latter. I sense his irritation about the sharp detour we've taken from our standard book club routine. I acknowledge having some guilt about going off topic from his precious *Quiet American*. But the rest of us have already turned the page. We're talking about nonfiction now – a possible real murder in a "quiet American" town! Marty needs to learn how to pivot.

"What if Max didn't send the suicide text?" Kathleen asks. "What if someone took his phone and sent it pretending to be him?"

"Claes told me the police found his phone in his pocket," says Paul. "But even if someone took his phone for a bit and sent the text as him, how would they have Max's passcode?"

Marty clears his throat. "No one took his phone. Max definitely had it right up until he died."

We all go quiet and turn to Marty.

"How do you know that?" I ask.

He takes a nonchalant sip of his wine. "I remember because we were having that silly drink that tasted like melted taffy."

"The *Bananavit*," says Paul. "I didn't like that one much myself, but Max wanted something tropical and sweet to show aquavit's versatility."

"Well, I remember he was holding that drink while he was on the phone. He was having a heated conversation. At one point he dropped his phone. After he picked it up, he looked angry, like he wanted to throw it at someone. Then he used that cremains key and got into the elevator by himself."

"What time was this?" I ask.

"No idea," says Marty. "You told me to focus on the little details, so I did. But I wasn't watching the clock. I just remember the candy taste of the drink coating my mouth as I watched all this happen, and that was the second to last drink. He wasn't around for the *Fikatini*, remember?"

I nod, as something from my conversation with Rosetta clicks into place. "Wait a minute. I have an idea," I say, walking over to the whiteboard. I take the eraser and wipe it clean. "Let's reconstruct a timeline based on the cocktails. We can match people's recollections to what happened during which drink." I uncap a marker and draw a grid on the board. "Marty just gave us important information that occurred during the *Bananavit*, and earlier today, Rosetta gave me clues that happened during that same drink, and also the *Primeval Forest*." I pause and look to the group. "Five suspects. Eight cocktails. If each drink was served at precise fifteen-minute intervals, we can use them as our time stamps. We can't expect people to know the exact time of night when they witnessed something, but there's a chance they might remember what drink they were having."

Paul leans down and pets Noodles, who is asleep at his feet, snoring softly in a steady rhythm. "This is great. And we know Max died sometime between the *Bananavit* and the *Fikatini*, so that window will be critical to explore when we're talking to people."

With Paul's assistance, I write down the eight cocktails, in order, on the left-hand side of the grid, and create columns for each of the five suspects.

	Claes	Daniel	Rosetta	Tess	Edith
Malmo Fizz					
Primeval Forest					
Aquavit Negroni					
Tempus Fugit					
Carmel Sunset					
The Haunted Lingonberry					
Bananavit					
Fikatini					

I add three more columns for Paul, Marty, and me to record our accounts. "If we map out everyone's recollections against the timings of the cocktails, pretty soon we'll have a full picture of the evening. And we can use my phone footage to cross-reference any clues." I write down Marty's recollection into the *Bananavit* square linked to his name. In Rosetta's square, I add her story about going to the bathroom to dump out the same cocktail. I point to my column. "I'm going to rack my brain later and write down everything I can remember using the footage I took at Mysa to guide me."

Marty cuts into the lemon cake and serves each of us a slice. "Don't you think we should just leave this to the police?"

"They don't seem to think Max's death is suspicious, Marty. I think we're on our own."

I run my finger down the list of drink names, stopping at the *Primeval Forest*. I take down a few notes in the square that intersects with Rosetta's name, careful to fill it in as neatly as possible with all the details she shared with me. I steal a glance at Kathleen, who has turned to chat quietly with Paul. She slaps his shoulder as he whispers something in her ear and folds over with laughter. Kathleen is always such a flirt. Then again, so is Paul.

I tap Edith's square on the board with my marker. "If Edith is pregnant ... maybe it's with Max's baby? That would explain why Tess seemed so upset. Impregnating another woman would—"

Marty stabs a piece of lemon cake with his fork. "Do you hear yourself? Theorizing hypothetical melodramas about people we hardly know?"

Ignoring him, I turn to Paul. "Shall we start with our own recollections and go chronologically? Marty and I arrived late, so we didn't make it in time for the first cocktail, the *Malmo Fizz*."

"Ah. Too bad, that's my favorite drink," says Paul. "It's

an homage to Max's hometown, a variation on a gin fizz." He slouches back in his seat and stares at the whiteboard, tapping his fingers against his lips in thought. "I was running around a lot for the first hour of the party. It was kind of a blur. The only thing that sticks out in my mind is the way Daniel was behaving." He turns to Kathleen to explain, "Daniel was Max's financial adviser."

"Is that Daniel Williams?" asks Kathleen. "I groom his yellow lab, Bill Barkworth."

"His dog sounds like a financial adviser, too," says Paul.

She giggles and they share a smile. Yep, there is definitely a spark there.

"I noticed he was acting standoffish," Paul continues. "He was buried in his phone and not really socializing with anyone. His wife seemed annoyed with him, too. When I was making the rounds, asking everyone how they were liking the first drink, Daniel could barely bring himself to look up from his phone and talk to me."

I write this down in the cocktail grid.

"And then, when a server offered him a drink, he snapped at her. It was really rude. I almost said something because I get protective of the staff."

"I know Daniel had a problem with alcohol a while back," Kathleen chimes in. "His wife always keeps their liquor cabinet under lock and key. Maybe he was stressing that he might fall off the wagon?"

I add a few more notes to the squares on our cocktail chart as everyone contributes further information. Even Marty manages to muster the energy to add a few more details.

"The one thing that I remember distinctly was that weird little hoarse scream I heard," I say, turning to Marty. "Do you remember that? It was during the *Bananavit*."

"I vaguely remember you commenting on it. But I didn't hear the scream. You're the one with the preternatural sensitivity to sounds."

I write down the scream in the *Bananavit* square under my name. Then, off to the side of the chart, I write *BRONWEN??* in red. "We still need to figure out what this Bronwen thing could mean. Marty, are you sure you can't have Tim trace the license plate for us?"

He gives a firm "no" headshake. "That's overstepping."

I give a defeated sigh as Paul gets up and walks over to the board. He holds out his hand and I give him the marker. Below the grid, he writes: *MOTIVES*. Underneath that, he adds:

Claes: Jealousy over Max's wealth? Something to do with Bronwen? Affair?
Daniel: Off the wagon? Gets drunk and loses control?
Rosetta: Strange Tinctures business relationship gone sour?
Tess: Edith's pregnancy?
Edith: ???

Kathleen leans forward. "Money is a likely motive. You could find out who the beneficiaries of Max's will are from Daniel?"

Paul nods in agreement. "If the farmers' market mystery woman really is Bronwen, and she's not dead, then that means she's the one who has something to gain, if she and Max were still legally married."

Marty takes another bite of lemon cake, eyeing Paul suspiciously. "You're awfully quick to assess others' motivations, Agatha. But what about yours? You were Max's business partner. Is there anything you want to tell us?"

Immediately, I feel uncomfortable. "Marty, what are you driving at?" I give a nervous laugh and look to Paul, who seems to be taking it all good-naturedly.

Marty sets his fork down and wipes his mouth with a napkin. Silently, he gets up and walks over to the board. Selecting the red marker, he uncaps it and writes *PAUL* underneath the other names.

I'm beginning to realize this evening may have been a mistake. Now it's Marty who has the overactive imagination.

Paul smiles at me. "It's okay. It's a perfectly logical thing to consider."

I give him a sympathetic look. "You are many things, Paul Hammond. But you are not a killer."

Marty taps the marker against his cheek. "We established that the killer is likely to be someone close to Max. We also agreed that it must be someone who had access to the roof. I'm just noting the fact that Paul was Max's business partner, and he had access to the staff key via Edith if he wanted to use it."

Kathleen meets my gaze and we share a look of concern.

Paul laughs. "If I were the killer, why would I be here helping you?"

"That sounds exactly like something the killer would say."

"Okay, you two!" I snap, taking the marker from Marty. "Let's please get back to more plausible scenarios, shall we?"

A silence falls over us as we all stare at the whiteboard in thought.

"What if it was some kind of organized crime hit?" I offer. "I've been watching a lot of Scandi noir lately. Swedish gangs are definitely a thing."

"Oh, please," says Marty. "This is not about the Scandinavian mob. Have you been to Sweden? Their prisons are nicer than our airports."

"This Bronwen thing is bothering me," sighs Kathleen. "How can we confirm whether or not the woman in the photo is Max's dead wife?"

Paul shakes his head. "I don't know."

A pensive frown twitches between Marty's brows. "I might know someone who can help us."

15

"Nina Hernandez," says Marty, holding up his phone to show us a Getty Images photo of an attractive Hispanic woman in her forties. "She used to be one of my clients. Formidable businesswoman. She lives on a vineyard in Jolon. They make a remarkably good sparkling wine. But primarily, she's known for her liquor empire."

"I remember you talking about her," I say, grateful for Marty's sudden shift into helpful mode. Perhaps he had been feeling left out. "You told me she's kind of an adventurer, right?"

He nods. "She's a real character. Flies her own plane, climbs the highest mountains around the globe. Also has a penchant for dating younger men. And she knows everything and everyone in the world of alcohol. I have no doubt she's crossed paths with Rosetta and Max before, and it's possible she might even have known Bronwen."

"Sounds promising," I say.

"Where's Jolon?" asks Kathleen. "Never heard of it."

"It's just over an hour's drive south of here." He gives a

small smile. It might be the first time I've seen him smile all night. "Here, I'll give you a visual." Leaning forward, he places his wine glass on the counter. "So, if this is where we are in Carmel," he reaches for a crystal bitters bottle and places it a few inches away from the glass, "this is where Jolon is."

"Actually," Paul interjects, "I've been to Jolon. Lovely place. Quite small. It's a bit farther south and east than that." He reaches for the crystal bottle and nudges it away from the glass.

"Uh, no," snaps Marty. "I know exactly where Jolon is, and it's *here*." He reaches for the crystal bottle and pushes it back to its original location.

This competitive streak in Marty is usually only something I notice when he's playing pickleball. Sensing his growing irritation, I interrupt. "This is silly. I'll just look it up on my phone."

"We don't need to look it up," Marty says firmly. "Jolon is *here*."

As he reaches for the crystal bottle, his arm knocks over the glass of wine. It spills all over the counter, and some of the liquid drips down onto the carpet. An awkward silence falls over us like a weighted blanket as Paul reaches for a napkin and begins to wipe it up.

Marty gets up from his barstool. "It's apparent that no one came here tonight to discuss Graham Greene." He clears some of the glasses and marches out of the room.

I feel my cheeks flush with embarrassment as Paul gets up

and gathers an armful of empty cake plates. I give him a small "thank you" smile. He winks at me and walks out the door to follow Marty back into the house.

Kathleen turns to me sharply and lowers her voice to a whisper. "So, Paul's your ex-husband? You never mentioned how . . . attractive he is. You're back in touch? How did I miss this?"

I laugh. "I hadn't seen him in ages before last night. He knew about *Sips and Whispers*, so that's why he invited me. Just a marketing thing." I stop. *Was it really?* Was this fate or . . . by design? I begin to wonder if something else might be going on. He did look like he wanted to tell me something at Mysa . . .

"Is he single?" Kathleen asks.

With the glass of wine half-raised to my mouth, I freeze. Taken aback by the question, I pause to take a long drink. "Yes, I think so."

"Sorry. Gosh, I mean . . . I know he's your ex. Probably off limits, right?" she says, with a tone in her voice that suggests she wants me to respond otherwise.

"You know he lives in San Diego, right?"

"You say that like it's a bad thing. A long-distance relationship is the dream."

I stroke my earlobe in thought. "It is?"

"Oh yeah. Larry was around *too much*, you know? We were in a rut. That level of familiarity, it's stifling. I never had the opportunity to *miss* him."

"But you two were so *in it* together. I always saw you as true partners. Best friends."

"Ha," she laughs. "Best friends. That's the real kiss of death for any romantic relationship."

I take a long sip of wine as I consider Kathleen's words. I feel a sting of something. Is it concern about my own marriage? Or jealousy at the idea of Kathleen dating Paul? I'm not entirely sure.

We leave the Drinks Cabinet together and go downstairs into the house. Paul and Kathleen gather their things and head to the foyer, where he helps her with her jacket.

"So, what's our plan then?" I ask, turning to Paul.

"I think I should go over to the rental house tonight. Noodles and I can stake it out for a while. See if anyone shows up with the key."

"Good," I say, nodding. "Maybe I can go back to Mysa tomorrow and look around while it's still closed? See if there are any clues that the police missed?"

"Perfect. I can give you the code to get into the building and tell you where Edith keeps the staff key to the elevator."

"Okay," I say. "We have a plan."

16

I walk over to the nightstand and set my steaming mug of hot cocoa on a coaster. As I slide into bed, I revel in the exquisite sensation of the cool, silky soft sheets against my bare arms and legs. I've never once regretted the premium price I paid for them. I adjust the pillow tucked behind me as I lean against the tufted linen-upholstery headboard and open the lid of my laptop. I stare at the yellow sticky note reminder I've placed on the screen again: *Buy anniversary gift*.

For several weeks, the perfect gift idea has eluded me. Why can't I come up with something that would prove my devotion and yet knock his socks off? A personal trainer? No. Too insulting. Custom bobbleheads of us for his den? Uh, no. A David Yurman black rubber and sterling silver woven bracelet? Seriously? For a thousand dollars? No. *Is Marty putting the same effort into thinking of a gift for me?* I drum my fingers on the lid of the laptop, thinking . . . thinking . . . I reach for my hot cocoa and take a contemplative sip.

It's only 10:45 p.m., still early by my standards, but Marty is already sound asleep next to me. I always get energized at nighttime. This is when I do some of my best brainstorming and research for *Sips and Whispers*. I have so many questions popping into my head after the day's events. Why did Rosetta get so upset earlier? Who was the woman with Claes at the farmers' market? Could it really be possible that it was Max's wife Bronwen, who everyone believed to be dead?

I realize I feel even more confused than when I started this investigation. Nothing is crystallizing in my mind. Not like it does in crime dramas where there's an *aha* moment. I'm only having a *huh? wha?* moment.

Marty's feet begin moving wildly back and forth, and his breathing becomes irregular, as though he's running. Probably having his usual childhood dream of being chased by a "growl bear." This animal of his nightmares continues to pursue him into adulthood. I place a well-practiced, calming hand on his chest. He makes a small grunt and soon settles back down.

Taking a deep breath, I go back to my laptop and pull up the Mysa footage I saved to my desktop. I scroll through the various photos and videos. A picture of Rosetta catches my eye.

I shake Marty awake. "Marty! Marty!"

He jerks. "What is it? What's happening?" He sits up and puts on his glasses. "Where's my Swiss Army Knife?"

"Wake up! Look at this." I point to the photo on the screen. "Rosetta told me that she dumped out the *Bananavit* in the bathroom sink because it tasted so disgustingly sweet. But see this photo?" I show him an image of Rosetta holding a full, creamy yellow drink in her hand. "And then this one a few frames later," I narrate as I toggle forward to an image of Rosetta standing near the fireplace, talking to a man with a service dog. She's holding the half-drunk *Bananavit* up to those voluminous lips of hers, wrapped sensually around the straw. "She's drinking it here in this picture, and it's half full. That's contradictory to the statement she gave me."

"So, she lied to you about drinking a drink. You interrupted my R.E.M. sleep cycle to tell me this?"

"The *Bananavit* was served right around the time of Max's death. Don't you think that's strange? That she lied about not drinking *that* drink?" I turn back to my laptop screen.

"You've become obsessed. It's not healthy. What about *Sips and Whispers*? Won't your followers be wondering what's happened to you?"

He has a point. I haven't posted anything since Wednesday morning. Tomorrow is Sunday. Over the years, I've found Sundays and Mondays to be my lowest engagement days, so I usually avoid them. That means the soonest I could post would be Tuesday. Nearly a week of inactivity is not good. But then again, if I lose a few followers, so what? This mystery is what's calling me now, and I need to see it through.

"Today was exciting, Marty. Following a mysterious woman. Taking surreptitious photos. Interviewing suspects . . ."

"I think I've heard enough about the wonderful time you've been having with your ex-husband."

I frown. "I'm talking about the excitement of a new experience. There's no reason to be jealous."

"Ha! Jealous? Of Mr. Barely-Has-His-Life-Together-For-The-First-Time-At-Middle-Age-With-His-Tiny-House-And-Blind-Dog? No, I'm pretty sure I'm just fine." He lays back down and punches his pillow to fluff it.

My phone buzzes. It's a text from Paul:

No visitors to the house yet. I'm going to stay in the truck overnight and watch for as long as I can. Maybe you could take over sometime tomorrow?

I text him back a thumbs up and turn to Marty. "Paul says there's no action yet. He's over at Max's rental, watching the place."

"He's staking it out?"

"Yes, just for twenty-four hours or so."

Marty groans and we lapse into silence. He closes his eyes, although I can tell he is nowhere close to falling asleep. Normally, I would know exactly what he's thinking, but this time I'm not so sure.

He speaks to me without opening his eyes. "I don't like your ex-husband hanging around like this."

"I understand why you might feel that way. Really, I do," I say, heaving a deep sigh. "Please understand, I'm just wrapped up in the intrigue of this thing. Paul is charismatic, sure, but there's nothing between us anymore."

A MURDER IN EIGHT COCKTAILS

"That's the second time you've noted his charisma," he says, sitting up. "You know who else had charisma? Ted Bundy. Haven't you read that book by Ann Rule? I think Paul's a bustard."

I turn my head sharply to face him. "That's out of line, Marty. You hardly know him. Now you're comparing Paul to Ted Bundy and calling him a bastard?"

"Not a bastard. A *bustard*. They're a bird species known for performing unusually spectacular mating displays. They inflate their air sacs and puff up their chests before they jump and twirl around all over the place. They're ridiculous birds, frankly."

I sigh. "It's all just taxonomy to you, isn't it? Categorizing people and giving them labels."

Marty turns away from me and lays back down. A long silence stretches out between us.

Realizing I've probably tested his patience one too many times today, I soften and choose my next words carefully. "Babe, I'm glad that you've found your birding passion at this stage in life. But I'm still exploring mine, okay? Today it's ASMR. Once upon a time it was interior design. And it might be something completely different tomorrow."

"So you want to pursue a degree in criminology, is that it?"

"Don't be facetious. Aren't you concerned at all that middle age isn't going to be interesting? I am. I refuse to be bored."

"Well, I'm sorry I can't be more exciting for you, Madame Bovary. You know, you have to cut me some slack here. This whole 'thing' you have going on . . . this attitude . . . it's new. You weren't so restless before."

"What is this 'before' you're referring to, Marty? There was no different 'me' before." I pause. "The other day, on NPR, I was listening to this interview with a sociologist who was saying how marriage, as an institution, was initially created when people had much shorter life expectancies. Here we are, together twenty-five years, and we're only starting the second *half* of our adult lives."

"Wait a minute. You don't think we've been happy these last twenty-five years?"

I shrug. "We were too busy to know. We both had full-time jobs and a child to raise. There wasn't time to ask questions about what we wanted other than whatever a situation called for in that moment. But now that we've retired, *all we have is time*. So. Much. Damn. Time."

Marty gives a subtle nod. "It does feel like time has, I don't know, slowed down lately."

"Do you think we did the right thing? Retiring early? Maybe we should have worked longer. I could have done more with my interior design business. Or tried something else. Don't you want to blaze new paths?"

"Do we really have to 'blaze' new paths? Can you use a slightly less scary word? Sure, fine. Let's wander some new paths. I'm happy to amble around, see what's out there. But all this talk of 'blazing' is inflaming my head." He wrestles with his pillow and tries to settle back down. After a minute, he reaches over to the nightstand drawer and pulls out an eye mask and arranges it over his eyelids.

I gaze over at the framed photo of Zack on my nightstand. When Marty and I got married, I was initially ambivalent about having children. Motherhood simply wasn't on my radar. I thought it would be wiser to devote our energies to keeping the marriage intact. I didn't want to fail again. Children would add chaos and distraction to our lives. But Marty very much wanted a little Keane or two. He was persistent, so we struck a deal — we'd have one child. It was the right decision for us, and how lucky we were when Zack came into our lives.

Now that he's away at college, I sometimes find myself dwelling on what he might be doing at any given moment. I wish I could press a button and see where he is on a screen somewhere. I'm not a helicopter parent. I simply miss knowing what he's up to. The little mundane things, like what he ate for lunch. Even though we talk or text a few times a week, it's not the same. Being a mother means everything to me. I get emotional just thinking about how fortunate we are to have Zack. I had wrongly assumed a child would test our marriage. Now I worry he might have been the glue holding us together. Those eighteen years went by so fast. Why have the months since he left felt so agonizingly slow, as if we were drowning in quicksand?

I shift against my pillow. "Do you ever feel like Zack doesn't need us anymore?"

"It's his first year away at school. He's just at that age." Marty sighs. "I miss him too. Why don't you ask him to come home next weekend?"

"No, no. He's having a good time. I don't want to be one of those mothers who cajoles their kid into visiting more than they want to. And anyway, we'll see him plenty this summer."

He touches my arm. "You should be proud that he's so independent. We raised a good kid."

I nod. "Well, I might as well tell you that I'm planning to go back to Mysa tomorrow. Paul gave me the entry code."

Marty sighs and pulls up the eye mask. "Please, I'm begging you to leave me out of this. I need to get some sleep. I have the Frog Pond hike tomorrow."

"I'll take that as an 'Okay, dear.'"

"Go ahead. Now, are you ever going to go to sleep? The glow of that laptop is burning my retinas." He puts the sleep mask back on and pulls the duvet up over his head.

"In a minute. But first I need to ask you something."

A muffled voice grumbles from under the duvet. "Oh God. What now?"

"I want you to help me stake out Max's rental house tomorrow night, okay? Paul said he can handle it for twenty-four hours, but he'll need a break after that."

Marty doesn't respond.

"Babe, don't you see? The three of us, you, me, and Paul, we could be . . . we could be like an investigative supergroup!"

He throws back the duvet and sits up. "Sorry, but no. I'm going birding tomorrow."

I persist. "You know what a supergroup is, right? It's when members of a band, each with an individual talent, come together to form something bigger. Aristotle's thing about the 'whole being greater than the sum of its parts' or whatever. Like The Traveling Wilburys or—"

Marty holds up a hand. "Um, excuse me, I know what a supergroup is. No supergroup has ever surpassed its antecedents. The Traveling Wilburys were probably the best of the bunch and they only released two records. Pretty sure no one is still talking about Squackett."

I raise an impressed eyebrow.

He gives a self-satisfied nod. "If you'd like more supergroup history, I can give you a tour of the supergroup section of my record collection. It's in 42E."

"Marty, don't you see? That cataloging mind of yours could be brilliant at this detection stuff. With all your paramilitary birding equipment and your skills of memory and observation, you could be better than Paul and me combined!" I close the lid on the laptop and look him straight in the eye. "Will you please just come with me on the stakeout tomorrow?"

"Don't you think round-the-clock surveillance of an empty rental house is overkill?"

"Please? It would mean so much to me."

He runs his hand along his chin. "I'll probably be too tired to go to the Frog Pond tomorrow anyway." He turns to me.

"If I go, will you make me a pecan pie? You haven't made one in a while."

I break into a beaming smile. "Absolutely."

"With the bourbon-vanilla whipped cream?"

"Deal."

Marty meets my eyes, then shakes my hand. Suddenly, he pulls me tightly to him in an extended hug. As if he's afraid to let go.

Sunday

17

In the daytime, Mysa looks foreboding against the dreary, overcast sky. Its sharp, modern angles dramatically cut into the steep cliffside, and I can hear the frothy waves crashing against the rocks below. I feel a sense of trepidation as I turn the car into the entrance. The harsh reality of what happened here just two days earlier settles over me like cold, murky water. I get chills as I cross the parking lot. The evening of Max's death scrolls through my mind like a slideshow as I climb the steps to the entrance and punch in the security code that Paul gave me.

"Hello?" I say, edging the door open as I cautiously enter the space.

There's no answer. It makes sense that the place would be empty at noon on a Sunday, two days after the owner died so tragically. But I don't want to take unnecessary risks, so I call out again. No reply. I cast my eyes around. Most of the furniture has been pushed out around the perimeter of the main room. I scan the pristine bar, the hallway leading to the elevator, the ticking clocks on the walls. Nobody is here. The whole atmosphere of the place has shifted since the night of the party. All the glamour and mystique is now tempered with a deep and silent sadness.

I close my eyes and try to visualize Max strolling around, admiring this gorgeous property he restored to its former glory. His California Dream. I wander into the bathrooms. Everything, even a small back area for staff only, is immaculately presented, right down to the smallest details.

Thoughts flash through my mind of Max plunging from the rooftop ledge. Skull cracking as his body slams onto the rocks of the cliff below. The image chills me. I need to see for myself if there is any evidence of a struggle up there, but first I want to explore the lower level.

I walk toward the spiral staircase that leads to the floor below and survey my surroundings as I make my way down. The lower level is windowless, except for a pair of sliding glass doors to my right on the north side of the building. There are a couple of offices, a cloakroom for staff, and a large storage area. As I wander around, I note a set of metal, pull-out art racks. I go over and begin to flip through them.

There are about fifteen works in total. Evocative, black-and-white photographs of different people. They all have a similar, cinematic style, and are signed by an artist whose name I don't recognize, *Riis*. There isn't much to see otherwise. A few old tables and chairs. No records or documents anywhere. This level is strictly utilitarian, meant for storage and staff belongings. Satisfied with my examination of the space, I now have a fairly good grasp of the layout and decide to go explore the rooftop. I turn around to head upstairs.

I pause. It's almost imperceptible at first, but I feel the distinct crunch of a few grains of sand under my feet. I take another step and feel another crunch. I pause, reminded of how I used gently crunching sand underfoot in a beach-cocktail-themed video for *Sips and Whispers* last summer. Perhaps I'm just being hyper-sensitive to my environment, as I always am, but this is strange. Why would there be sand in this room? It's squeaky clean otherwise. Mysa appears to be perched on a rocky outcrop of cliffside, and there is no beach nearby that I can see.

To my left, I catch sight of two tiny piles of sand behind one of the curtains of the sliding glass doors. I lean over and study them. It looks as though someone emptied sand from their shoes right there and tried to hide it behind the curtains. I reach into my purse for my phone and kneel down on the floor to take a closeup photo. I snap several more from different angles.

I try the glass doors and, surprisingly, they are unlocked. I open them and step outside. In the distance, there's a narrow wooden staircase built into a rocky slope that leads down to the water. I make my way over to the top of the stairs and look down. I can see they are steep, weathered, and treacherous. I slip off my flats and begin the descent.

As I make the trek down, the steps give way to sand, leading to a small beach. It's a little cove nestled inside the base of the cliff. I turn back and look at the steps, which were probably there long before Max bought the property. A secret exit for celebrities and lovers to sneak down to this private area unobserved. I kneel to scoop up some sand and let it run through my fingers. The texture is soft and fine as sea salt. I note a variety of rocks and shells in the sand, and a few cigarette butts as well. My ears tune in to the loud, rhythmic sound of the foamy waves. I stand back up, brush my hands together, and put them on my hips as I scan the area.

My eye catches a glint of something on the cliffside stairs. I walk over and crouch down to get a closer look. It appears to be an antique watch. The brand says Minifon, which I've never heard of before. I pick it up. Its face is partly smashed. The time reads 7:53 p.m. I go to my phone and scroll through photos until I find one where Max's arm is in the shot. I zoom in closer. It's tough to tell, but from what I can see, it could be the watch Max was wearing the night of the party.

I look up, studying the angle of the cliff, noting the distance from the rooftop above down to the cliffside stairs. Max's body was found on the west side of the building, and the watch is on the north side. Could it have somehow slipped off his wrist during the party and bounced down to land on the stairs? No, that's impossible. It landed so far away from the roof that it either had to have been intentionally thrown or placed here. But why would someone do that?

I close my hand around the watch, grasping its cold metal to my skin. How did the police miss this?! Then I gasp.

Fingerprints! Damn. I consider slipping it into my purse. No, there's all kinds of "purse pollen" rolling around in there, intermingling with my DNA molecules. The soft lining of my linen trousers would probably make for a more sterile and secure place, so I slip the watch into my pocket. I'll have to stop by the Carmel police station on my way home and talk to someone there.

I work my way back up the cliffside stairs and re-enter Mysa's ground level. Heading back up the staircase, I arrive at the main level again.

Time to get the staff elevator key. I open the door to the aquavit library with another security code Paul gave me. It's a large, octagonal room lined with mahogany shelves, topped with ornamental cornices. Aquavit bottles of every shape and size are elegantly displayed and lit from underneath. I admire the artfully designed lighting, which gives the room a majestic glow.

Paul explained to me that Edith keeps the elevator key in a small porcelain tray on the table in the library, since they keep it locked after hours. I prepare myself for the possibility that it might not be there, given that Max's rental house key has disappeared. But as I approach the table, I can see it's there. I take the key and slip it into my purse.

As beautiful as the aquavit library is, there isn't much else to see, so I turn back around and head toward the elevator. I note its position, directly across from the library's entrance. Inserting the key, I summon the elevator. As I ride it up, I look around. Something small and plastic is on the floor in the corner. I kneel down and pick it up. It's a long cap, like you might find on a tube of glue. I take a quick photo of it and place it in my pocket.

The doors ding and I step out onto the roof. I make my way over to the ledge, to the place where we found Max's body. Taking a deep breath, I edge myself closer so I can look down. I half expect to see some kind of marker or remaining police tape. But nothing is there. Just jagged gray rocks. No evidence of the horror of just two days ago. The world has already moved on.

I put on my reading glasses and examine the railing. No cracks. No blood. Nothing that shows any evidence of a struggle or fight.

Stepping back and keeping a safe distance from the edge, I reach into my bag and retrieve a pair of binoculars that I borrowed from Marty's stash of birding gear. Scanning the area, I note the ocean waves way down below crashing onto the cliffside. I can now see that because of the way the beach cove is positioned inside the cliff, it's not possible to view it from above. It truly is a secret beach. I can make out the faint outline of the cliffside staircase, but it blends so perfectly into the cliff that it would not have been obvious to the naked eye that night.

I step gingerly away from the ledge and make my way toward the long wall of the backbar, spotting a door that says "Fire Exit Only." I open it and look out at the narrow landing of the metal fire-escape stairs leading down to the ground. I hold the spring-loaded door open as I check the back side and note that there is no handle for re-entry. A door of this type is made to lock so that no one can re-enter the building. Obviously, the killer could not have used this as their way up to the rooftop to kill Max. But they could have used it as their exit. Unless, perhaps, the killer was Tess. She could simply have pretended to "discover" Max after pushing him off the roof, and no fire-escape exit would have been required.

Because I know I will be locked out once the door swings shut behind me, I decide I'll take the fire-escape stairs down to check if there are any clues that indicate the killer exited via this route. Then I'll re-enter Mysa through the main entrance.

I feel something cold and hard press against the back of my head.

"Don't move," says a voice behind me.

18

My heartbeat pulses in my ears as I freeze in place. It's as if my joints have fused together, and I can't move. Who is pressing a gun into the base of my skull?

"Who are you?" asks the deep, male voice behind me.

A droplet of sweat rolls down my back. Mustering resolve, I suck in a shaky breath and pull myself together. "I'm . . . I'm Willa Keane. I was one of the guests at the soft opening two nights ago."

"What the hell are you doing here?"

I weigh my options. One route is to make something up, but what if I'm not convincing? What if I upset him more? Knowing that my answer means life or death, I decide to go for a version of the truth that omits my investigative intentions. "I was just having a look around because Max's death has really affected me. I thought maybe coming here would help give me some closure."

No reply.

I quickly try to deduce who it could be. Obviously, it has to be the killer, whoever he is. Why else would he be here in the daytime with a gun? Returning to the scene of the crime, no doubt. I think I detect a slight accent, but his voice is so clipped with intensity, it's hard to tell. I consider turning around to take a quick look-see. But discretion is the better part of valor, they say, so I stay put.

I ramble on in the hopes it will calm him down. "I live in the area," I say, taking on a conversational tone. "I have a YouTube channel about cocktails, *Sips and Whispers*. That's why Max invited me. He wanted me to promote the bar." I think I detect the faint odor of cigarette smoke.

"You shouldn't be here."

Finally, I'm able to identify the accent. Blunt consonants and throaty vowels. Swedish. It's Claes. I feel the gun ease off from my head and hear him step away. I'm still standing there, not moving, as I hold the spring-loaded fire-escape door open.

"It's depressing up here. Let's go to the bar."

I let go of the door. It closes behind me as I slowly turn around. It is indeed Claes, wearing a short-sleeved powder-blue polo and khaki pants. He looks like a golfer who's just lost his ball in the rough, and does not appear as threatening as he sounded a few seconds ago.

A long, uncomfortable silence stretches out between us. Seemingly annoyed at this unexpected situation, he shifts his weight, then turns toward the elevator and, together, we get in. As we ride it down to the main level, I keep my gaze fixed on the floor while I consider the fact that I'm in an empty building with a man carrying a gun. What the hell am I doing?! At least we're leaving the rooftop, so he obviously isn't planning to push me off the ledge. Maybe he's thinking a bullet in the head will be quicker? Sure, now that I've cut my hair into a stylish bob, lost ten pounds and am feeling like I've achieved "peak Willa" — *now* is my time to die? Hopefully Marty gives *The Carmel Pine Cone* a recent photo of me.

"Sorry," Claes says, finally breaking the silence. "I didn't recognize you. I thought you might be the killer coming back to clean up evidence."

The elevator dings and we exit, heading toward the bar. He looks back at me. "Do you like Pappy Van Winkle?" he asks, placing the gun on the counter and selecting a couple of drink glasses.

My mind is still spinning, trying to orient myself to this sudden 180. A minute ago, I feared he was going to blow my head off like I was in a Martin Scorsese movie. Now, here we are, sitting at this gorgeous bar like old friends, preparing to toss back some expensive bourbon.

"I've never had it before, but I'd like to try it," I say, eyeing the gun.

He pulls the cork off the bottle and pours two fingers' worth for each of us. "Here's to life's mysteries," he says, handing me a glass.

Hesitantly, I take it. I swallow a small sip and purse my lips as the fiery sensation of the whisky warms my throat. "Whoa. That is not what I imagined it would be."

He stares at me. It's unnerving. Trying to keep calm is a struggle, with the gun lying so close to his free hand.

I decide to address the Max issue head-on. "You said 'killer' a moment ago. You don't think Max committed suicide?"

Claes tilts the drink toward his lips, then pauses. "Of course he didn't," he responds, seeming to snicker at the thought. "He had a beautiful life."

"I agree with you," I say cautiously, not sure where this might be heading. "I want to help you find out what happened to your brother."

He takes a swallow and smiles appreciatively. "Now that's an exquisite drink. Far better than aquavit, don't you think?"

As he enjoys its complexities, I study him up close. He's very different from his brother. His face is handsome but ruddy, and a little puffy. Probably from a lifetime of too much alcohol and smoking. His nose is crooked, as if it had been broken in the past and did not heal correctly. Although his overall demeanor has mellowed, something behind his clear blue eyes remains combative. I am looking at a complicated man.

My eyes drift over to the wall filled with clocks of every kind. "Why did Max have such a fascination with time?"

He sighs. "Max and I were raised by our father. He worked in the operations department of Sweden's railway system." He nods toward a beautiful gold railroad chronometer pocket watch displayed on the wall. "That was our father's watch."

"What about your mother?"

"She died when we were very young. He was hard on both of us. Abusive. He was so rigid that, if we didn't get out of bed the moment the alarm clock rang, he would beat us. Or if we committed some other minor offense, we weren't allowed to have dinner." I watch his fists clench and unclench as he speaks. "Our lives were rooted in trauma, but Max and I each took very different life paths."

"How so?" I ask, doing my best to act clueless about his criminal history.

"Max became obsessed with punctuality and success. Everything was an effort to prove something to our father. To out-earn, out-succeed him. When Max made his fortune, he bought himself an Audemars Piguet. It was a watch our father always coveted but could never afford. That watch was Max's prized possession. It was older and more expensive than anything our father owned. Max acquired an extensive watch collection over the years. Each one he bought cost five or six figures, and he wore different ones around our father. Right up until he died. It was the ultimate 'fuck you' to him."

I think about the art I found in storage on the ground floor. Could this be a motive for Claes wanting his brother dead? Jealousy that Max could acquire any art he wanted? While, he, the no-good convict brother, had to steal art in order to get close to it?

Cautiously, I reach into my pocket to ensure that the Minifon watch I found in the sand is still there. It is. I feel the cracked face and pinch a grain of sand between my fingers. I wonder how Claes might react if I show him the watch and ask him to confirm whether it was Max's. Or is it possible that he was watching me when I went down to the beach? Could he have seen me pick it up? I decide on a wait-and-see approach.

I want to ask him so many more questions. About the woman who is possibly Bronwen. About Millie Hagerty, the Wisconsin art collector. The secret beach, too. But I feel too nervous to do it. I'm alone with a man who pulled a gun on me only moments ago. So I stay silent.

"When I was a kid," he continues, "I wanted to be an artist, but our father didn't approve. So, I gravitated toward some bad people in the art world who convinced me that there was a way to make big money by stealing art instead of making it." He averts his eyes. I can tell this brief moment of vulnerability has surfaced some dormant shame.

I nod and take another sip of Pappy in solidarity. "Did you ever get caught?"

He nods. "I went to prison for three years. It wasn't so bad. In some ways, it was the best time of my life. I didn't have to make any decisions, and I was able to reflect on what I wanted to do differently. You see, when Max was in his early twenties, something just clicked into place for him. He realized that if he didn't take control of his life, nobody else was going to help him. He inherently knew how to steer himself in the right direction – toward all of this," he says, gesturing around the room.

"And you?"

A wry smile slowly creeps across his face. "I'm sure you're sensing an emerging theme here. I messed up my life but managed to survive and move on, in spite of our father's tyrannical behavior. And Max . . . well, he flourished and became a huge success, not despite our father's abuse, but because of it."

I feel a deep pang of sadness for Claes and his lonely childhood. In a way, he reminds me of Rosetta, both of them lost souls who could never overcome perceived inferiority to their sibling. "Were you two competitive as adults? What was your relationship like?"

He takes a moment to consider the question, then nods toward his drink. "I think we were like this bourbon. It was the aging process that really deepened things over time and created an intense bond between us." He takes a sip. "We weren't always close, though. When I was in prison, we didn't speak at all. I reached out and asked him to help me get a better attorney, and he refused. He told me he was ashamed of me."

I nod in silent understanding, not sure what else to say.

"But that was many years ago. After I got out, he asked me to forgive him for being so cold, and he helped me start *Deathsmith*. Things had been good between us for a while, although I will say I sometimes felt like another part of his collection."

Furrowing my brow, I make eye contact with him. "What do you mean exactly?"

A MURDER IN EIGHT COCKTAILS

He twists on the barstool. "Max was a collector. First, of watches. Then of people. He liked broken, lost souls. People he could manipulate and control."

I flip through my mental dossier of the other suspects: Rosetta, Tess, Daniel, Edith. This description certainly seems to apply to Rosetta. I'll have to see if it lines up with the others, too. Although I'm not sure psychoanalyzing them will get me any closer to uncovering who killed Max.

"So what's next?" says Claes, brightening into an almost cheerful tone. "Are you going to continue on with this investigation of yours?"

"Investigation?" I ask, hoping my feigned bewilderment is convincing.

"Come on," he says. "Why else would you come here? You must be digging into this. Like one of those true crime podcasters."

I shake my head. "That's not me. True crime isn't my brand. I'm just a retired interior decorator who makes relaxing cocktail videos on YouTube."

"Look, I'm glad you care. No one else seems to. Certainly not the police."

"Well then," I respond, seizing the opportunity. "I guess I'd like to know if you remember anything strange from Friday night?"

Claes pauses. He appears to be taking a moment to reflect and replay the night's events in his head. I watch him flinch as he concentrates. "I can't remember anything that seemed out of the ordinary." He drains the rest of his drink. Suddenly, his coldness has returned. "Are we almost done here?"

"Of course," I say, nervous that the tension in the room has resurfaced. "I'll head back home. Just one last question for you. Do you remember anything distinctive about any of the eight cocktails that were served?" I ask, hoping my gentle prodding might stir a memory.

He goes quiet while he considers the question. "I remember how delicious the *Aquavit Negroni* was. Simple and classic. It was the only drink that I liked."

I can sense that Claes is holding back, and I won't get much more out of him. "Okay. Well, thank you for talking to me."

"Sorry about the whole gun thing."

"Don't apologize," I say. "I want to lead an interesting, unpredictable life. And you've made today . . . exciting."

I catch an ever-so-slight smile pull at the corners of his lips as I wave goodbye to him and hustle out to the parking lot.

The sky is fading into a blend of pink and gold as the sun lowers on the horizon. As I reach into my purse for my car keys, I have to clench my hands to stop them from shaking. I get into my car and pull out my cocktail notebook and pen. I've copied down all the latest information from our whiteboard grid onto it. I look at the empty squares in the Claes column. He had few recollections from the night of the murder, and has given me little that's useful, other than a glimpse into Max's psychology. I tighten my grip on the pen in frustration as I jot down everything I can recall him sharing.

Then I turn to a fresh page and write down the three things I've learned in the past hour:

1. Max's watch was removed from his wrist and thrown from the rooftop at 7:53 p.m., well after he died.
2. Sand is on the lower level of Mysa, meaning someone took the cliffside staircase up from the secret beach. Probably after smoking a cigarette.
3. Claes is definitely hiding something.

19

The Carmel police station is smaller on the inside than I imagined it would be. There are no perps handcuffed to benches or hookers in miniskirts milling around waiting to be booked, as I've seen on television. Just a small reception desk, some notice boards, and several plastic chairs lining a wall. The seventies décor and sunlight streaming in give it the feel of a high school principal's office.

I'm unsure how to approach the officer stationed at the front desk behind a glass screen. As I walk toward him, I decide that I need to sound authoritative, like a woman not to be messed with. I think of the bustards Marty mentioned that puff up their chests to impress. I take in a breath and lower my voice an octave.

"I need to talk to a detective," I say. "Now."

"Uh," says the cop behind the desk.

I squint to read his name tag: Sergeant Fowkes. He's a rotund man, in his sixties, with a long forehead, made even more so by a severely receding hairline. Though his bushy mustache proves his head is still capable of growing hair. I clear my throat and channel my best *Dirty Harry*. "Sergeant Fowkes, I'm here to discuss Max Magnussen's death. I think it was a murder."

He gives me a once-over that I detect to be equal parts fear, scrutiny, and befuddlement. "Okey-dokey."

I check my reflection in a nearby mirror. Maybe it's the short hair that's giving me "Don't mess with me, buddy" vibes. Whatever it is I am now giving off, I like it and decide I should run with this new persona.

He turns around and reaches above his head to a shelf lined with folders. He pulls one down and hands me a form. "Have a seat and fill this out, please."

I'm a little disappointed that I have to deal with red tape first, but decide it's best to comply. He gives me a clipboard and I take a seat. I fill out my name, driver license number, and address in block letters on the form. I get up and slide it under the glass screen.

I return to my seat and pull out my phone to text Paul:

I'm at the police station now. Hopefully the cops give this thing a closer look after I talk to them. Btw, I ran into Claes at Mysa, and he pulled a gun on me ... but I'm fine, I swear! He thought I was an intruder. Don't tell Marty or he'll freak out! Oh, and I found Max's watch!! Someone threw it from the roof AFTER he died.

I put my phone away and, for a brief moment, I feel a tug of something. I realize it's sadness. I'm sad that Marty, the first person I usually share everything with, is not the person

I want to immediately text about the day's events. I sigh and stare at the walls. Posters that look like they were hung in the 1980s decorate the space. Curled at the edges, they warn me against drugs, smoking, human trafficking. Nothing warns me against trying to solve a murder on my own. Ten minutes of twiddling my thumbs later, a tall female police officer appears in front of me.

"Hi, Ms. Keane," she says. "What brings you here?" She has creamy, round cheeks and a matronly figure that's stuffed into an ill-fitting uniform. Her nametag says "Officer Landry." I sense that she enjoys peering down at me from her nearly six-foot perspective. Her tawny mop of hair, permed into tiny curls, reminds me of alpaca fur.

I stand up and produce the watch from my pocket. "Hello, Officer Landry. You might recognize me. I've been a resident of Carmel for many years, and I was at Mysa the night Max Magnussen died. I went back there today and found this." I hand her the watch. "This was Max's watch. It was lying on the ground, on the north side of the building, far away from where his body was found. It appears that it had been thrown or planted there. And the time stopped at 7:53." I pause, partly to catch my breath and partly for dramatic effect. "I believe Max died sometime between the serving of the *Bananavit* and *Fikatini* cocktails, which means approximately 7:30 to 7:45. This watch was removed from his wrist and disposed of after his death."

She frowns at me, then down at the watch.

"I believe he was murdered." I add, as calmly as I can manage so she doesn't think I'm some unhinged woman playing amateur sleuth. I continue on, recapping my further suspicions about why and how Max's death might be foul play. I outline the five main suspects and highlight Claes' history as an art thief. Landry's face is tough to read. "And then," I continue, "Claes pulled a gun on me. I do think he's the primary suspect. Although it's possible someone else—"

She holds up her hand. "Hold on. He pulled a gun on you? When was this?"

"Earlier today. I showed up at Mysa unannounced and he mistook me for an intruder. But I don't want to press any charges. We talked. He didn't hurt me."

She raises an eyebrow. "Come with me. Let's sit down."

I follow her down a narrow hallway. Anticipating a cold, windowless room with a metal table and a bare light bulb, I clutch my bag close to me. To my surprise, we enter a clean, L-shaped office with potted plants and a small window. I sit down across from her and proceed to recount the last forty-eight hours in further detail as best I can. She listens to me, stone-faced and silent. I pause to take a breath.

"Oh! And I found this in the elevator," I say, producing the small plastic cap from my pocket. "I did some Googling, and it looks like it's a needle cap. There were also some cigarette butts in the sand, close to the area where I found Max's watch. Claes and the farmers' market woman – who may or may not be Bronwen — are both smokers! Don't you think there could be a connection?"

She clears her throat. "Ms. Keane, nearly one in five people are smokers."

I hesitate, trying to read her. Years of practice in hiding my true thoughts from my interior design clients allowed me to keep my expression neutral while I listened to their sometimes ill-judged instincts and coached them toward better choices. Officer Landry is doing the same thing to me right now, I can feel it. "Yeah, but come on, in Carmel? Nobody smokes in Carmel!"

She sighs and shakes her head, as though she's annoyed at even having to explain this to me. "The coroner has ruled this a suicide. Max had been drinking, and his ex-girlfriend told us he had been depressed about their recent breakup. She believes suicide makes sense. Not to mention the note sent to his friends from his password-protected phone."

"Ex-girlfriend?" I say. "At the party, Max spoke about her like they were still together. Don't you think that's strange?"

Landry sits back in her chair and folds her arms. "Ms. Keane, California's death investigation system is a complex machine. It's a patchwork of police officers, emergency workers, medical examiners, freelance experts, and coroners. We work together in concert on any suspicious death to determine what happened. Everyone I work with on these things is professional, dedicated, and serious."

I take a breath. I've read how police officers don't take

kindly to "proactive" members of the public, but it's entirely different and very frustrating encountering it in real life. It feels like I'm screaming into a void. "Look, I understand why Max Magnussen's death was ruled a suicide. The text message makes it seem definitive that he did it. But let me give you the watch at least, as evidence?"

Landry looks up at the ceiling. Pursing her lips, she blows out a slow stream of air. Then she directs her eyes back down at me. "No thanks." She produces a business card. "Look, I appreciate you taking the time to come here and tell me what you know. Call me if you come across anything else."

My emotions are bouncing around in my head like tennis balls in a dryer as I grip the steering wheel on my way home. I cringe at the way Officer Landry dismissed me, as if I were some sour woman who's exceeded her "Best if used by" date.

I pull into our driveway. How much should I tell Marty? I manage to unlock my fingers from the steering wheel and walk into the house, resolve flowing back into my veins. I plonk my purse down on the kitchen counter.

Marty comes in and eyeballs me for a minute. He's adept at reading my moods after twenty-five years of doing life together. "No luck today?"

I decide to give him the broad strokes. "It was fine. I found some clues. Including Max's watch," I say, holding it up. "It was thrown from the building *after* his death."

Marty raises an eyebrow. "Really?"

"But the police don't care. I offered to let them keep the watch, and this woman, Officer Landry, her exact words to me were, 'No thanks.' Can you believe that?! *No thanks??*"

"The watch thing is interesting. I'll give you that."

"Maybe this is all part of a big cover-up. That rooftop could have something to do with it. Maybe Max bribed public officials so he could open Mysa and that's why he was killed. Landry could be protecting the local government from some big exposé. If this ever got in the papers, it could ruin her career."

Marty shakes his head. "Listen to you. I think you've seen *Chinatown* too many times. This is Carmel. We don't even have house-to-house mail delivery, let alone a 'system' that can bring somebody like Max Magnussen down."

"I guess you're right."

"Don't you think all of this is a dead end? The police don't think there's a problem. What more can you accomplish?"

I tense up. "Listen, we had a deal, Marty. We're doing the stakeout tonight. You love Dashiell Hammett, come on! We'll be just like Nick and Nora in *The Thin Man*. Don't you want to be a fun-loving couple that solves crimes together?"

He sniffs and doesn't respond. We are having a marital standoff.

"Fine. If you're not coming with me, I'm going solo. But you're going to have to lend me those big-boy binoculars of yours, and I want the night-vision goggles, too."

He gives me a look that says, *You cannot be serious.* I return his look with a look that says, *I am dialed up to maximum seriousness. Is this really the hill you want to die on? Because you will die on it.*

The staredown lasts about three seconds before he caves. "It's almost six," he says, looking at his watch with a resigned sigh. "Let's eat the leftover tomato salad and crab puffs, and then we'll go."

The Stakeout

Ingredients:

1.5 parts wood-aged rum
0.5 parts banana liqueur
0.25 parts yellow Chartreuse (green works well, too)
0.25 parts honey syrup (equal parts honey and warm water)
3 dashes black walnut bitters

Method:

Add all the ingredients to a shaker filled with ice and shake vigorously for 15 seconds
Strain into a Nick & Nora glass

Legendary New York City bartender Dale DeGroff, founder of the Museum of the American Cocktail, popularized the usage of the Nick & Nora glass. It's a delicate, spill-resistant alternative to the martini glass, which he named after the main characters in Dashiell Hammett's fifth and final novel, *The Thin Man*. Published in 1934, the book features a fun-loving, cocktail-drinking couple, Nick and Nora Charles, who solve mysteries together. The glass has a long stem and a bowl shape, which keeps drinks cooler longer due to its small surface area. Ideal for serving drinks "up" (without ice), a Nick & Nora glass is often used for liqueurs, vermouths, and aperitifs.

20

Max's rental home is only a short drive away, just two miles north of Carmel. I checked it out online. A 4,000-square-foot Craftsman ranch that looks surprisingly low key. I spent several minutes clicking through the home's photos, admiring its lovely coastal California interiors and bungalow-inspired coziness. All natural wood floors, Mission-style furniture, beamed ceilings, and bookcases filled with knick-knacks. I wonder if Max intentionally chose it out of a desire for an authentic Monterey experience during his stay or if an assistant selected it for him. Probably the latter.

It's a dark night, and the moon is obscured by clouds. Marty slows down at a sharp curve and turns onto the street ahead of us, Magnolia Avenue. It's a narrow residential street that, according to Google Maps, will soon intersect with the home's private driveway. I look at my phone to check our exact location. It isn't loading. Cell service is always spotty in this area. If we get lost, I might have to dig out the folded-up map in our glove box.

I haven't touched that map in probably twenty years, back

when Marty and I were younger and took weekend road trips to wineries up and down the state. It was a busman's holiday for Marty, whose job was advising vineyard owners on how to keep their grapevines thriving and producing, but we always had a great time. They felt like little adventures. Long stretches of open road, listening to good music, and discovering hidden gems together.

Momentarily lost in thought, I recall how we would sit across from each other at a table in one of the vineyard's tasting rooms or out on the terrace overlooking the rows of vines, holding hands over the dinner table as we talked animatedly. I try to recall the last time we held hands, and I can't remember.

He rolls down the windows as we drive along the street. The soft night air wafts in, drawing me back to the present. I have been to this area a few times before. Once for a wedding and another time for a fundraiser. It's beautiful but somewhat isolated, filled with trees.

As we near the last intersection, we spot Paul pulling away from the stop sign. He swings over to our side of the street and rolls down his window.

"Greetings, fellow squad members," Paul says, smiling. Noodles' snout suddenly appears from behind his head in the passenger seat.

"How's Noodles doing?" I ask.

Paul shrugs as he gives him a pat on the forehead. "I think he's depressed. He misses SoCal. There isn't enough smog here."

A MURDER IN EIGHT COCKTAILS

"You get some rest. You've earned it."

He gives me a wink, and we wave goodnight.

Marty continues down the road and we reach the cul-de-sac where the rental is. He slows down. "Where do you want me to park?"

"Over there," I say, indicating the end of the cul-de-sac, a few yards past the house.

He parks beneath some overhanging cypress trees that provide the perfect vantage point. He turns off the car for a moment and we sit quietly together in the dark. I know this will likely be a drawn-out endeavor, perhaps an all-nighter. But I feel exhilarated. Here we are, staking out a house!

"Now what?" asks Marty.

"We watch and wait."

He sighs and shakes his head, reaching into the backseat for a canvas tote bag.

"C'mon, babe. Don't you think this is just a little bit fun? We're on a stakeout!"

His head swivels toward me and he gives me a look that says, *You're kidding, right?* He sits back and runs his hand over his head. "What are we going to say if someone comes by and asks us why we're parked here?"

"Easy," I say with a wink. "We'll say we're making out."

Marty gives a sharp laugh that's a little too harsh and a little too dismissive.

We sit in a tense silence. I pull out my notebook and stare at the cocktail grid. My mind races as I consider the key suspects:

Claes, the ex-convict and artisan of ashes. Daniel, the financial adviser in recovery. Mistress of mauve-ness, Rosetta Rawling, aka The Bitter Woman. Tess, the love of Max's life, who doesn't seem to love Max at all. Edith, the taskmaster of timeliness. Which one of these people is the killer?

A loud crinkling sound makes me jump. I turn to see Marty opening a large bag of shelled pistachios he stashed in the canvas tote.

I frown. "I thought you didn't like pistachios. How come whenever I put pistachios in a cake, you freak out?"

"Pistachios are salty snacking goodness," he responds matter-of-factly. "They do not belong in sweets."

"You have too many rules. Pistachios can be a wonderful addition to many desserts. You would love my pistachio flan if you would just open your mind and try it."

"Trust me, I am getting enough nuttiness in my life from you, babe."

I shake my head and return my attention to the driveway.

Wordlessly, we watch and wait for something to happen. The street remains empty. Most of the homes' lights are off and the neighborhood is quiet.

"Shall we listen to some Puccini?" asks Marty, breaking the long silence.

"No. We need every one of our senses directed toward the task at hand."

"Fine." He plunges his hand into the pistachio bag again.

I slowly turn my head toward him. The bag-crinkling is

causing overwhelming sensations in my brain. "Do you mind doing that a little more quietly? You're ruining my stakeout experience."

He shrugs and grunts an inaudible dissent under his breath.

"Can I have the binoculars?" I ask, giving a weary sigh.

Marty reaches back into his canvas tote and hands them to me. "Would you rather be here with Paul?"

The way he says Paul's name has a sharp sting to it. I resist the urge to snap at him, even though I'm frustrated. Why does Marty keep getting worked up about the wrong thing? I don't want him to be jealous of my ex-husband. I want him to stop obsessing about birds and care about making the second half of our lives more interesting.

I take a calming breath. "Babe, Paul is just more into this kind of stuff than you are. Okay? Please don't be worried. This whole thing, it's an adventure, don't you see? We're in the middle of a genuine murder mystery."

Marty shakes his head. "Paul with his literary bon mots and his adorable blind dog. I promise you, he only keeps that dog around to get women." He munches on another handful of pistachios, and we sit in a charged silence.

For a moment, I consider letting his attitude slide, but then I decide that airing my grievances is necessary. We need to get it all out in the open. "This isn't about Paul, okay? I just wish you were open to new experiences. Didn't Kathleen and Larry's divorce shake you at all?"

"Larry's an egomaniac." He reaches for a bottle of water from the bag. "Kathleen can do better."

I throw my hands up. "That's not the point. The last time I saw them, they seemed okay."

Marty frowns. "Then what is the point you're trying to make?"

"I'm just saying that it feels like *The D Word* can happen to even the most solid, grounded couple. It's like there's this invisible fault line in every marriage. Unpleasant and unpredictable as it is, it only causes tremors from time to time, and we just accept that it's there. Until one day, all of a sudden, big tectonic plates shift, and it just splits wide open. Doesn't that scare you?"

He inhales deeply and touches my hand. "We have a good foundation. You don't have anything to worry about."

I rub my temple with my forefinger. "I wish that were true, but you don't know that for sure. I think we need to talk about what we both want to do with the next half of our lives."

A pair of headlights appear in the distance.

"Get down! Get down!" I shout.

We both scrunch low in our seats as the bright beams of the turning car pass over the windshield like a wandering searchlight. I peer over the dashboard, watching as the car turns slowly into the home's long, tree-lined driveway. It's a vintage Mercedes convertible. Just like the one that was parked in The Bitter Woman's driveway. From the security lights lining the entrance, I can see what appears to be a female driver wearing a mauve headscarf sitting low in the seat.

"Who is that?" Marty whispers sharply.

"I think it's The Bitter Woman! Rosetta! What do we do now?!"

Marty drops his head a little, sighing. "Give me the binoculars." He brings them up to his eyes and trains them on the house, making a few adjustments until he has a clear view. "Lights are going on in a few rooms. A person is moving from one room to another. It could be The Bitter Woman. Looks like her." He switches over to his night-vision goggles. "These have thermal imaging," he explains. After a long silence, he gasps. "Okay, I can see her now!"

"What's she doing?"

"She's turning on lights in two different rooms."

"Why did you gasp?"

"Sorry, I was just excited. These gadgets really work so amazingly well."

I roll my eyes and look at my phone. Still no cell service. I can't call Paul. Damn.

Marty lowers the goggles. "What could she possibly be doing in there?"

A muffled cry pierces the night air.

I grab Marty's arm. "What was that?!"

We wait in silence. I cock my head, straining to listen. All I can hear are the eerie sounds of crickets chirping and the gentle breeze tickling the leaves on the trees.

Another scream.

"Please tell me you heard that." I grasp the handle of the car door.

Marty grabs onto me. "Stop right there. You're not going anywhere."

I feel a tight knot of resentment high in my chest. Why does Marty keep stifling the high-octane thrills that this investigation is bringing into our lives? I am determined not to let his stubborn antagonism affect me. I open the car door.

"We're law-abiding citizens, Willa. What you're about to do is . . . I don't know what it is. I don't know if it's illegal or not. But I know it's dangerous. We're not going up there." He gives me a desperate, pleading look as he fumbles for his cell phone. "I'm calling the police."

I fold my arms across my chest. "And what are we going to tell them? A woman we barely know has pulled into the driveway of a dead man's rental house we're staking out? I was at the station three hours ago trying to convince them to help me. Officer Landry acted like I was creating drama out of nothing. They are going to be suspicious of *us*, not her!"

Marty tries punching 911 into his phone. Nothing. He shuts it down and turns it on again. He dials 911 again and hits send. Nothing. He slams the phone down on his lap.

"There isn't any service up here, Marty. I've already tried. We'll have to drive back down to the highway if we want to call the cops." I take in a deep breath. "I'm going up to the house to check it out. You can stay here and leave the car running, okay? Be ready to take off when I come back out."

"What are you talking about?" Marty's owl eyes are really bugging out from his head now. "You are not going up there alone. And I am not your getaway driver. This is insane."

"Listen, Marty," I begin, softening my tone, "just do this for me, okay? Come with me up there to check it out. We heard someone scream. We can't just drive off like nothing happened. After this, we'll go home, and we'll have a quiet night in with a movie and talk. Okay? Just do this *one thing* for me."

Marty looks down and slowly shakes his head in silent protest.

I steel myself. "Fine then. I'm going up there. And you can't stop me."

21

I feel my pulse quicken as we creep toward the house. I turn around and make eye contact with Marty, who's trailing along behind me. After some further back and forth, he reluctantly agreed to come along. He gives me a quick *be careful* look as we cross the front lawn. Fortunately, there is enough greenery to obscure us from view as we make our way to a large bay window. I crouch down and ease my head up enough to peer inside.

The lights are on, but I don't see anyone as my eyes glance over the spacious living room. Farther back, I recognize the home's open-plan kitchen from the online listing I reviewed earlier. I note a pair of sliding glass doors that lead out to the backyard and gesture for Marty to come have a look. He scowls as he sidles up beside me and takes a peek inside.

I turn my head and give him a nudge. "Do you see that?" I whisper, pointing to the Mercedes parked in the driveway. A bumper sticker with the words *Bitter Is Better* is illuminated by the yellow light of the home's lampposts. "That's definitely The Bitter Woman's car!"

Marty nods. "Yes, I see it. So what? I think we should go. I have a bad feeling about this."

"We heard her scream. What if she's injured? She might need help. We're just being upstanding members of the Carmel community."

"I don't like this," grumbles Marty.

I grab his arm. "Come on, we have to check on her."

He looks up at the sky, as if summoning courage from the universe. I hurry up the flagstone steps of the porch, cautiously approaching the front door, and knock.

"Hello? Rosetta?" My voice pierces the night air. "It's Marty and Willa Keane!"

"Why don't I get you a bullhorn? I don't think you yelled our names loud enough!" hisses Marty.

I press my ear to the door and listen. No response. "We're coming in!" I call out.

"Great. Now they know that the Keanes are polite cat burglars who announce their presence before breaking and entering!"

"Shhhh!" As I reach for the knob to turn it, Marty grabs my hand.

"Are you nuts? You're really going inside? A neighbor has probably already called the police! We need to leave. Seriously, I cannot survive a day in prison, Willa. I can barely eat regular food."

"It's unlocked. We're just going in to check on her. We have probable cause, you know."

"Probable cause?" he chokes out a laugh. "That's a legal rationale used by law enforcement. Not by retirees trying to add a little zing to their lives!"

I knock again and ease the door open. "Hello? Rosetta?" I call out into the house. "We're here because somebody sent us over from Mysa to get something."

Marty shakes his head in exasperation.

I call out into the house again. "Rosetta? Hello?"

No response.

I open the door wider and slip inside, gesturing for Marty to follow me. The light cast from the living room into the foyer is enough for us to see. All my senses are on high alert as I look around. The house feels unnaturally silent. I shiver. We move through the living room into the kitchen and pause to listen. Just the hum of the refrigerator. I turn to him and mouth the words, *What now?*

He shrugs and mouths *I don't know!* back to me.

We walk farther into the kitchen. I scan the edges of my sight for anything that's amiss or out of place, but everything is clean and tidy.

A chair scraping across a floor breaks the silence. Chills creep up my spine.

I grab Marty's arm. "Did you hear that? It's coming from down there!" I say, pointing to a long, darkened hallway to our right.

"Oh God. I think my muscles have locked up," says Marty, panic in his voice. "I . . . I can't do this. Let's go back to the car."

A MURDER IN EIGHT COCKTAILS

"Pull yourself together! Follow me."

I will my body to move forward, and we proceed stealthily toward the long, unlit hallway together. Doors are spaced intermittently along each side, like a hotel. The only light comes from a room with an open door on the left side, toward the far end. No sound is coming from it. For a moment, I consider the possibility that I am leading both of us to the edge of hell.

As we arrive at the doorway, I clear my throat and softly call out, "Anyone in here? Hello? Are you okay?"

Slowly, I inch forward into the room. Marty grabs onto my waist and follows directly behind me, making for a very short conga line.

In the shadows of the back corner, a figure is slumped in a chair.

We freeze. The figure isn't moving. Every hair on my body stands up like I'm caught in a lightning storm. I feel a sudden sense of dread, tentacles of it uncoiling and spreading in my gut. I whip around and look at Marty. Our horror is mirrored in each other's faces. I turn back around and step closer. An iciness tingles my skin. I can see a curtain of thick blonde hair is matted over the figure's face.

"Rosetta?" I ask softly, voice trembling.

As we get closer to her, I can feel my breath sawing in and out of my lungs. I stop still and my stomach plummets. She's motionless. I note her pale mauve leggings, matching gauzy blouse, and the unmistakable bouffant adorning her head. A pair of beady eyes look back at me from above her shoulder. It's Orson, quivering on his tiny leash pinned to her blouse.

I reach out and touch her shoulder. The body slides sideways and falls off the chair onto the floor, revealing that she has been strangled with a wire. It's wrapped so tightly that it's cut into her skin and bloodied her neck. A reflexive gurgle escapes from the open mouth. Her bulging eyes are passive, empty.

A high-pitched, other-worldly squeal comes from behind me. It's Marty, his hands gripping his face as he screams in horror, just like the Edvard Munch painting.

Terror has frozen me to the spot. As air rushes back into my lungs, I begin screaming too. I grab onto Marty, lock eyes with him, and we simultaneously turn back to look down at Rosetta's body. Then we turn to face each other again and scream in unison.

In my panic, I let go of him and he sways awkwardly, stepping backward as he tries to regain his balance. I hear a sickening snap.

Marty gasps as he looks down. "Oh my God!!!" he shrieks, hopping away from the body. "I stepped on her hand!" He points at her splayed out body on the floor, the pinkie finger on her right hand bent at an odd angle. "Look! I broke her finger!!"

Orson, frightened by the chaos, pulls his body backward until he's able to release his head from the leash and scurries away.

A MURDER IN EIGHT COCKTAILS

Marty grasps his chest, panting. "Thanks to your midlife crisis I'll never sleep again."

"Let's get the hell out of here!"

We charge down the hall together as fast as we can. When we reach the front door, Marty yanks it open and we scramble out of the house. Sprinting down the driveway to the car, I can feel my heart pounding in my chest as adrenaline courses through my body. I can't remember the last time I've ever run so fast.

Marty fumbles for his keys.

"For God's sake, hurry up!" I shout.

"I AM HURRYING!"

We throw ourselves into the car and Marty hits the ignition. We speed down the street and the tires squeal as he peels out onto the highway.

"What the hell just happened?" gasps Marty, his knuckles bone-white as he grips the steering wheel. "Two dead bodies in one week. Do you realize I actually laid rubber back there?"

I place a firm hand on his arm. "Marty, calm down."

"How did Carmel become such a hotbed of crime? We should move to San Francisco. We'll be safer."

"I hope you finally believe me now. That my 'murder theories' about Max aren't just theories?" I fumble with my phone. "I need to call Paul. We have to think through who would want to kill both Max *and* Rosetta!"

"Are you joking? Paul is the person who got us into this mess. We need to stop this now, before one of us gets hurt. Let's go to Mexico or something. Lay low for a while."

"Do you hear yourself? 'Lay low for a while'? This isn't a spaghetti western, Marty. Just drive."

After a quarter of a mile, my phone displays two bars of cell signal as Marty pulls into a gas station. I dial 911. "Hello? We need to report a dead body."

"You go ahead and talk to the cops," says Marty, opening the car door. "I'm going to go buy a pallet of Rolaids."

I grab his arm. "Stop. Stay here." I go back to my phone. "Yes, that's correct. We found a dead body. There's been a murder."

22

"I'm sorry, what?" I say, touching my forehead. "I . . . I don't understand."

"There is no body, ma'am," declares the unsmiling police officer standing in front of me.

The words echo in my ears. We have just arrived back at Max's rental. One squad car is parked in the driveway and the other is parked on the street.

I glance nervously at Marty, reading his mind with the look he's giving me. *Are you happy now?* I turn back to the officer. "Have they checked the entire house? Are you sure? Listen, we saw a dead body. She was strangled with a wire. This was less than half an hour ago! She has to be in there."

"Can you please check again?" asks Marty, his voice crescendoing into a high, husky squeak. I know that sound. Marty is reaching the end of his tether.

Officer Landry comes out of the house and walks toward us. She comes to a halt and folds her sturdy arms across an ample bosom, studying us both through narrowed eyes. "There is no dead body anywhere in that house."

"That's . . . that's not possible," I stammer.

"Willa, right? I want to believe you. But you're making it very challenging for me," she says, popping a stick of gum in her mouth. "This fella your husband?"

"Yes. I'm Marty Keane." He offers his hand and she gives him the once-over, sizing him up as she shakes it.

Two other officers emerge from the house and head toward our group. One of them snaps off a pair of disposable gloves while staring at me in silent judgment. It's clear they've completed their search and found nothing. The other one is speaking into the radio on his shoulder while eyeing both of us.

I turn back to Landry and try to articulate my thoughts, but nothing meaningful is coming out. Any hope of them taking me seriously has disintegrated. I look to Marty, seeking some kind of reassurance.

He looks back at me blankly, obviously still in shock himself. "It just doesn't make any sense. None of it does."

"Could you check on Rosetta? We have her address," I say. "I promise you, we saw her body. That Mercedes is her car. It's still parked in the driveway but the garage door is open and it's empty. Doesn't that seem odd to you? I think the killer must have put her body in the trunk of whatever car was parked in the garage and driven off . . ." I stop talking because I notice something. There's movement on the porch. I squint, and my eyes grow wide.

Orson is perched on the cushion of a small wooden bench.

There's something forlorn about his small figure, now motherless, staring back at us.

"Orson!" I shriek.

He watches me move toward him. Cautiously, I reach down and gently scoop him up.

"It's okay, Orson." I place him in my purse and turn back to Officer Landry. "Don't you see? Now we have definitive proof The Bitter Woman was here! This is her pygmy chameleon!"

Officer Landry turns to the other two cops and they all look back at me blankly. "Who?"

"Rosetta! The woman we found dead who is now missing. She's also known as The Bitter Woman. This chameleon is her emotional support animal. He rides around on her shoulder. She had him with her on a tiny leash hooked to a brooch pin on her chest."

"Come with us," says Landry.

They lead us back into the house. I feel my entire body tremble as we go into the room where we found Rosetta's body. It's pristine. Neatly arranged and tidy, no body, no sign of the violence we saw earlier. I look to Marty in disbelief. His face is ashen.

"This can't be," he says. "We saw her, she was right there. Can't you go by her house? Check on her? She won't be there, I'm telling you."

Officer Landry looks unconvinced. She takes out a notepad and jots something down. "What did you say her name was again? If she's lived in the community for as long as you say, I'm surprised I don't know her."

"Rosetta Rawling," I say firmly. "I'll give you her address. She's a recluse, so that's probably why."

Landry stares at me, expressionless. There's a long, uncomfortable silence. "Listen folks, it's late. I think you both need to go home and get some rest." She turns to me. "Especially you. Drink some chamomile tea and turn off that brain of yours. Tomorrow morning, come down to the station. File a report. We'll do a welfare check on her then." She writes down a few more notes and adjusts her notepad so it isn't possible for us to see what she's writing. "Before you go," she says, looking up, "we just need to be certain we have a handle on this, so I'm going to ask you something else. Okay?"

I look to Marty and then back at Landry. I nod eagerly. "Yes. What is it?"

"Are either of you taking any new medications? Or experiencing any memory issues?"

I roll my eyes and shake my head in exasperation. "No. We certainly are not. Listen, please write this down in your notepad in case *you're* having memory issues. We found a dead body. In this house. Someone took it, and they are now driving whatever car was parked in this home's garage."

Officer Landry nods slowly. She exchanges a surreptitious

glance with one of the other officers. "Bill," she says, turning to the officer who was speaking into his radio earlier. "Did you check to see if there are any security cameras in the house?"

"There's an alarm system, but it wasn't set. No cameras."

"Maybe the neighbors saw or heard something?" I offer. "Shouldn't you ask around? Don't you think it's possible that this could somehow be connected to Max Magnussen's mysterious death?"

She heaves a sigh. "Ms. Keane, we've been over this. We're a small police force, but we're good at what we do. We get people like you a few times a year. You want to play amateur sleuth because you listened to a podcast or saw a Netflix documentary that made you think, 'Gee, maybe I could do that some day too.' People want to believe that they can somehow become the main character in a bigger story." She takes a breath. "The point is, we care about the residents of Carmel. We are part of the fabric of this community, and we want to believe you. But what you're telling us . . . it's just not lining up with the facts."

Considering the lunacy of this whole situation, I understand where she's coming from. But I need to somehow convince her that Marty and I are not, in fact, lunatics. Marty puts his hand on my arm. *Stay quiet. Let's go home*, his touch says.

I look down and nod. No use in arguing any further. Marty

puts his arm around me, and we say goodnight to them before walking silently back to our car.

I sit in the passenger seat and set my purse on my lap. Cautiously, I open it, and Orson pops his head up. Hanging his arms over the edge, his frightened eyes look around. "What do chameleons eat?"

"Willa, if you think we're going to keep that goggly-eyed reptile, you better think again."

"He just lost his mother."

"Give him to Saint Paul, The Animal Samaritan."

"No way. Noodles would eat him for lunch. Give me your water bottle." I unscrew the cap and pour a little into it. I hold it in front of Orson, who hesitates for a moment, then takes a few drinks with his long pink tongue.

As we drive home, my thoughts drift. The Carmel Police Department is writing me off, but I'm not giving up. As crazy and dangerous as this entire situation is, I feel possessive of it now. It's a hot mess. But it's *my* hot mess, and I am determined to figure out what the hell is really going on.

I take out my notebook and leaf back through my pages of notes. "Let's consider motives again. What could have led someone to murder both Max *and* Rosetta?"

Marty doesn't respond. I can tell he's exhausted. The rest of the car ride is silent. We arrive back home and park in the driveway.

"I know this has all been a lot. But you must believe me now, right? Don't you think Tim Kluver can find someone to run the license plate so we can figure out who the mysterious farmers' market woman is? Or at the very least, he can tell us more information about Max's autopsy?"

Marty takes off his glasses and rubs the bridge of his nose. "You're in luck, because tomorrow is Monday, and I happen to know exactly where he spends his Monday nights."

Monday

23

After a cursory online review of chameleon care, it dawns on me that I need to create a safe, temporary haven for Orson now that his mom is gone. Climbing the narrow steps up to the attic, I find exactly what I am looking for: Zack's old aquarium. We stored it up there years ago after his goldfish, Nettie, died. I carry the rectangular glass vessel down to our bedroom, set it on the window seat, and close the shutters to keep the sun out. After I line the bottom with old newspapers, I put in some small, nontoxic plants and a tree branch for Orson to climb. I find some wire screen mesh in the garage and bend it around the top as a makeshift roof. Then I step back to admire my handiwork.

I scowl. It's functional but not homey. Not much of a step up from the covered shoebox he's currently sleeping in. Orson deserves a more feng shui environment until better accommodations can be made. Hm.

Oh yes, I have just the thing! I run back up to the attic and rummage through Zack's old toys to find his canister of Lincoln Logs. I return to my project and build a miniature log cabin for him to hide in. I make a little Lincoln Log table and bed, with a fuzzy blue washcloth as a duvet, then place them both inside the aquarium. In a final burst of inspiration, I take a small mirror from my purse and hot-glue it to the back wall of his new habitat. Now, Orson can admire that handsome scaly face of his whenever he pleases.

I lift the lid from the shoebox. He's awake. I set my hand palm-side-up in the box. Hesitantly, he crawls onto it. I raise him up and stare into his beady eyes. "We're going to find out what happened to your mom, buddy."

I carefully lower him into his new accommodations. He must be overwhelmed because he doesn't move.

"You're the first rescue animal we've had in a long time. I'm not sure whether we can keep you. But if not, I promise I'll find you a great home."

He closes his eyes. I give him and his surroundings a two-minute misting – as recommended by Wikipedia – with a spray bottle.

"You know, I used to design cozy spaces for a living. I miss it."

His eyes open and he looks up at me. Something about sitting here with him is helping me process all the insanity of the night before. I take a photo and send it to Paul:

Orson is settling into his temporary digs. Fyi, Marty booked us a table at The High Note tonight at 7:00 p.m. Tim the medical examiner is meeting us there.

He responds with a thumbs up. Apparently, Marty's birding friend is a medical examiner by day and a jazz musician by night. I'm pleased that Marty has finally agreed to help out.

I look into Orson's eyes. "Can I talk to you for a minute?"

He stares back at me.

"Why is it that when we get older, life requires us to make decisions that narrow our experiences? Settle down or stay single. Retire or keep working." I sigh. "I'm always wishing there was another option. One that expands my life."

I think back to Kathleen's comment at book club. *Best friends. That's the real kiss of death for any romantic relationship.* I wonder if I agree with her. Marty's balanced, solid companionship has made him a wonderful husband and father. But we've lost that sense of fun we once had. I feel wistful for those days.

Orson gives me a slow blink.

"Thanks for hanging out with me. You're a good listener."

He turns and walks into his new Lincoln Log cabin.

I head downstairs and find Marty seated in his favorite armchair in the living room, reading a book.

"Orson seems to be enjoying his new setup," I say, putting on my sunglasses. "Paul is meeting us at The High Note tonight." Marty stays buried in his book. "Alright, well . . . I'm heading off to Lyle's to show them Max's watch." Lyle's is a local antique shop that specializes in watches and jewelry.

Marty looks up from his book. "You say that like it's just

another normal day. Have you forgotten that we discovered a corpse last night? A corpse that vanished into thin air?"

"Yep. Our second corpse in a week, lest we forget. And I'm going to have the watch the first corpse was wearing examined by a watch expert. Do you want to come with me, or . . ." I pause to glimpse the book's cover, "do you want to keep reading *Why Bold Birds Make Bad Choices*?"

"I sense that my answer should be yes." He inserts a bookmark between the pages and gets up from his chair.

As we embark on the short walk downtown, Marty's mood seems to lighten with every step. Carmel is a picturesque haven brimming with hidden passageways, secret courtyards, and green spaces. Everyone is out and about – families, tourists, people walking their dogs. But I find it difficult to reconcile the cheerfulness of my surroundings with the grisly events of the last few days. I feel myself drifting above it all because I have a secret that no one else in this warm hug of a town knows – that a murderer is lurking in our midst.

We turn onto Ocean Avenue and soon turn again, arriving at Piccadilly Park, a petite oasis of green serenity thanks to the efforts of the local garden club. We halt, as we always do, so Marty can spot any interesting birds perched in the trees. I tug on his arm, and we continue on our way.

Lyle's is an antique shop that has flourished in downtown Carmel since the 1980s. It's a nostalgic sanctuary located on Dolores Street, near the library. I've known the eponymous owner for years. He's helped me find a number of unique pieces for my clients, and I know that he also has a particular expertise in jewelry and watches.

As we approach the storefront, its familiar striped awning greets us. I pause to peer in the window. It's always filled with an array of interesting objects. The current display is an Art Nouveau vase, a pair of brass duck head bookends, an oil painting of a ship, and a Victorian boot scrape.

Marty holds the door open for me and we go inside. The place hasn't changed much in all the years I've been going there. It isn't a big Aladdin's Cave like some of the other antique shops in the area. Instead, it's cozy and tastefully stuffed to the gills with carefully selected objects, well-illuminated by a variety of chandeliers hanging from the ceiling. Making our way through a maze of tables and chairs, we approach Lyle's desk at the back.

He's seated there, tinkering with something and wearing a jeweler's loupe over one eye. Plump and bald, Lyle has a deep, gravelly voice and a thick Louisiana accent that makes him instantly recognizable in the local community. He knows his stuff, but he's also deeply honest. If I ever ask him a question he doesn't know the answer to, or request a piece he can't find, he tells me right away rather than eschewing the question or trying to sell me something else, as so many vendors are prone to do.

"Willa!" he says, his face lighting up. "You've owed me a visit for a while now. How long has it been?"

I smile at him. "Probably not since I retired. Three years at least. Although, didn't I see you at the Fourth of July fireworks last year?"

He laughs and takes the loupe away from his eye. "If you did, I was probably having too many hard lemonades to remember. What can I do for you?"

"Well," I say, gesturing to Marty, "I've brought my husband with me today because we want you to have a look at a watch for us."

Lyle introduces himself to Marty. I hand him the watch and he takes a seat to examine it carefully. I'm practically holding my breath, so I'm relieved when he finally looks up at me after a minute or so.

"I've seen a couple of these before. Minifon made them in the fifties. They were used by spies and the police."

"Really?" I say, intrigued. "Anything else special about it? Is it worth a lot of money?"

"Not really. Probably a couple thousand."

I frown in thought. "The thing is, this watch was Max Magnussen's."

Lyle looks up at me. "Is that right? Terrible tragedy what happened to him. Did he give this to you?"

"No. We found it on the ground, outside his cocktail bar, after he died. I just wanted to know if there's anything strange or distinctive about it, given the circumstances. We'll give it back to the family, of course." As the words leave my mouth, I realize that this probably sounds rather sketchy on my part, so I divulge a bit more information. "We showed it to the police and they didn't seem to care. But we thought something about it was odd, so that's why I want an expert opinion before I hand it back to the family."

"Let me have a closer look," says Lyle. He studies it again, fiddling with something. "Hm."

"What is it?"

"It appears there's a secret compartment in the watch," he says, smiling. "It's nifty. Look at this design." He shows me the back of the watch and twists a small metal dial on the side, causing part of the watch to slide open. There's a click, and a mechanism releases to reveal a small compartment inside. He closes it again, and it retracts back into the watch, perfectly concealed. "The compartment stored a microphone so the wearer could record conversations." Smiling, he shows the inside of the empty compartment to me. "See that?" he says, holding it up. "There's an engraving."

I narrow my eyes to read the engraving: *Tempus Fugit*. "Time flies," I say. "That was Max's motto."

"Max used to come in here whenever he was in town. Intense guy. Always asking about what antique clocks we had, and when we would acquire more."

"Really? And you never noticed him wearing this watch?"

He shakes his head. "Not that I remember. Last time he was in here, he got a mahogany 'eight-day' duration wall clock with a wood rod pendulum. It was designed by the foreman who oversaw the construction of Big Ben."

"Does anything else stand out in your memory about Max?"

"He always came in here with a woman."

"What did she look like?"

"Kind of nondescript, really. Blonde hair. Thirtysomething."

I consider this. Tess is in her twenties, quite striking, with dark hair, so that doesn't fit. The description only aligns with one person. "Did she have a brusque, humorless demeanor?"

"Yes indeedy. First time she came in she told me to sit up straight. Said I was developing a buffalo hump on the back of my neck from hunching over my work. She always had a burr in her undies about something."

"That's Edith Stonewall. She's the hostess at Mysa, and I believe she's also a massage therapist at Redwood Ranch."

As he continues to examine the watch, another customer enters the store.

Lyle walks over to the counter. "How may I help you, ma'am?"

As he speaks to the customer, I digest this new information. It makes sense. If Max and Edith were in fact an item, her expensive Verdura pineapple watch was probably a gift from him.

The customer, a young woman, holds out what appears to be an old silver baby ring. She smiles at Lyle and makes a circular motion around her neck with her other hand.

"Uhh. This is a little ring for a baby, ma'am," says Lyle nervously.

She nods, points to her neck again, and launches into a flurry of sign language.

"Hmm. You want to know if it's real silver?"

She looks frustrated and shakes her head vigorously as she tries to communicate with Lyle.

Marty steps toward her and begins signing to her. With ease, he moves his hands animatedly. I stand there, astounded as she smiles at him and they continue a silent conversation for several minutes.

Marty turns to Lyle. "That's her late mother's baby ring. She wants to buy a thin chain so she can wear it around her neck."

Lyle nods and they continue a brief discussion, then the woman thanks Marty. He waves goodbye to her as she leaves. When we finish our visit with Lyle, we head outside.

I stop and put my hands on my hips. "Martin Keane, how do you know sign language?"

"My college roommate, Neil, was deaf. He taught me. Great guy."

"How did I not know this about you?"

He shrugs. "I guess it just never came up."

My brow furrows. I thought I knew everything about Marty. Apparently not. Even after all these years, he can still surprise me.

As we walk back home, my mind swirls with everything we've just learned from Lyle. Edith's relationship with Max and potential pregnancy have to somehow play a role in all of this. Perhaps I've been focusing on Claes and *Maybe-Bronwen* for too long and need to direct my scrutiny elsewhere. I look back at Marty, who has fallen behind. He jogs to catch up to me.

"Would you slow down?" he says, huffing and puffing.

"Come on, Marty," I say. "We need to talk to Edith Stonewall."

24

"Imagine Edith and Max together," I say, as we drive toward Redwood Ranch. We're in our SUV, and Marty is in the passenger seat next to me. "Do you think Max liked her for her punctuality? Could have been his kink?"

Marty laughs. "The thought of that is both appalling and fascinating." He frowns in concentration. "So, if we think Edith is pregnant with Max's baby, how does that make her a suspect? Why would she want to kill the father of her child?"

"No clue. Did you get the trackers, by the way? Can you put them in my purse?"

He sighs and nods. "Yes. I have two."

Before we got in the car, I convinced Marty to go into his birding gear and retrieve the small GPS devices he uses to track some of his favorite species. My plan is simple: I want to plant one on Edith because she is the only suspect we know almost nothing about. If we're successful, we can find out where she lives and track her movements.

"Do you really need both of them? They're kind of expensive."

"I want a spare so we can plant one on another suspect if the opportunity arises. You can buy more."

He places the trackers in my purse. "Oh, sure. I'll just stop by GPS Tracker Mart tomorrow. Because it's right around the corner and I have all the time in the world."

We turn off the highway and drive up a scenic road through a pristine forest area to arrive at the Redwood Ranch, a hidden, restorative sanctuary just south of Big Sur. I've never been here before, but I know its rustic elegance draws visitors from all corners of the globe. It's an exquisite place. Nestled into the landscape, it appears as if it naturally sprouted into existence under the sheltering trees. We park our car and go inside. The front desk clerk greets us warmly.

"Hello there," I say. "Can we see a spa menu? I'm a friend of Edith's, and I told her I'd come in for a massage today."

"Oh, sorry, madam, but spa experiences are for hotel guests only."

I turn to Marty, doing my best to feign irritation. "Going to this spa was your twenty-fifth wedding anniversary gift to me, and you didn't plan ahead and book a room?"

Marty scowls in confusion. Then the implication of what I'm saying dawns on him. "Oh, uh, right, I mean, well . . . Sorry, darling," he says, switching into performative mode as he gives a sheepish look to the clerk. "I've never been that good with gifts."

"It's no problem at all," says the woman. "We have some availability. We can book you into one of our hotel suites, and then we do have one slot open today for a couples' massage."

I watch Marty's pupils narrow into pinholes. The clerk's phone rings, and she's momentarily distracted while she takes the call.

"Abort mission!" Marty whispers. "Couples' massage? That sounds weird."

"Oh, stop it. You're acting like we're in Times Square in the seventies. We'll be fine. And you know," I say, giving him a flirty look, "it might be quite fun."

"Interrogating a murder suspect while I get oiled and pummeled on a table is not my idea of a turn-on."

I dig deep into my argument arsenal. "Marty, do you realize the countless times I've put your and Zack's needs ahead of my own, day after day? How many meals I've made for our family over the years? The piles of laundry I've washed and folded? The untold number of errands I've run? And yes, agreeing to retire when *you* wanted to, before I was ready?"

His face softens.

"I just want to see this thing through to its conclusion, whatever it may be. Please. Consider it your wedding anniversary present to me, okay? A little adventure."

For a moment, he hesitates. I'm certain he's going to protest further, so I'm pleasantly surprised when he pulls out his wallet and signals to the desk clerk. She hangs up the phone.

"We'll take a room, please. And let's book the massage."

25

A woman clad all in white leads us along a series of wooden walkways through the spa at the Redwood Ranch. After weaving our way around bamboo plants and over rippling streams, we finally reach a room labeled "Couples' Treatment Suite" and enter a small waiting area.

In the corner is a large champagne-glass-shaped kinetic sculpture fountain. Pale "champagne" bubbles up through the stem and into the bowl of the coupe, spilling over the rim and down into a pool where it's recycled back up through the stem again. The soft sounds of the little bubbles popping inside the champagne glass mesmerize me, sparking an idea for a *Sips and Whispers* video. I can set a crystal coupe in front of the camera, hold a champagne bottle up high and slowly tip it to splash the liquid down over the sides of the glass while I whisper about the history of champagne. I'll call it *Dream Bubbles*.

The woman hands us two fluffy white robes before turning to leave. "You may get undressed. Your massage will begin momentarily."

Marty cringes. "What if I don't want to get undressed?"

I shrug. "I don't know how these things work either. Now, strip!"

As we take off our clothes and put on the robes, Marty turns to me. "I thought breaking into a house was the craziest thing we've ever done, but I was wrong. This is the craziest thing we've ever done. Happy anniversary."

"Thanks, babe," I respond. "I promise I'll think of something thoughtful to get you in return."

We enter the massage suite, and a spectacular view greets us from huge glass windows facing the Pacific. The sun is making its late-afternoon descent, casting silver shimmers onto the ocean's surface. I note two large massage tables covered in towels and blankets set up outside on the balcony.

There's a gentle tap at the door. I pad across the teak floor and peer through the peephole. Edith Stonewall and a burly older man are standing there in fitted polo shirts embroidered with the Redwood Ranch's logo. I sigh, annoyed with myself that I didn't consider there would of course be two massage therapists. Hopefully his presence won't create too much of a challenge.

"You can come in now," I call out, as I retrieve one of the trackers from my purse and slip it into the pocket of my robe.

They enter the room and I note Edith's large tote bag, with a water bottle peeking out of the top, slung over her shoulder. Her Verdura pineapple watch dangles from her wrist. She tosses the bag down by the end table next to the couch, and we all walk out onto the balcony.

"Hello, I'm Mike and this is Edith. You can remove your robe and lie down on the table, face down, please," the burly man says to Marty.

He reluctantly unties his robe and obeys the command.

I sit down on my massage table. "Beautiful timepiece," I say, nodding to her watch.

"Thank you," she says, reaching for the clasp to undo it. She removes the watch and sets it aside. "It was a gift."

"A gift? Really? From whom?" I ask, trying to sound blasé and not too curious.

"Someone special, that's all." Her tone is standoffish. She gestures for me to lie down, and I comply.

As she begins to knead my shoulders in silence, I realize I am going to have to abandon my nonchalant approach and try a different strategy to get her to open up. "You know, my daughter is pregnant and has some questions about prenatal massage," I lie, hoping she might find the connection to me and my fictitious daughter heartwarming enough to volunteer that she's pregnant too.

She remains silent and works her way down my arm to my hands.

I look over at Marty, whose pale white body is stretched out on the table while Mike the Mauler hammers his back into meatloaf.

I clear my throat, thinking about my next move. I sit up

and pull my robe around me. "Don't you think we could chat a little first?"

"Your massage time is ticking away, ma'am." A small twitch of recognition flickers across her forehead. "Wait a minute. I know you."

"Oh, yes," I stammer. "We were at Mysa the other night. The night Max Magnussen died."

Her face hardens. "Yes. I remember you two. The truants who missed the first cocktail."

"Terrible what happened to Max, isn't it?" I say.

Edith stiffens. I look into her eyes. It feels as though she's let her guard down for a moment. I can detect a faint vulnerability there.

"It's difficult to talk about," she says. "Now please, lie down."

I comply, and pretend to be absorbed in the massage while considering how I'll plant the tracker in the tote bag. As subtly as I can, I catch Marty's eye and signal with my head toward the inside of the suite. *We need to go inside,* I mouth to him.

Marty exhales through his nostrils and turns his head up to Mike. "I've decided I can't be naked out here in this baking sun. I'll look like a boiled ham tomorrow."

"We can move the tables inside if you feel exposed."

"Yes, thank you," Marty responds.

We get up and wrap the robes around us as Mike and Edith lug the tables inside the suite. I reach for the tracker in my bathrobe pocket. As I pull it out, it slips out of my hand and skids across the floor and under the couch. *Dammit!*

I gesture to Marty, but he hasn't seen what just happened. Quickly, I pull off one of my earrings and stuff it in my robe pocket. "Uh oh! Babe, can you help me? I think I lost my earring!"

Marty looks at me and his eyes widen. He stares back at me, confused.

"It flew off, and then, I think it landed over there. Help me look!" I signal to him and kneel on the floor.

Lifting the long sheet that's draped over the massage table like a curtain, I stick my head under it for a private audience with Marty. He gets on the floor and lifts up the cloth on the other side and frantically whisper-shouts to me under the table.

"What the hell are you doing?!"

"I dropped the GPS tracker. It's under the couch!"

"Oh, good God."

"Are you guys okay?" asks Mike from the balcony.

"Distract them, Marty. Please? While I go and get it."

"Distract them? How?!"

"Get creative. Step out of your comfort zone! Hurry!"

Edith and Mike come back into the room, rolling the carts filled with spa products and towels. Hoping I won't be spotted, I commando-crawl behind the couch. I hear Marty speaking animatedly to them.

"Hey, do you guys see that Laysan albatross out there?"

Silence from Edith and Mike.

"They're amazing birds," says Marty loudly. "You see, they dance with each other in order to find the perfect mate. Like this."

I crane my neck around the couch to see Marty bobbing his head rhythmically to a silent beat. I suppress a laugh. He looks ridiculous.

"They also point their bills to the sky and do mating calls — sort of a mutter or a moo, like this."

As Marty makes a strange guttural sound, I reach under the couch but my fingers can't quite touch the tracker.

"After two albatrosses realize they like dancing together, they commit to becoming partners for life. They're the most steadfast couples of all bird species."

I peer over again to see Edith and Mike looking on in amused horror as Marty "wing flaps" his way over to them and makes a clicking sound with his tongue. He is really selling this, without a shred of self-consciousness. I'm impressed, and also touched that he's making such an effort.

"For a short, stocky man you have the grace of a ballet dancer," says Mike.

I reach under the couch again and strain hard. Finally, my fingers make contact with the hard plastic corner of the tracker and I clasp onto it. Quickly, I crawl over to Edith's tote and drop it in. I give the bag an extra shake so the tracker drops farther down. I back away, still hugging the floor.

Suddenly, I see a pair of shoes.

"What are you doing?" says Edith.

Swallowing hard, I look up. She's glaring down at me, her eyes flashing with menace. This isn't fair. I really thought I was getting quite good at this detective-spy thing. Now Edith is probably going to punch my lights out with those strong hands of hers.

I take a moment to think and catch my breath. "Oh, hello. I dropped my earring and it rolled under the couch." I retrieve the earring from my robe pocket and show it to her. "But I found it! Let's finish up this massage, shall we?" I get to my feet. "Sorry, I'm just not myself today. Max's death has me so upset."

We go over to the massage table and I climb back on. Relieved that she seems to have bought the fabricated lost-my-earring-under-the-couch story, I lay on my stomach and wait for the massage to resume.

"I'm just trying to understand what happened. I can't even sleep."

She sniffs but doesn't comment as she works on my right leg.

"Does anything about that night stand out to you? Anything strange that happened with Max, or anyone else?"

A silence passes as she moves over to the other side of the table and starts on my left leg. Finally, she breaks the silence. "There was something odd that happened, yes. Now that I think about it."

"What was it?"

There's a chill in her voice. "I caught Claes snooping through Max's art collection in the downstairs storage area."

I raise an eyebrow. "When was this?"

"It was exactly 6:30 p.m. because we had just served the *Aquavit Negroni*, and I knew it would take fifteen minutes to go up and down the stairs several times to get more ice for the bartenders. I needed to be back upstairs in time for the next drink to be served."

I take a moment to appreciate that Edith Stonewall, the paragon of precision, is, of course, the only suspect so far who remembers the exact time stamp of a memory. Over Pappy Van Winkle at Mysa, Claes told me that the *Aquavit Negroni* was his favorite drink. But, if he was downstairs looking at the artwork when it was served, that means he was lying. This is new and important information. My suspicions about Claes are reignited.

"Did Claes say anything to you?"

"He said one of the pictures had special significance to him and he hadn't seen it in a while. But he was acting nervous. Like he had been caught."

"Did you notice anything else? Anything strange about the rest of the evening?"

She massages me in silence while she considers the question. "Only that horrible lizard thing."

"Orson?"

"Yes. It was near the end of the night, when I was gathering up the take-home aquavit gift baskets from the aquavit library. That icky little thing ran past me. I nearly dropped a bottle I was so scared."

"Did you scream?"

"Yes, I think I did."

Aha. So that was the hoarse scream I heard during the *Bananavit*. Another puzzle piece has snapped into place.

"Did you get to enjoy the final drink? The *Fikatini*?" I ask. "That one was my favorite."

She looks at me as if the suggestion offends her. "No. I was busy working. I went back to the library to get the gift baskets and handed them out to the guests who were leaving."

I decide to press my luck with one final question. "I noticed that you had the elevator key on a lanyard around your neck. Did you ever let the key out of your sight at any point?"

"No. I did not."

I believe her. If no one else had access to the rooftop, then the killer must be one of the people who had a key.

"You didn't give it to Paul?" Marty chimes in from the other table.

I roll my eyes. I can't believe he still thinks it's possible that Paul is the baddie. What an obvious cliché twist that would be. This mystery is bigger than that.

"No," she says firmly. "I take my stewardship of the elevator key very seriously."

I have a sense that our conversation is coming to an end, and that Edith isn't going to let us probe any further. So, I finally relax and enjoy the rest of my massage in silence next to Marty, who is obviously not enjoying his.

When we're finished, we thank Edith and Mike, who make a quick exit. We gather up our things and change back into our clothes. We settle our bill and make our way toward the car. After we both climb in and shut the doors, we erupt into laughter.

"I hope to God you got that tracker planted," says Marty.

"Mission accomplished." I give his hand a squeeze. "I liked your albatross dance. You really know how to shake your tail feathers, baby."

He shrugs. "I guess that means I'm devoted to you for life, babe."

26

We've been back home for a couple of hours, enough time to recover from our spa adventure. I'm in the kitchen, seated on a barstool munching on a pain au chocolat. Stress-eating pastry has always been a reliable coping mechanism for me. I'm going through the Mysa footage on my laptop again, cross-checking the images with the cocktail timeline grid. It's hard to believe that after studying this footage so many times, no additional clues are popping up. I need a fresh pair of eyes.

"Marty, can you come in here?"

He enters the kitchen and comes over to me.

"Can you tell me if you notice anything in the Mysa footage? I've been staring at it for so long, my eyes are going crossed."

He sits down and goes through the content for several minutes while I prepare a charcuterie board of grubs, crickets and mealworms for Orson.

"Okay. Look at this," says Marty.

I wash my hands and go over to him. Peering over his shoulder, I see a photo of Max, standing next to Tess and holding *The Haunted Lingonberry*. The drink is full. Tess's dress is still pristine and white. It hasn't been ruined by the spill yet. "Okay," I say. "I'm looking. What do you see?"

"The berries," says Marty. "Look at the drink in the other photos." He toggles through a few other pictures. That's when I notice it too.

I gasp. "Max's drink only has two berries and the rest have three!"

Marty nods. "Yes. You know, I read once how the mafia used the number of beans in an espresso martini garnish to communicate coded messages."

I frown in disbelief. "The mob drank espresso martinis?"

He shrugs. "Just saying. Maybe it was a poisoned drink, and that's how it was labeled?"

"It's possible." I give him a hug. "Thank you."

I take my laptop and head up to the Drinks Cabinet. I go to the whiteboard and write down Marty's two-berry discrepancy observation about *The Haunted Lingonberry*. Suspects and potential motives flit through my brain as I take a few steps back to look at the whole board, where I've charted out further theories and taped photos of Claes, Edith, Daniel and Tess.

I write METHOD in a new section and list out:

Poison or drugging (Haunted Lingonberry?)
Shoving off roof
Attack with needle (cap found in elevator)

I consider how Rosetta was strangled, which somehow feels less premeditated than the methods above. What's still bothering me is why someone would want to kill Max *and* Rosetta. Was she just in the wrong place at the wrong time? What is the link between them? I think about the drama with *Strange Tinctures*, and her jealousy over Max dating her sister Lola in high school. Rosetta said Lola lives on the East Coast, and I've pored over the guest list enough times to know she definitely wasn't at the party, so Lola can't be a suspect.

I sigh and check my phone. Normally I'd be greeted with a string of *Sips and Whispers* notifications from YouTube at this time of day. But the screen is blank. It makes sense, considering I haven't posted anything in nearly a week. I feel anxious. Tomorrow, I'll have to make a video.

A text message pops up from Paul:

Check your email. I got the staff list and forwarded it to you. It has all their addresses and phone numbers. One of the bartenders, Nick, is Claes' friend who I mentioned to you. I know the rest of the staff pretty well. Don't think any of them could have done it.

I go to his email and find Nick's name and information in the staff list. *Nicholas Coates.* Why does that sound familiar? I

A MURDER IN EIGHT COCKTAILS

think for a moment. *Aha!* I Google the article about Claes' art theft conviction and find what I'm looking for:

> Earlier this year, his accomplice and getaway driver, Nicholas Coates, was convicted of a lesser charge and sentenced to one year in prison.

Holy hell. One of Mysa's bartenders is Claes' partner in crime? Maybe he and Claes plotted to kill Max with the poisoned cocktail. I check my watch. We need to leave for The High Note soon to meet Tim Kluver. Paul will be there. I can't wait to see him and tell him about this latest development.

I catch myself. Is it okay that I'm looking forward to seeing my ex-husband? Am I feeling something more . . .? No. No way. I am merely attracted to the fact that he is happy to embark on this murder mystery adventure. Fate has brought him back into my life at a vulnerable time, that's all. I have to stop overthinking it.

Locating Nick's number on the staff list, I dial it. As it rings, I consider what I'll say. Coercion is the only thing I have in my arsenal. The call goes straight to voicemail.

"Hi, um . . . Nicholas . . . Nick, hello. My name's Willa. I was a guest at Mysa the night that Max Magnussen died. Listen, I have some information on you. I know what you did with *The Haunted Lingonberry*. Garnishing Max's drink with two berries and not three? So, yeah . . . let's talk. Call me back." I leave my number and hang up.

Wow. Did I really just do that? I am so badass! Hopefully, even if he doesn't know what the hell I'm talking about, it's enough to prompt him to return my call.

I turn the ringer volume up on my phone so I won't miss the call. I go downstairs to the house and enter the master bathroom, then check myself in the mirror. My worry lines are looking more relaxed, and my complexion is glowy. I can't believe only a few days have passed since Max's death. While the horror of it is still gnawing at me, I'm also amazed at how quickly the days seem to be flying by. Every nerve in my body is vibrating with a mix of fear and excitement.

"I've got movement from Edith!" Marty calls out to me from the kitchen.

"Okay, babe! Hold on!" I touch up my lipstick and gather my purse.

My phone buzzes with a text from Kathleen:

Hey. I need to tell you something. Paul asked me out. Is that okay? I don't want to say yes without running it by you first . . .

Her text lands like a rock in my gut. I take a deep and steadying breath. Maybe I am still attracted to Paul . . . a little. Or am I just jealous that someone close to me is feeling butterflies? That exciting, mysterious feeling that new romance brings. As much as I want to triage my emotions and figure out if I am really feeling anything other than a little youthful nostalgia for Paul, I can't. There's too much on my mind to delve deep right now, so I reply to Kathleen with what I know I *should* reply. What a good friend would reply:

A MURDER IN EIGHT COCKTAILS

Of course!! By the way, Paul is meeting us tonight at The High Note. We're going to talk to Tim Kluver there. Want to join us?

Typing bubbles appear as she responds:

I'd love to but I have to groom a pair of Maine Coons. Report back with any intel. Either on how Paul feels about me, or on Max's death. Both mysteries!!

Marty is seated in front of his laptop as I enter the kitchen. He's got that serious, inquiring look on his face that he gets whenever he's concentrating.

"Edith lives in Salinas," says Marty. "She stopped at an address there about an hour ago, and I checked it out. The property listing online says she bought the house twelve years ago." He looks up from his screen. "I've got it set up to record her movements while we're at The High Note, so we can play it back later."

"You're a great stalker, babe."

I put on my jacket and we head out the door together. Like everything in Carmel, The High Note is only a short stroll away. It's a local favorite, a dimly lit jazz club hidden in the basement of a longstanding pizza establishment.

Paul greets us at the entrance. As we head downstairs, I get him up to speed on the two-berry discovery, along with the realization about Nick Coates being Claes' accomplice.

He nods. "The Mysa recipe definitely calls for a three-berry garnish. I agree this could be something. Good work, Marty."

Marty shrugs indifferently.

Together, we enter a low-ceilinged room with exposed brick walls, leather booths and small tables. The place is crowded in a way that's pleasant, not stifling. Red glass candles run along the well-stocked bar and table tops. I take in the ambient chatter and clinking glasses around me and feel my hairs stand on end from their ASMR effect. To the side of the bar is a small raised stage where a grand piano and drum kit are positioned under a single bright spotlight. We make our way to a corner table, well-worn from years of contact with customer elbows and drink glasses. Marty stops to chat with a neighbor he knows. Paul and I continue to our table and sit down.

"You know, I probably should have mentioned this to you before I did it, but I asked Kathleen out," says Paul. "I hope that's alright."

I pat him on the shoulder. "After all these years, this may be the first time you ever asked if I was alright with something you were doing. I'm not your keeper, Paul, and I'm not Kathleen's either."

He laughs, and we share a smile. Marty arrives and takes a seat with us.

"So, how do you know this medical examiner guy? Tim, is it?" Paul asks Marty.

I note how Marty doesn't make eye contact with Paul when he talks to him. "*Jinx* is what he goes by here at The High Note. He's in my birding group. Except he's a twitcher, which means he focuses on the pursuit of rare birds. Twitching is an offshoot of regular birding. It's too extreme for me."

"There's extreme birding?"

"Yep. They're real fanatics."

We take our seats and a server with a silver nose ring approaches us.

"An old fashioned for me," says Paul.

"Same for me," I say, looking around. My mind wanders, trying to imagine what Tim might be like. I've never met him, only heard Marty's occasional stories. I picture him to be tall, bald and dour. All business and tight-lipped. I turn back to Marty, who is studiously examining the menu. I sigh and lean toward him. "Just order something."

Marty looks up at the server. "The bar menu says 'red' or 'white,' but I would like to see your wine list, please."

"You're looking at it."

Marty ignores my fingernails tapping impatiently on the table. "Well then, what label is the red? It must be quite good if you're selling it at that price point. Is it astringent or smooth? Jammy? Assure me it's not cloying."

"It's red."

"Marty!" I hiss. "This isn't The French Laundry. Order a flippin' drink and let this man get back to his other customers!"

"I'll just have a Diet Coke," grumbles Marty.

As Paul leans over the table and tries to draw Marty into a conversation, I study them both. How could the two men I'd married be so different? Fastidious Marty, the Cranky Owl, and Hunky Paul, the Golden Retriever. Now the most unbelievable set of circumstances have brought us all together.

"There he is!" says Marty, his voice interrupting my contemplation. He nods in the direction of a short, heavy-set man wearing a navy blue suit, who's awkwardly lumbering onto the stage.

I watch Tim make his way over to the piano, with a large oxygen tank attached to a two-wheeled cart rolling along behind him. He bows modestly to the scattered applause. The drummer and vocalist speak to one another in a hushed tone while Tim wrestles with the tank. Once he's settled, he nods to his bandmates and, on the downbeat, moody notes begin to float out over the crowd.

"Do you think anyone else here knows Tim's a medical examiner?" asks Paul.

"Jinx," snaps Marty.

"Huh?"

"I told you, at The High Note, he only wants to be called Jinx. It's his alter ego. He prefers to compartmentalize."

"Sure, man. Jinx it is," says Paul.

I can sense Marty's growing irritation as he leans over the table to speak to us in a low voice. "Listen, if you want this guy to help us, we need to play by his rules. Let's keep the discovery of Rosetta's body to ourselves and focus on Max questions only. I don't want Tim, or any of my birding friends, thinking I'm nuts."

I nod in agreement. The server returns with our drinks.

More people are beginning to arrive, slinking past us as they take their seats. We sit brooding together in the syncopated atmosphere of the club, listening to the sounds of Tim's piano and the patrons chatting around us.

"Hey, you two," Paul says, raising his glass. "Here's to our inaugural investigative adventure."

I join in. Marty looks askance, then takes a tiny sip of his Diet Coke. I can tell he's unsettled that Paul is with us. I'm annoyed. He had finally started to loosen up and help me, but now it feels like we're back to square one.

27

After the first set wraps, I watch Tim/Jinx ease down from the stage and make his way toward us.

"You must be Willa. Hello!" he says, approaching me and pumping my hand vigorously. "And you're Paul?" He shakes Paul's hand too and looks around. "I'll sit here on this chair, where I can push this damn tank out of the way." He looks up and smiles at us. Even with the cannula attached to his nostrils, he's very pleasant-looking. "Emphysema," he says, nodding toward the tank. "Too many cigarettes over the years. Never thought they would turn on me, but they did."

I'm fascinated. This large teddy bear of a man has seen death in all its forms. Natural. Violent. Accidental. Tragic. But he has a gentleness to him, an almost Norman Rockwell quality. Like you want to sit with him by a fire while he reads a story to children on Christmas Eve.

"Jinx here runs *Feathernet*," explains Marty, patting him on the shoulder. "It provides up-to-date information on rare birds along the Monterey coast. His authority in the world of seabird twitching is unparalleled."

A MURDER IN EIGHT COCKTAILS

Tim/Jinx sighs. "Have to put all my energy outside of work into the site now. Can't do much of anything else these days. I used to hike miles and miles or go out on daylong boat trips just to get a glimpse of a great-winged petrel or a hooded merganser. No longer can do. So I compile information from other sources instead. Still gives me the thrill of the chase."

A waitress comes by and delivers a creamy cocktail with a candy bar garnish on it to Tim/Jinx.

"That looks delicious," I say.

"It's my signature drink, although it's basically just liquid dessert. They make it for me here." He smiles as he unwraps the candy bar and pops it in his mouth. "I'm enjoying every moment of life, while I still can."

"You should write a memoir about your work as a medical examiner," says Paul, taking a sip of his old fashioned.

"Yeah, I certainly have tales to tell. I sleep in a recliner in the living room every night. Two reasons: one, so my wife doesn't have to hear me wheeze, and two, so when I'm called out on a case in the middle of the night, I can just push the button on my armchair to raise myself into a standing position. I sleep in my clothes, including shoes and socks, so I can leave the house at a moment's notice."

"So," I say, doing my best to casually segue, "I know Marty told you why we're here. Do you think someone can run that plate for us?"

He sits back in his chair and looks at the three of us as though he's seeing us for the first time. "Yes. I'm having someone look into it. Should be able to get you something tomorrow. How else can I help?"

"Well," I say hesitantly, "we want to know about the autopsy. We know they've concluded it was suicide. No suspicious cause of death. But we want to learn more about the specifics of what you found, if we can."

He leans in closer and lowers his voice. "I could get fired for talking to you. But to be perfectly blunt, who knows how much longer I'll be around? Once you're tethered to one of these things," he says, gesturing to the tank, "your days on this earth are numbered anyway."

His words make me think of Max's motto, *Tempus Fugit*. I nod in sympathy, realizing I already feel an affinity for him. I can definitely understand why he and Marty are friends.

"Were there any signs of a possible poisoning?" I ask. "We have reason to believe he might have been poisoned."

"No, but I'll tell you this," he continues, "there was a big gash on his right temple. And his skull was dented. Blunt force trauma. That was a steep drop. He fell at least thirty feet. Everything is consistent with a fall."

Paul looks at me, then presses him further. "But isn't there a way to tell if he was pushed, or somehow involved in a struggle before the fall? There's no chance that the gash could have been caused by a murder weapon of some kind?"

He takes a deep lungful of oxygen, or at least as deeply as he can. "There were no defensive wounds, no. Nothing strange in the toxicology results. Just a BAC of .15 percent which was normal considering it was a cocktail party."

"You really don't think there is any chance it was murder?" asks Marty.

"Speaking from thirty-five years of experience, no. I don't. Especially not with a carefully composed suicide message that was sent to several people from his password-protected phone." He sighs and folds his arms. "A murder hasn't happened here in twenty years. This ain't Modesto, ya know."

I sigh. If only he knew that *two* murders have happened in our quaint little town over the past few days.

Paul interlaces his fingers and places his hands on the table. "But Max wasn't acting like someone whose life wasn't worth living. Quite the opposite. He was making plans for the future."

"Listen, I perform autopsies of the human body, not the human mind. In my experience, people who are suicidal are often very calm once they've made that decision. If you really believe that he was murdered, then I think you need to look into his private life. See what was really going on. You'll find your answers there."

I nod. He's right. "The police aren't taking us seriously at all. We've been trying to talk to Officer Landry and she says the coroner's ruling is definitive."

He gives a small laugh. "I know Landry. She's a tough buzzard. Does not want to be told that she isn't doing her job right. If you keep going to her with questions and concerns, she's going to buckle down twice as hard that this was a suicide. Hate to say it, but she's the defensive type, so I think your best bet is to see what you can uncover yourselves. But don't tell anyone I said that."

I sigh. "Okay."

"There is one more thing," says Tim.

I notice that both Paul and Marty lean forward a few inches to listen in closely.

"It appears Max was in the process of getting a neck tattoo removed." He takes out his phone. "Now, I could *really* get in trouble for this, so take a quick look and then promise me you never saw it."

We all nod in solidarity. He shows us a closeup photo of Max's neck tattoo. I recall seeing a brief glimpse of it above his shirt collar at Mysa. It starts below the ear, and I can clearly read the letters *TE*. The rest of it looks faded, and the skin around it is red.

"The bumps and irritation are consistent with laser tattoo removal."

I look at Paul. "Did you know about his tattoo being removed?"

Paul shakes his head. "Max was a private guy."

"From what we could see, it looked like the tattoo originally read *TESS*, followed by a heart. He was having most of it removed but keeping the *TE*."

I nod. "That makes sense. *Tempus Fugit* was Max's motto.

He might have been in the process of changing the tattoo to say *TF* instead of *TESS*."

The drummer approaches our table. "Jinx, next set starts in five minutes. The tip jar is pretty damn full, man!" He gives a thumbs up and negotiates his way back through the tables toward the stage.

Tim nods and rises to stand. "Look, I respect what you're doing. Trying to be good citizens. Poking around, asking questions." He leans forward and taps his forehead. "If you really think something happened to your friend, you've got to look into it yourselves. But be careful."

"Thanks for talking to us, Jinx," I say, as he turns to leave.

"You got it," he responds, looking down as he unwinds the oxygen cord from an entanglement with a chair leg. "Investigation is like jazz," he says, wresting the cord free. "You have to consider your options and make a choice. Pick a path, and then you gotta play through the changes." He pauses to look at Marty and me. "Just like marriage. You gotta play through the changes."

Jinx's Drink

Ingredients:

2 parts cream*
1 part Frangelico
0.5 parts Chambord
Candy bar (fun size) or a chocolate truffle, for garnish

Method:

Chill a cocktail glass

Add the first 3 ingredients to a shaker filled with ice and shake vigorously for 15 seconds

Strain into the chilled glass

Skewer candy bar or truffle on a cocktail stick and rest over glass

*Oat milk works well as a nondairy substitute.

The Central Coast of California offers some of the finest birdwatching in the world, particularly seabirding. This is partly due to Monterey Canyon, an enormous underwater geological feature in Monterey Bay that goes as deep as 12,000 feet. The canyon's cold, nutrient-rich water is teeming with life, which attracts an astonishing variety of seabirds. Organized boat trips leave at dawn, providing the best chance at sighting "pelagic gold." In the summer of 1961, a large flock of seabirds called sooty shearwaters consumed toxic algae and became disoriented, causing them to go berserk and attack people and homes in the Monterey area. This incident inspired Alfred Hitchcock's 1963 horror classic, *The Birds*.

Tuesday

28

"That's it from me today, gentle friends," I say softly, while looking into my Leica camera and presenting the *Tempus Fugit*. I take a sip. "Mmm. This makes for a great aperitif before dinner. Alas, there's so much more that I want to share with you all, but the sun is hugging the horizon." I tap my nails on the cocktail glass. "I do believe this cocktail has performed its mellowing magic as we bid one another a golden goodbye."

I always end my videos with these words, whispered with a smile. After switching off the camera and the large pair of softbox lights, which give warmth to my complexion, I sit down at my laptop to edit the video.

There's a knock at the door of the Drinks Cabinet. I look at my watch: it's 2:30 p.m. I open the door to find Paul holding a crate of aquavit. I've been expecting him, just not expecting him to be exactly on time.

"Have you ever been this punctual in your whole life?"

He gives me a wink. "I guess I'm a changed man." He sets

the crate down next to the bar counter. "This aquavit is more dill-forward than some of the others."

"Speaking of, I just finished making your lovely *Tempus Fugit*. Before I post the video, I just want to check . . . do you really think I should? Is it in bad taste to continue promoting Mysa?"

"No," he responds, "I think Max would be pleased. You know what a stickler he was. He would have wanted you to fulfill your contract."

I nod. "Why don't you stay for a minute? I'll serve you one of my nonalcoholic specialties, *Bohemian Iced Tea*. It's Earl Grey, blackcurrant syrup, essence of elderflower and a star anise infusion."

He takes a seat as I make the tea. I place it in front of him and sit down on the opposite side of the bar.

Paul lifts his glass and stares at the drink. "Listen, I wanted to tell you that one more thing came to me after I racked my brain for every little detail."

"Do tell," I say, raising an eyebrow in anticipation.

"Max didn't let me use *Strange Tinctures* products in any of the eight cocktails."

I frown. "He didn't? Why?"

"I don't know. I figured it was superstition, since he was selling off the brand. He had all of Rosetta's products cleared out of the bar. I had to redo some of my specs."

"Hm. It might mean something."

He turns to me. "There's something else I've been wanting to talk to you about, too. It's not about Max or Mysa."

I pause. So my instincts were right. He *did* have something to tell me. I'm nervous, unsure where this might be heading. My twentysomething ego would have wanted it to be a romantic overture. A grand apology for letting me go, and a declaration of his undying love for me. I hold my breath.

He reaches into his jacket pocket and unfolds something. "I wanted to give you this."

I look down. It's a check.

"I had planned to give it to you at Mysa, but obviously, I couldn't. Not after everything that happened. Anyway, I wanted to tell you that I always felt guilty about the money I owed you. From the loan you gave me after we separated."

I exhale. Somewhat relieved, somewhat disappointed. "Don't be silly. That was years ago. I don't even remember how much it was."

"I do. I remember the exact amount. It was very generous of you, and I want to repay you."

I take the check and my eyes widen. Forty thousand dollars! Paul, that's *way* more than I ever gave you. I can't accept this."

"I've adjusted for inflation."

"I don't want it. Truly." I try to hand it back to him.

He waves it away. "Keep it. I insist. You'll make me feel

better. It's bothered me for years. I don't want this hanging over my head." He slides his hand across the table and covers mine, giving it a gentle squeeze. "I also want you to know I'm ashamed of how I treated you." His eyes are brimming with emotion. "I admit that inviting you to Mysa was a way for me to see you again. I wanted to heal old wounds."

I'm struggling for the right combination of words to respond. "Paul . . ."

"You don't have to say anything, Wil." He fiddles with his glass and takes a few more swallows of tea. "These last few days have been just like old times. And I'm happy for you. I mean that. You've really made a beautiful life for yourself here."

"Thank you." I exhale a long sigh and shift in my seat. "You know, sometimes I think you were smart not to get remarried. Marriage is long. Sometimes I think I'm not built for it at all. Before you go thinking my life is perfect . . ."

We share a silence, and he smiles at me.

He drains the rest of his tea and pops up from his chair. "One more thing. Before I forget. I asked around about Tess, and a server told me she's a tour guide at the Hearst Castle."

"Oh, really?" I find myself struggling to focus on Paul's information about Tess. I'm still reeling from our conversation.

"I think we should go down there and talk to her."

"Great idea."

I walk him to the door. Just before he leaves, he turns around and looks at me, then gives me a kiss on the cheek. It takes me by surprise. He lingers there slightly, as if considering whether to do it again. Then obviously thinks better of it.

I wave goodbye to him as he pulls out of the driveway, unsure how to process this moment. My phone buzzes, and I jump, startled. It's a number I don't recognize. I answer.

"Willa Keane?" says a male voice on the other end.

"Yes?"

"This is Nick Coates. I got your message." His voice is tight and firm. "Let's meet."

"Okay. Can we talk first?" I squeak. Damn. I'm trying to sound tough but failing miserably.

There's a long pause. So long that I think perhaps the call has dropped.

Finally, he speaks again. "I'd prefer to discuss this face to face. I have something I want to show you."

Could this be a trap? I'll need to meet him somewhere safe, somewhere familiar, where there will be plenty of people around. "Okay. How about we meet at Mr. Fluffington's? It's a cat speakeasy on San Carlos."

"A cat speakeasy?"

I lower my voice so he knows I'm serious. "Yes. You enter through a secret door at the back of the wine shop on the corner. They serve drinks while you pet rescue cats that are up for adoption. Do you have a problem with that?" I realize the way that I deliver the last line is less "tough guy" and more "crazy cat lady."

"Fine. I'll see you there in an hour."

"Okay."

I consider texting Marty to tell him where I'm going. But I don't want to aggravate him any more than I already have. Then I think about calling Paul. He could easily turn around and come with me to meet Nick. But he's technically Nick's boss. Unlikely that Nick will want to open up to me with Paul present.

I decide I'm on my own for this one.

29

It's early evening, and Mr. Fluffington's is busy, filled with people of all ages petting cats, sipping drinks, and tapping away on laptops. The place is lined with booths on either side, and several comfortable chairs covered in floral fabrics form a seating area in the middle. A strange man wouldn't murder me in the middle of this cozy feline watering hole . . . would he?

I approach the bar and order a whisky neat because a whisky neat feels like the drink a badass vigilante detective would order.

"Neat means no ice, right?" says the flummoxed young man behind the bar. He's barely out of his teens, probably a student working part-time.

I nod and help him identify the right type of glass for the drink, immediately nullifying the "feeling cool" effect of my drink order.

I take a booth by the window. I've been to this place a few times before with Kathleen, who provides free grooming services for their furry residents, all rescues from across

Northern California. A portly tuxedo cat with a collar that reads *MERLE* pads toward me. When he realizes I have no treats, he flicks his tail and turns away.

My mind wanders to Paul. He'd love this place. Our shared love for animals was always a powerful glue. Just as I begin to contemplate what that surreal moment we shared in the Drinks Cabinet could mean, the door jingles and I look up.

Nick Coates walks in. I recognize him from a few photos I found online. Slim, with thick glasses and greasy hair, he doesn't look threatening. As he makes his way toward me, I can see there's a bag slung over his shoulder. He could be armed with a weapon. I need to keep my guard up.

I tense as I give him a subtle wave, and he slips into the booth, opposite me.

"Willa, right?"

I nod.

He looks at me through the lenses of his dark-rimmed glasses, assessing me. "Okay. So, who the hell are you?"

I swallow. We aren't off to a good start. "I'm just a concerned MOP."

"MOP?"

"Member of the public. Isn't that the street term?"

He rolls his eyes. "I wouldn't know. I grew up in Vermont."

"Vermont? How did you ever find yourself stealing art in Sweden?" I catch myself. His expression is stark and determined. I can tell my conversational tone isn't appreciated.

"I'm not here to tell you my life story. Look, I only have a few minutes. I need to know more about *you*. Why exactly do you want to talk to me?"

"I only want to understand why you served Max that particular *Haunted Lingonberry* with a different garnish. That's it."

"Shouldn't you just leave all this to the police?"

I huff. "Why does *everybody* keep asking me that?!"

He looks me up and down with narrowed eyes, still unsure what to think of me.

Suddenly, a gray kitten leaps onto my shoulder. I look at the cat's nametag: *MAVIS*.

Nick looks at Mavis and his seriousness melts away. "I had a cat once. Henrietta. She was the best."

A waitress appears and Nick orders a tea. Mavis jumps down onto the table and walks toward him. She purrs with pleasure as he gives her a few chin scratches. Suddenly, he's less antagonistic.

"Cats can read people. She definitely likes you," I say with a smile.

We make eye contact. His eyes have softened. In some strange way, we've found a connection.

The waitress returns with a flowery china cup and saucer filled with tea, and places it in front of Nick.

I decide to lean on some old skills from my interior design career. Carefully offering prompts that suss out what's on the client's mind. Even if they don't always know how to articulate it for themselves. "Listen, I know you were Claes' accomplice in the art theft years ago. But that's ancient history, right? You aren't a thief anymore. Can you please just help me understand why you were working at Mysa? What brought you to Carmel after a life abroad?"

He sips his tea from the delicate china cup. "It's tough to get a job with a criminal record, you know. Claes was just helping me out."

"Okay. That makes sense. So, you said you have something you want to show me?"

He nods. Slowly, he reaches into his pocket and produces a brown glass bottle with a smiley face sticker on it. Placing it on the table in front of me, he nudges it forward so I can get a closer look. The smiley face is creepy.

"Two weeks ago, I got an email from somebody offering me cash to spike Max's drink with LSD the night of the party. A few days later, I received an anonymous package with this glass bottle and five thousand dollars in cash. They said if I spiked his drink and served it to him successfully, they'd wire me another twenty thousand."

I raise an eyebrow. "Did you tell anyone about this?"

He shakes his head no. "I thought it was weird, but I wanted the money."

"Why would anyone want to do such a thing?"

"They said it was a little prank they wanted to play." He continues to pet Mavis.

"Can you show me the email?"

He hands me his phone, and I scan the email. It's pretty straightforward, and says exactly what Nick has just told me. There are precise instructions for him to mark the spiked drink with a different garnish so there are no slip-ups. I note it's from tempusfugitmax@gmail.com and to nicholas@deathsmith.com.

"Wait," I say. "You work at Mysa and you *also* work for Claes at *Deathsmith*?"

"Yes. I'm one of their artisans. Many art thieves are passionate art lovers themselves, you know. I paint memorial portraits, mostly. I mix dead people's ashes into my acrylics."

I grimace. "How did they have your email address? It must be someone who knows you."

"Not necessarily. I have a website for my art, and it links to my *Deathsmith* profile. So, yeah, very easy for someone to Google me and get my email."

Mavis jumps off the table and lands gracefully on the floor.

"So . . . did you spike the drink?"

"Yes," he replies. "Listen, I may be a thief, but I'm not a killer. When I found out Max died, of course I felt horribly guilty. I figured maybe he fell off the roof after getting disoriented from the drugs."

"Did you tell Claes then?"

"No. I still haven't told him. But he mentioned to me that you've been looking into Max's death because you think he was murdered. He does too. So, that's why I came here." He taps the bottle with his finger. "I'm thinking maybe this isn't LSD. Maybe it's poison."

I take the bottle and place it in my purse. "Thank you. I'll look into it. But I won't tell anyone you gave it to me."

"I hope you get some answers." He stands up and nods to me, then reaches down to give another cat a final chin scratch before he leaves.

I continue to sip my drink in the booth as I contemplate what all of this could mean. Claes somehow appears less guilty now. Nick wouldn't have talked to me if he and Claes were in cahoots to kill Max. Something is telling me I need to stop giving so much mental space to Claes and start considering the other suspects more seriously.

Suddenly, I notice a car's bright headlights in my peripheral vision. I squint out the window. It's a black sedan, idling in the parking lot. The headlights are too blinding for me to see inside the vehicle, but I have the sudden instinct that I'm being watched.

I feel a chill as I silently stare out at the car. Is someone following me? It stays there, and it feels like a warning. I wait a few minutes. Finally, the car backs up and drives off.

On my phone, I pull up a ride-hailing app. Even though it's only a five-minute walk, I decide to order a car home just to be safe. As I wait, I check YouTube for comments on the *Tempus Fugit* video that I posted an hour ago. I see that a flood of notifications have come in. After my unplanned hiatus, reading through them is affirming:

A MURDER IN EIGHT COCKTAILS

We missed you. I'm feeling more relaxed already!
Can you do another one just whispering the ingredients, no other sounds?
You should do more garnish videos. Just garnishes!!!
You have no idea how much I needed this video today. Terrible headache and you helped so much.
Zzzzz soooo soothing!

It pleases me that my cozy little corner of the internet is such a kind and supportive community. I start to put my phone away when I get another notification. I glance at the screen again. A new comment has popped up, from a user named *Tempus-FugitMax*. I frown. That's the same handle as the person who emailed Nick about spiking Max's drink.

Whatever you think you're doing, stop.

I freeze. My heart begins to race. I blink a couple of times and reread it. Some creep has tracked me down on *Sips and Whispers* in order to threaten me? Could this really be happening? Then, another comment appears:

You're next.

30

Lavender-scented steam fills my nose as I settle into my clawfoot bathtub and let the warm, bubbly water slip around me. I lean back and drape my arms on either side of the tub. My nerves feel taut after noticing the ominous car in the parking lot of Mr. Fluffington's. Not to mention the threatening YouTube comments.

Who the hell is this *TempusFugitMax* person? Is it the killer, or just some prankster? The thought of him or her watching my ASMR videos, peering into my home through their phone, makes me shudder. It's becoming difficult to discern where my instincts end and paranoia begins.

I inhale some deep breaths through my nose and close my eyes. Relaxing my anxious, easily excitable mind is something I've refined to a science over the years. My surroundings play a part in that, too. Several years ago, I redesigned our master bathroom to be an appealing, restful harbor in which to decompress from the rigors of the day. A shimmery, cerulean tiled floor lines the walk-in shower. Soft blue wallpaper and sparkling light fixtures give the room a peaceful glow that reflects my love for the Pacific Ocean.

A night to myself is a rarity. Marty is off with "the bird herd" for their monthly Cluster Flock gathering at a local pub. I have no dinner to cook or errands to run. My mind wanders to Paul, and that moment we had earlier in the Drinks Cabinet. That's all I can think of it as, "a moment."

An undeniable attraction is there, yes. Some wistfulness and nostalgia. Even regret. Age has turned Paul into a good, reliable man. Is it possible our timing was just off? If he and I met now, would we have a successful relationship? His personal growth has me wondering if perhaps I was also a bit childish in our marriage. Stubborn, possibly. Maybe a little flighty. Somewhat intense. Yes, I was certainly all of those things. And maybe those things are affecting my marriage with Marty now, too . . .

Taking in a deep breath, I exhale slowly and sink lower into the bubbly water, its warmth surrounding me.

A distant noise of breaking glass pops my eyelids open, like a window shade snapping up. I sit up and strain to listen. There's only silence. But my inner alarm bells are ringing.

I hear the rhythmic sound of footsteps in the downstairs hallway.

My throat constricts and my mouth goes dry. Someone is in the house. Could it be Marty? No, he would have called if he was coming home early. And besides, that isn't what Marty's footsteps sound like. After twenty-five years of marriage, I know his gait.

My nerves twinge. I am definitely not alone. What is happening? I stand up, sloshing water over the sides of the tub. A wave of adrenaline rushes through me and goosebumps prickle my skin as I step out. I wrap myself in a robe and tiptoe over to the door. As my fingers grasp the door handle, I hesitate. Where is my phone? I squeeze my eyes shut to think. Usually, I put it on the nightstand, but I think I left it charging downstairs in the kitchen. I curse under my breath.

The house is silent as I edge open the door. Blood thuds inside my ears. The bedroom is dark, but the hallway light is on, providing enough illumination for me to see that the room is empty. I look over at Orson, sound asleep on his little bed.

For a moment, I consider every possibility other than an intruder. Could it be a mouse? Did a tree branch hit the window? Is this just my overactive imagination at work? I continue to listen in silence. No, something is definitely wrong. I can feel it.

Fear twists in my gut. I need to call the police. Should I scream? I take a tentative step and look around for something to use as an improvised weapon. Marty's golf clubs are in the garage. The knives are in the kitchen. I turn to the nightstand. The lamp will have to do. I move silently over to it, unplug it, and take off the lampshade. I wind the cord around the heavy crystal base, then lift it, gripping it with both hands like a baseball bat.

A MURDER IN EIGHT COCKTAILS

Armed with the lamp, I creep softly down the hallway toward the stairs, holding the lamp base up in the air, ready to clobber anyone who steps in front of me. I pause at the top of the stairs to listen again. I hear the sound of drawers opening and closing. My grasp tightens on the lamp. I'm weak in the knees. Am I going to pass out? My whole body is shaking. Should I hide? Yell for a neighbor? Confront the intruder? I visualize where my phone should be in the kitchen – plugged into the charger on my little built-in desk by the doorway.

I make my way silently downstairs. As I reach the bottom and enter the foyer, my bare feet pause on the hardwood floor. I note that the front door is still deadbolted. They must have entered through a window or the French doors on the side of the house. I hear footsteps again. It sounds like they're out on the patio, running away.

As I turn toward the kitchen, my stomach tightens in knots of anxiety. I observe shards of glass scattered across the floor. The French doors leading out to the patio are wide open, the curtains billowing in the night breeze. Someone has shattered one of the panes and unlocked the door handle from the inside. My purse is lying open on the floor. The room is empty otherwise. Whoever was here has now left.

I exhale and set the lamp down on the counter. Stepping carefully over to my desk, I fumble for my phone and dial 911 with trembling fingers.

A dispassionate male voice answers. "911. What's your emergency?"

My voice is raspy. I can hardly form words. "My house has just been broken into."

"Ma'am, what's your location?"

My eyes drift to the kitchen island, and immediately I realize what's missing.

Max's watch. It's gone.

31

Police cars outside wash the house in flashing blue and red lights. I have a blanket draped over my shoulders, and I'm drinking a mug of hot tea. Marty made it for me after rushing home in a panic once I called him. He's been speaking to Officer Landry for several minutes, trying to tactfully remind her of the events leading up to all this in the most logical way possible. Although I can tell from her facial expression that she is deeply skeptical of every word coming out of his mouth.

"I understand that we are not currently the most well-regarded people among your staff at the Carmel Police Department," says Marty. "But we think this break-in could be directly linked to the . . . incident from the other night with Rosetta Rawling."

"The 'incident' of the nonexistent dead body?" asks Landry. "You know, I waited for you two at the station on Monday morning. Offered to have you come down and fill out some forms, remember? But you never showed."

"Sorry about that," I say, jumping in. I feel sheepish. Given their lack of interest in the case, going to the station didn't feel like a priority at the time, so it didn't occur to me to actually go. But I realize now that might seem suspicious on our part.

"We ran a welfare check on Ms. Rawling. She didn't answer her door or her phone. But that's not uncommon. For all we know, she's just out of town."

I sigh. "I know you think we're making all of this up. But why would we do that?"

"I don't know. I meet a lot of strange people in this job."

I nod along sympathetically. Then I stop nodding, realizing Landry considers me to be one of those strange people.

She smiles in my direction. "Ms. Keane, in the Carmel Police Department, we think of ourselves as an integral part of this community. Accordingly, we lend each resident a certain amount of goodwill in any situation. You can think of it as your own individual 'benefit of the doubt account.'"

"Oh, well, that's nice, I suppose."

Her smile fades. "Your account is about to go into overdraft."

Marty places his hands on his hips. "Don't you think we should have someone here overnight? In case they come back? Should we stay at a hotel?"

"You can do whatever you want, Mr. Keane. But as far as we're concerned, this is a nonviolent petty crime. The intruder must have heard you coming down the stairs and decided to flee. You're lucky you weren't hurt." She gives us a *What can I tell you?* shrug. "They rummaged through your purse and took an antique watch that was sitting out on your counter in plain sight. Seems like an opportunist looking for a quick smash and grab. Are you sure nothing else is missing? Jewelry, passports, any other valuables?"

"Not from what I can tell," I say. "Although I haven't checked my purse yet. The 911 operator told me not to touch anything." I gesture toward my purse on the floor.

Landry nods. "Check it for me, then."

Feeling the untrusting scrutiny of Landry's eyes on me, I reach for my purse and take in a few breaths, trying to calm myself down as I look around inside it. Everything appears to be there. My wallet, my makeup, my emergency stash of candy and chocolate. Except . . . wait a minute. The brown bottle of LSD with the smiley face. It's gone.

"Damn," I say, as I root around in the bag again to be sure it's not there.

Landry exchanges a look with another officer. "What is it?"

"A bartender at Mysa was given a large cash payment and a bottle of some substance, either drugs or poison, to spike Max's drink the night of the party. They came forward and gave it to me. I was going to give it to you to have tested. But it's not here. They took it."

Landry gives me a blank stare. "You expect me to believe that the thief who stole an expensive watch from your home left your wallet safely in your purse after rummaging through it, and only took a small brown bottle of an unknown substance?"

"*Yes*!" I huff an exasperated sigh. I don't consider myself a confrontational person, but it's infuriating that Landry isn't taking me seriously. "Look, I know you think we're just a couple of bored suburban retirees, but this all really happened!"

The other officer gives me a judgmental scowl. "You know, we haven't had a burglary in this area for months. It's extremely rare. The last case was a family whose daughter had broken into their house to steal money for drugs. Are you sure this couldn't be someone known to the family? You mentioned you have a son, Zack, is it? Is Zack having some problems? Is that why you're stressed out? Maybe he wanted some of that 'substance' for himself?"

"No, it's not possible. Zack would never do that."

Marty throws his hands up. "Couldn't you at least dust the kitchen for prints?"

Landry shakes her head dismissively. "I don't think we're going to go full *CSI* on a nonviolent petty crime."

We talk to them for a few more minutes, but it's clear we're getting nowhere, so I tell them we want to go to bed. They say goodnight to us, and Marty walks them to the door.

My energy is completely sapped as I trudge back upstairs to check on Orson. He's in his Lincoln Log cabin.

"Orson? Are you in there?"

After a few seconds, he peeks out. His body color has

changed from his usual brown-green to almost black. His mouth is open, which I have never seen him do before. He seems frazzled, too.

Marty comes in. "I called Tim and told him what happened. He's going to have a sheriff park outside our house for the night."

"That's very kind of him. Tell him thank you."

He unbuttons his shirt. "I really don't like sleeping in the same room as that creature. Can't we move the aquarium to another room?"

"No. He's actually very sweet and has quite a little personality. There's a knowingness behind his eyes. Don't worry, though, I'm just keeping him safe until we can find a good home for him." I reach out and squeeze Marty's hand. "Come on. You have to admit, this is frightening, but . . . it's exciting, too. Right?"

"Exciting? We're way beyond that. People are breaking into our home because you're out crimefighting on the mean streets of Carmel. We have moved into all-out hysteria."

I march over to my laptop and open the lid.

"Oh God. What are you doing now?"

I pull up the website for Hearst Castle. "We're going undercover. As tourists. I'm going to book a private tour of the castle with Tess. She told the police that Max had been depressed, and she believed it to be suicide. If she's the only person close to him who thinks he *did* kill himself, we need to talk to her and find out what she knows."

Marty rolls his eyes at me as he gets into bed. "We're not going undercover. Have you met us? We couldn't blend in if we tried. All this mystery stuff makes you hyperactive, and Paul's seven feet tall with a blind dog. We're like some traveling vaudeville act."

"I think it could work if it's just you and me. I'll play it cool, I swear. Paul can come with us if he wants, but he and Noodles can stay in the car. Tess might not even recognize us." I turn my attention back to the site. "The only private tour available tomorrow with Tess is an evening tour. It says there are 303 stairs, and it's a three-quarter-mile route. Okay with you?"

"Can I wear orthopedic shoes?"

"I'm being serious."

"Hearst Castle is in San Simeon. That's over two hours' drive from here."

"Yep. And Daniel's house is on the way there. We need to interview him, too. Didn't you say that Nina Hernandez's vineyard in Jolon is also in that direction?"

Marty sighs. "Yes."

"We're going on a road trip."

Wednesday

32

I wake up to the sound of Marty zipping up a duffel bag. I open one eye and stare at him. "What are you doing?"

"Packing. We've got a big agenda. First, we're going to see Daniel, then we have to track down Tess at Hearst Castle, followed by a visit to Nina Hernandez's vineyard. That's a lot of drive time. It makes more sense if we stay overnight at a B&B. We can talk to Daniel and Tess today and go to Jolon to see Nina tomorrow morning before we drive back."

I smile. "Thank you. I told Paul we'd pick him up around nine. You did book two rooms, right?"

Marty sighs. "How could I forget? Yes, and I checked to make sure they allow dogs." He pulls down a small suitcase from a shelf in our closet and brings it over to me. "After you get dressed and packed, let's get going."

I cock my head to the side. "How have you gone from 'please stop this madness' to 'let's pack up and go'?"

He dips his head to make eye contact with me. "Because I realized I might as well help you organize this whole thing so we can move on with our lives. And . . . I don't want my wife going on a road trip alone with her ex-husband."

I give a nervous laugh. "Marty . . ."

"I'll see you downstairs."

I sigh and throw back the duvet. Checking myself in the floor mirror, I'm pleased to see that my haircut still looks fresh and bouncy, as though I've hardly slept on it. I quickly put on a comfortable sundress and my favorite earrings, a gold pair that belonged to my mother. After packing my suitcase, I carry it downstairs and take out my phone to text Kathleen.

Key is under the mat. Thank you so much for watching Orson!! You're the best.

Marty calls out to me from the garage. "Willa! Let's go!"

I slip on my low-heeled sandals and flip off the lights as I hustle out through the door and into the garage. Marty loads my suitcase into the car and opens the passenger side door.

I notice a little basket is resting on the seat. "What's this?"

"It's a road trip care package that I made for you: CARBS. C: Coffee in a travel mug; A: Animal crackers; R: Rolos; B: Bananas; and S: Strawberry scone. After twenty-five years of marriage, I know exactly what you need for a long car ride."

My eyes sweep over the basket. There's a tenderness in how carefully the items have been arranged. I note that there are tissues, cough drops and hand wipes tucked into the corner.

Deeply touched, I give his arm a "thank you" squeeze. Sweet, thoughtful Marty.

Gray clouds are screening out the sun as we pull onto the highway and drive south a few miles. My phone buzzes with a text from Zack.

Good video yesterday. I was getting worried ... you hadn't posted in a while. Everything okay?

I smile. Even though he's busy building his own young adult life, Zack still checks my channel. Considerate and caring, just like his dad. I respond:

Thank you for being my biggest fan. We've just got a lot going on this week. Nothing to worry about. Your dad and I are going on a little road trip down to Jolon for a vineyard visit.

He responds to my text with a thumbs up. Omitting the whole murder investigation thing is the right move. No need to involve him in the current insanity of our lives, and I know Marty would be upset if I brought Zack into this. Besides, it will be better to tell him about it in person later, when he comes home over the summer break.

I pull up the directions Paul texted me and read them aloud. "We're looking for a sign on the east side of the highway." Marty slows down. "There! I see it," I say, pointing ahead.

We turn off the Pacific Coast Highway and onto a narrow gravel road, passing under a sign suspended on tall wooden poles that says *Welcome to Peaceful Pines RV Park*.

Marty frowns. "He lives at an RV campsite?"

"Well, I don't think you can just haul a tiny house into downtown Carmel and park it at the curb like it's a food truck."

The road leads into a forested area that becomes denser as we drive farther into the park. We pass various RVs, pitched tents, barbecue grills and campers in lawn chairs as we continue deeper into the trees.

"We're looking for lot twenty-seven."

"I see it," says Marty. We pull up, and he turns off the engine while we wait for Paul to appear.

It's strange to be sitting here, staring at the life of the man I walked away from. I'm pleasantly surprised by how nice-looking the place is. It's obviously been designed to fit in with nature. Rustic, yet modern, with gray-stained wood-plank siding, a black metal roof and large windows that invite plenty of natural light inside. I imagine the thoughtfulness and ingenuity required to design its interior so that it's cozy, not cramped.

Paul waves as he steps outside with Noodles, under an outstretched awning that shades a couple of wooden folding lawn chairs and a tray table. He turns and locks the door behind him.

"Morning, you two," he says, as Noodles squats for a quick potty on his way to the car.

Marty raises the index finger of his right hand, which is resting on the steering wheel, in silent acknowledgment. Paul lifts up the rear hatch of the SUV and sets his duffel bag and canvas tote of dog food and water for Noodles inside.

"Your place looks lovely," I say cheerfully, as they climb into the backseat.

"Are we ready to get this traveling circus on the road?" asks Marty, as he puts the SUV in gear.

We head back to the highway and turn south for a mile, then west to Daniel Williams' house, a sprawling Art Deco mansion located about ten minutes south of Carmel. Situated on an immaculate lawn at the end of a picturesque cul-de-sac, it looks just like the kind of stately home that a successful financial adviser would live in.

"Wonder whose birthday it is," says Paul from the backseat, nodding toward a bunch of brightly colored balloons tied to the mailbox.

We turn into the wide semi-circular driveway and park behind several other cars: gleaming Bentleys, Porsches, and a white Maserati. Marty shifts the car into park and turns off the ignition.

I take in the home's magnificent exterior. "Look at those curved walls and the steamship railings. This place is an Art Deco dream."

We walk up to the entrance together. As Paul is about to press the doorbell, the door swings open and a young boy who looks about seven years old answers, smiling up at us expectantly. He has tightly braided hair arranged in intricate cornrows.

His smile fades. "You're not the cake."

"Oh. Sorry," I reply, stammering as I consider what to say next.

"Where's my cake?" he presses on. "It's late."

"I . . . I don't know kiddo."

He looks down at Noodles and his face lights up. "Doggie!! Can I play with him?"

"Sure," says Paul. "We're here to see Daniel Williams. Is he your dad? Is he home?"

He gestures for us to follow him. Paul hands him the leash and he takes Noodles along for a walk ahead of us down a long hallway. The squeaky sounds of his sneakers on the shiny floor are pleasant and soothing. Posed family photos filled with bright smiles line the walls. The entire Williams family looks like a Ralph Lauren ad.

We pass through a stunning living room with rounded curves and corners everywhere, punctuated by patinas of gold and silver in the lamps and coffee tables. A breeze coming in through the grand open windows brings the soft scent of gardenias with it. We continue on to the back of the house, through a pair of open glass doors and out onto an enormous terrace that's been ornamented in elaborate Alice-In-Wonderland-themed décor.

Marty gives me a nudge and points to an artfully painted sign with the words *Curiouser and curiouser* on it. "That's you."

I shrug. "Alice was an intrepid explorer. So am I."

A MURDER IN EIGHT COCKTAILS

Several pink flamingos wander about aimlessly on the vibrant emerald lawn. One dips its neck to the ground and nibbles on something. Croquet equipment is set up, and a woman dressed as the Queen of Hearts is doing a magic trick for a group of children. Someone wearing a large white rabbit suit is handing out treats in a beautiful rose garden that runs along one side of the house.

"Dad's over there," says the little boy, pointing to Daniel, who's holding court on the grass with a group of adults clustered around him. They're standing near a table displaying an ice sculpture and an assortment of food and refreshments labeled *Eat Me* and *Drink Me*.

As we step off the terrace, I remove my sandals to prevent the heels from sinking into the ground. Planting my feet on the close-cut grass, the blades tickle the spaces between my toes. The sensation triggers warm memories of playing with Zack in our own backyard when he was young. I make a mental note that this memory might inspire a *Sips and Whispers* video. Maybe a grass-themed cocktail. It would have to involve gin. And maybe freshly squeezed cucumber juice for flavor and muddled cilantro for color.

We make our way over to the refreshment table. The birthday boy wanders over to select a treat. One of the flamingos gives a nasal honk.

Marty smiles down at the boy. "Did you know that a group of these birds is called a flamboyance of flamingos?"

He unwraps a jumbo-size rainbow lollipop and stares up at Marty from behind its large circumference. "Do you know when my cake is going to come?"

"Call the bakery, kid," sniffs Marty. "I'm not the cake scheduler."

He blinks back at Marty, then wordlessly turns away and walks over to his friends.

A server comes by with a tray of cocktails and hands each of us one. I look to Paul before taking a sip, and we share a smile. The drink is cool and crisp on my lips. It hits me again how unusual this whole adventure is. I'm investigating a fricking murder mystery, with my husband and my ex-husband! Here we are, an investigative supergroup. The Super Snoops. Together, we approach Daniel. Flanked by Marty, Paul and Noodles, I feel a long-repressed giddiness flow through me.

Daniel stops talking abruptly. Excusing himself from the group, he walks over to us. "Paul, hi. What are you all doing here?"

Paul gives an apologetic bow of his head. "Sorry to come over unannounced like this, but we're wondering if we could talk to you."

A flicker of apprehension crosses his face. "Well, this isn't exactly a great time," he says, gesturing to the party around us.

"We're very sorry," I chime in, smiling. "But this is important. It's about Max."

I watch his eyes look past us. Following his gaze, I can see that he's focused on a woman standing at a table near a trellis of clematis vine. I recognize her as the woman in the sequined dress from the Mysa photos. As she shares a look with Daniel, there's a potent mixture of understanding and irritation in her eyes. Must be his wife.

Daniel gives her a subtle nod and turns back toward us. "Okay. Let's talk," he says, looking around, then lowering his voice. "But not out here. Follow me."

33

Daniel leads us inside the house through a pair of heavy stained-glass doors and down a long corridor. We enter a wood-paneled library with an ornately carved ceiling. Hundreds of leatherbound books line the walls, mixed in with thoughtfully placed Art Deco accents. I'm distracted for a moment as I admire the great care taken by an obviously brilliant designer to honor this century-old aesthetic.

He shuts the door and turns the latch, locking us in. Was that really necessary? I feel myself tense as he turns to us. His whole demeanor has shifted.

"Interrupting my son's birthday party is a bold move," he says sharply. "What exactly do you want?"

Paul raises a conciliatory hand. "We just want to ask you a few questions about the Mysa party. We're trying to figure out what happened because we don't think Max was suicidal."

Daniel's eyes dart around, from Paul to Marty, over to me, then back to Paul. "I don't want any involvement with this. Whatever you're up to."

I exchange a look with Paul. *How the heck are we going to get this guy to talk?* We all stand around for a moment, sharing an awkward silence.

To my surprise, Marty speaks up first. His tone is confident and calm. "Listen, Daniel, we talked to the police yesterday and told them that we aren't ready to accept that Max's death was a suicide. They agreed to look at his phone records because I witnessed him arguing on a call with someone. We're relieved they're looking into it, but we figure that process could take weeks. It's fine if you don't want to talk to us, but the police will probably be interviewing everyone soon anyway. Can you please just help us get some basic information now, while that night is still fresh in your memory?"

I slowly turn my head to Marty, stunned. He gives me a subtle wink, and I respond with a smile and an appreciative nod. Of course, the police are definitely *not* helping us, but that entire spiel he just concocted was fairly convincing.

Daniel swallows and looks away, staring into the mid-distance. I can sense a reticence is still there. Hopefully, he decides it's better to talk so he can get back to his son's party. He turns his head back to look at us. "I'll give you ten minutes."

He leads us over to a scalloped-back sofa facing a pair of low-slung chairs.

After we take our seats, Paul leans forward. "Is there anything strange that stands out to you from that evening? Anything that seemed off or unexpected?"

Daniel considers the question. "I'm not sure if I remember anything in particular. I left early, so I wasn't there when they discovered him . . ."

I frown. "What time did you leave?"

"I don't remember exactly. My wife was annoyed and wanted to go home, so we did. It was just after they'd served that bluish-purple drink."

"The *Carmel Sunset*," I say, making a mental note that this means they left around 7:00 p.m. If he's telling the truth. "Do you have any idea what Max's phone call might have been about? Why he was arguing with someone?"

I can tell he's deciding how much information he wants to divulge. After a long pause, he continues. "After Bronwen died, Max buried himself in his work. He went on a big M&A kick. Buying up smaller businesses and scaling them was always his favorite thing to do. It was like therapy for him, watching them grow and conquer. But many of them had been underperforming lately, and Hyperion was having some financial troubles as a result. So, he decided he wanted to sell off some of his acquisitions. Run a smaller, tighter ship and focus on his core business. We were arranging a sale of *Strange Tinctures* to a private equity firm when he died."

"And that's why he was stressed? Was the deal falling through?" asks Marty.

"It was teetering on the edge. Max always freaked out when something was on the brink. He viewed himself as this master strategist, so he couldn't stand situations where he wasn't in control."

"Which private equity firm?" asks Paul.

"Peristyle Capital. The sale wasn't coming together as well as Max had hoped. We were in the middle of trying to close the deal at the party. That's why I was fine with leaving when my wife wanted to go. Most of the key people at Peristyle Capital are London-based. It was getting late, so I wanted to get home in time to revise a few documents and get everything over to them in an email by the time they woke up." Daniel pauses. Something crosses his face. Is it sadness? Regret? Guilt? It's hard to read him. "Then a little while after I got home, Max's text message came through . . . and I couldn't believe what I was reading."

"What did you do?" I ask.

"I called Claes, and he told me what happened."

"You two were close," I say. "Max gave you one of the keys and talked about how you were his most trusted adviser. How did you first meet?"

He clears his throat. "In my thirties, when I was divorcing my first wife, I developed a bit of a problem with alcohol. I didn't want to go to traditional rehab. So I went to this place, Hazelwood. Max was there too."

I frown. "Max had an alcohol problem?"

"No, no. Hazelwood isn't just for addicts. It's a 'life cleanse' retreat. People go there for all sorts of different reasons. Max was trying to work through some childhood trauma. That's how he met Edith. She was a massage therapist there."

I exchange a quick glance with Marty and then Paul. Now we're getting somewhere.

"I heard they were an item once, is that right?" asks Paul.

"I wouldn't say that, no. I'd characterize it as more of an occasional fling," he replied. "Edith worked for him for many years. It made their dalliances complicated. But it wasn't anything serious. He told me he wasn't in love with her. Said she was too controlling." He gives a small laugh. "I always thought that was kind of funny. That they were so alike."

"We've heard rumors that Edith is pregnant," I say, leveling my gaze at Daniel. "Do you know about this?"

He responds with a slow nod. "Yes. Max didn't want anything to do with the baby. He wasn't happy about becoming a father. In fact, he told me it was something he had intentionally avoided his whole life. He was trying to start over with Tess. She was the love of his life. Or so he said. Edith's pregnancy was going to interfere with that. He was terrified Edith would tell Tess, so he tried to keep her quiet."

"How? With money?"

"Yes. He got her to sign an agreement that arranged for the baby to be taken care of financially as long as she never used Max's last name or publicly acknowledged him as the father."

I raise an eyebrow. There it is. A potential motive for Edith to kill the father of her child. Jealous anger over Tess. Having to sign papers to keep their love child hidden away for life would have been painful. The key presentation and public declaration of love for Tess on the rooftop that night could have pushed Edith to her limits. She is now just as viable a suspect as Claes, perhaps even more so. Not that my suspicions about Claes are absolved yet.

"Can we go back to how you met Max? At what point did you become his financial adviser?" asks Marty.

"Hazelwood was expensive, and I was practically broke at the time, from my divorce. Max and I became friends and he ended up picking up the bill for my stay. It was six figures. He said he was paying for it on one condition: if I pledged to him that I'd reinvent myself. Stay sober. Become successful again. Find happiness. So, I did just that. Even changed my name."

"What did you go by previously?"

He rubs his temples. "Before, I was Danny. 'Danny' was the kind of guy who would rip off his clients or go out and drink all night, then lie to his wife about it. Danny was self-centered. But not Daniel," he says. "Daniel's a reliable family man."

"Was Max a tough client?"

He hesitates. "Sometimes. He liked to call me 'Danny,' like it was our little in-joke. To remind me that I was indebted to him. He also questioned my choices a lot. It always felt like he was testing me."

"Testing you how?"

"Sometimes he'd offer me a drink. Then he'd apologize

and say he'd forgotten I was sober. Even at Mysa, I noticed how the servers kept offering me cocktails after I refused countless times and told them I didn't drink. It was almost like he'd instructed them to do it."

I take in this information. Claes described Max as a collector of broken people, and his tendency to manipulate was becoming a running theme among his "friends." It seems Max grew up to be just like his father. I realize now that I can't solely focus on physical clues and the cocktail timeline. I also need to consider how Max's controlling tendencies, and the psychological effects of that behavior, could have driven someone to murder him.

"Can you tell us, did he make any recent changes to his will?" asks Paul.

Daniel shakes his head. "Not that I'm aware of. His will was put in place years ago. He was planning to leave the majority of his American assets to charity."

"What about the rest of his fortune?" I ask.

He presses the tips of his index fingers together and steeples them under his chin. "I will say that he made some moves before he died. Transferring assets. Changing trusts. Moving money to offshore accounts."

"Really? Why?"

"I don't know. He was working with an estate planner in Sweden when he died. For whatever reason, he kept me out of those conversations." He pauses for a moment, then blinks, seemingly to shake off whatever wistfulness had lodged itself in his mind. "Max wanted to sell his other homes and live in one primary home here in Monterey. That's why he was going to remodel the ground floor of Mysa. He wanted it to become his personal office, as part of his plan to downsize his 'big life' as he called it."

"So he was planning a future. Period," Paul chimes in.

"Yes. I definitely don't think he killed himself."

A quick rap at the library door causes all of us to jump.

"It's Harriman, sir," says a voice from the other side.

Daniel gets up to unlock the door, and a tall white rabbit in a blue waistcoat pops into the room. "Sorry to interrupt, sir," says a baritone voice emanating from the single-toothed smile on its furry face. He holds up a cartoonishly large pocket watch. "But it's time to open the presents."

"Start without me," he responds, annoyance dripping from every word.

"Can I please change back into my chef whites, sir? I need to start working on dinner, and I need a smoke break. This thing is pretty flammable," he adds, gesturing to his suit. "I'm afraid I'll set my fur on fire."

Paul stands up. "We've taken up enough of your time. Thank you for talking to us. If you think of anything else, call me, okay?"

Daniel nods and flashes his glossy magazine smile as we thank him for his time. I wonder what thoughts might be running through his mind as I try to line up my gaze with his, but a direct line to his pupils isn't there. A chill runs through me.

I realize Daniel, or "Danny" as he used to be known, reminds me of an *Alice in Wonderland* character: the Cheshire Cat. There's something enigmatic and artificial about him.

He escorts us back to our car, playing the part of polite host. But it feels as though he's really making sure that we actually leave.

As we drive south along the highway, we talk through the details of what Daniel told us, and I add them to the cocktail timeline in my notebook. We collectively agree that Edith's viability as a suspect has increased significantly, although something about Edith as the killer isn't working for me. She strikes me as too much of a rule-follower to commit murder.

I need a snack, so I reach for Marty's CARBS basket and take a banana. As I peel it, I note that he selected a bunch that was just starting to speckle, my preferred stage of banana ripeness. It's a small, thoughtful detail from someone who knows all my preferences and idiosyncrasies. Maybe this is an aspect of marriage that I haven't been appreciating enough. I take a bite, and its mellow sweetness hits my palate as I pull up Hazelwood's website on my phone:

> Reset your mind with a complete wellness experience. Escape life's stresses to focus on your personal transformation with sessions led by world-renowned therapists and health coaches. Break through your barriers, restore your inner self, and feel good again.

A MURDER IN EIGHT COCKTAILS

As we approach Hearst Castle, we agree that Paul will stay in the car with Noodles while Marty and I take the tour solo. Tess would immediately recognize Paul, but she might not know who we are right away, especially given my new haircut. The plan is pretty straightforward: we'll corner her for a private conversation once we get to a natural stopping point in the tour. I figure if we have the element of surprise on our side, we might be able to get her to open up.

34

Studying Tess Hitcham up close, I can understand why she caught Max Magnussen's eye. Doe-eyed and sultry, she carries herself with the fizzing, exaggerated energy of a stage actress.

We're an hour into the Hearst Castle tour, but we haven't broached the real reason why we're here yet. Tess is our guide, dressed in full 1920s flapper garb. I look down at her tasteful red nails and note the faint tan line on her ring finger, where an engagement ring had once been. My mind flashes back to the argument Rosetta told me she'd overheard between Max and Tess near the elevator. *I can't believe you gave it to her. How could you?* Perhaps the absent ring might have been the "it"?

She leads us into the magnificent dining hall of the main Hearst Castle residence. Tapestries hang on the walls and heavy brocade chairs surround a long table dotted with ketchup and mustard bottles.

"This is where we eat with WR, here at 'The Ranch,' as we call it."

I respect her determination to remain in the present tense. As if "WR" Hearst is about to round the corner with Charlie Chaplin and invite us all to join them for a game of bridge.

"WR likes to remind people that this place was originally a camping site for his family, hence the ketchup and mustard bottles." She speaks in a rehearsed, Transatlantic accent. The kind of clipped, faux-British English that Katharine Hepburn used in old black-and-white movies.

I look at Marty, who gives me a quick eye-roll and taps his wristwatch, indicating we should progress to our questions. I nod in agreement. We follow her into a large room.

"This is the Assembly Room, it's the social hub of the house, where we gather for lavish costume parties. Sometimes we clear all this heavy furniture away to make a dance floor," Tess says with a wink, tapping her heel on the floor. "WR loves it when his guests cut a rug. Anyone wanna do the Charleston with me? It's all the rage!"

"She's so committed," Marty murmurs under his breath.

"No, we're okay, thanks," I say.

"Alright. Well, now we're going to go have a drink by the Neptune Pool, where many of our legendary exploits happen here at The Ranch."

We follow her outside and onto the grounds of the enormous property, passing an array of classical statues, illuminated and glowing white. Whoever orchestrated the tours has done a brilliant job of timing the entries to ensure that any concurrent groups remain out of sight. It feels as if we have the place to ourselves and have traveled back in time. Actors in costume are sprinkled about, fulfilling a variety of 1920s archetypes. A pair of men in tuxedos stand by the cerulean pool while a flapper chats away at the bar with a honey blonde in a satin gown and matching gloves.

I've been to Hearst Castle once before, as a volunteer chaperone on Zack's school field trip, but to see it at night is magnificent. The place is a world of its own. Twinkling lamps and the faint outline of the ocean in the distance give me goosebumps. Crickets chirp, reminding me it's getting late.

I wait for Tess to finish her sentence about the history of the Neptune Pool before speaking up. "Tess, we have some questions to ask you. Not about this place, though. They're questions for *you*."

She frowns. I can sense her strong reluctance to break character.

"We were at Mysa the night Max died. We're friends of Paul's," I explain. "We're concerned that perhaps Max didn't kill himself, and we want to know what you remember from that night."

Her frown darkens, and she places her hands on her hips. "Why the hell didn't you say something sooner? And why should I tell you anything about my relationship with my dead ex-boyfriend?"

Ex-boyfriend. There it is again. Officer Landry had mentioned that they were exes, too. But at the party, Max had called Tess his fiancée and the love of his life. Strange. I would have to dig into this with her, but for now, I need to cover the basics.

"The police told us you believe it was suicide. But we don't think it was."

She hesitates. I notice she's practically quivering with emotion now. Her eyes have darkened, intensified. "I'm a volunteer docent, but I can still get fired, you know. I'm not supposed to break character."

"We just want five minutes to talk to you," says Marty. "Then we'll go, we promise."

"I don't know," she responds.

A server in a tuxedo appears with a tray of golden-colored cocktails in coupes. "Bee's Knees?" he offers.

Tess takes two glasses from the tray and hands one to each of us. "Ooh, look, I think that's Jean Harlow!" she says, feigning a theatrical gasp and pointing in the direction of one of the costumed actors. Once the server leaves, she lowers her voice to an angry whisper. "You're being too loud! If you want to talk, please be discreet. I take this job very seriously. I'm not supposed to go off-script."

"Okay," I say, lowering my voice. "When did you and Max break up? He introduced you as his fiancée, so we thought you were a couple."

She gestures to an actor nearby and glares at me, then projects her voice loudly for everyone to hear. "Marx? Yes, Harpo Marx once draped mink coats over that statue of the naked women over there so they wouldn't be cold. Harpo was a real card!"

"Tess!" I shout in a hushed whisper. "We get it. You can't talk freely here. Isn't there some place we can go where we can just talk for a minute? So you don't have to . . . you know, perform?"

She looks me up and down, hesitating. Then she looks to Marty. I can tell she's assessing us, deciding whether or not to confide what she knows.

"What time does your shift end?" I take a sip of the Bee's Knees, and its soothing, honey-sweet flavors hit my palate.

She shakes her head. "Listen, sometimes we take VIPs on a bonus tour of Hearst's bedroom. I'll take you up there for five minutes. But then you must go. Agreed?"

We both nod. "Agreed."

Bee's Knees

Ingredients:

2 parts gin
0.75 parts lemon juice
0.5 parts honey syrup (equal parts honey and warm water)
Lemon twist, for garnish

Method:

Chill a cocktail glass
Add the ingredients to a shaker filled with ice and shake vigorously for 15 seconds
Strain into the chilled glass and garnish with lemon twist on rim

Media tycoon William Randolph Hearst's palatial California estate, Hearst Castle, was designed in 1919 by master architect Julia Morgan. Morgan was the first female licensed architect in the state of California and designed more than 700 buildings throughout her career. Originally intended to be a family home, Hearst Castle became the raucous site of legendary parties. Before guests sat down to dinner, they would gather for cocktails in the Assembly Room, which at 2,498 square feet, was larger than the average American home. Phones were stationed at each end so that guests could call if they needed to speak to someone on the other side of the room. The Bee's Knees, a popular drink at the time, would likely have been one of the tipples served.

35

We enter a bedroom with an ornate fireplace and a canopied bed. The heavy chintz fabrics everywhere give the room a moody, suffocating feel.

Tess pulls off her long satin gloves. "These things get hot," she says, tossing them on the bed.

"I can tell you love working here," I say. "Your passion for the history of the place really shines through."

"I see myself as a human portal, leading you back in time." She leans against the bedpost. "This is where WR carried on his longtime affair with Marion Davies," she explains, waving a hand around the room. "We're supposed to talk about all the lurid details of their affair. Tourists love to hear how Marion was just a wild party girl, a hanger-on with no real talent. But the truth is, she was brilliant. And funny. Much more than just WR's mistress. She even helped Hearst with a million-dollar check when he ran into financial trouble. And they were completely and truly in love. For decades."

Tess seems to be loosening up, so I want to keep her talking. "That's a very empathic portrait you paint of her. What was going on in Hearst's marriage? Why was he cheating in the first place?" I realize the ridiculousness of my own question as the words leave my mouth. As if there is ever a clear rationale for cheating. But I've become hyper-curious about other people's marriages lately, especially since hearing the news about Kathleen and Larry.

"Millicent Hearst was living a separate life," Tess explains. "They didn't have shared interests anymore, and she was focused more on motherhood than her marriage."

I frown. "Maybe she thought Hearst was a fuddy-duddy."

"Maybe Hearst tried to get her to join in his interests and failed," grunts Marty. "Aviation and journalism are worthy pursuits, you know."

I roll my eyes and turn my attention back to Tess. "So, can we get back to your relationship with Max? When did you two break up? From the way Max spoke about you at Mysa, it sounded like you were still together."

Tess takes a seat on the bed and kicks off her heels, as if she's in her own bedroom. "I'd ended things between us a couple of weeks before the party. Max was deeply depressed about it. I think he was in denial, honestly. He wouldn't accept it. You should know that, before you go around assuming his life was perfect and he had no reason to kill himself."

Her tone is almost defiant. As if she wants me to know she devastated the man emotionally. I glance over at Marty, and he nods for me to continue.

"How did you two first meet?" I ask.

After a small hesitation, she answers. "I used to be a magician's assistant. It was a high-end show, one where they entertain celebrities and heads of state. I met Max at a charity event, when we were performing for the Swedish royal family."

There's something a little too polished in her delivery. It feels like a performance. I consider how a magician's assistant is only one step removed from an actress. It's easy to imagine Tess misdirecting an audience away from the trickery at work with her beauty and charm. It would be a handy skillset for committing murder, too.

"Things were great with Max for a while," she continues. "We were together for a couple of years. But Max wanted to control everyone and everything around him. He was a narcissist. Lovebombing me and all that. I wanted real love. So I ended it." A self-satisfied smile plays at the corners of her lips. "Do you want to see the break-up letter I sent him?"

I nod as she reaches into her purse and pulls out her phone:

My love, we can't do this anymore. It's obvious that you are just another magician, Max the Magnificent, and I am relegated to the role of assistant. You run the show on an international stage while I'm tied up ever tighter in your controlling knots. I fear if I don't escape my cage now, I never will. I was wrong to think we could make this work. It's time now for me to disappear.

On the nose, yes, but clear and direct. I wonder if Tess herself might be a narcissist, too. She seems to take pleasure in knowing she had such an effect on a wealthy, powerful man. I note the date on the email: April 27. The Mysa party was May 12. I think of Edith. If she is in fact pregnant with Max's baby, that means they were definitely carrying on their affair while he was still with Tess. I consider broaching this with Tess somehow, but decide against it. We've finally gotten her to open up, so I don't want to upset her and put her on the defensive.

She blows out a sigh. "Max was in total denial about the breakup. He begged me to attend the Mysa opening. He said that my being there would mean so much to him. When I saw him at the party, the first thing he said to me was how he wanted to try and make things work again. He'd bought a home in Carmel for us, and he wanted to live a simpler life that wasn't all about him." She shakes her head. "But I knew this was just another tactic to get me to stay. That's why I wanted to talk to him on the rooftop, privately. End it for good, so he understood it really was over."

I decide to switch to our more pressing questions, unsure of how much more time she'll be willing to give us. "Did you know he was in the process of having his neck tattoo removed? Why would he get rid of it if he was in denial about your breakup?"

Her face is blank. I was hoping the mention of this would elicit some kind of emotional response or facial expression that would help me read her better, but it doesn't.

"I think it was a desperate attempt to get my attention," she says, "to make me change my mind. But the crazy thing is, he never even asked me about getting that dumb neck tattoo in the first place. I hated it."

I nod. "Sounds like he was very possessive. Someone told us they heard you having an argument with Max in the middle of the party. Is that true?"

She tilts her head. "I was angry because I saw Edith wearing the watch Max gave me."

I raise an eyebrow. So the watch was the "it" that Rosetta heard them fighting about. "The Verdura pineapple watch? I noticed it myself, it's beautiful."

"Yes. I love pineapple everything. I collect little pineapple tchotchkes. The watch was an anniversary gift, so it had real sentimental value to me. A lot of my things are still at his house in Sweden. So, when I saw Edith wearing it, I knew he'd been sleeping with her. I mean, I haven't even fully moved out yet, and here he is giving her my favorite watch? It felt like a very intentional thing. Like he asked her to wear it so it would make me jealous."

Max is really starting to sound quite petty. It has me wondering about the Minifon watch. If Max gave Edith a watch as a signal to Tess, could the Minifon have been serving a symbolic purpose too?

"Anyway," she continues, "we were arguing, and I said we should go up to the rooftop so people wouldn't hear us. He agreed. So we went up there, and that's when I told him it was over for good. Let's just say he didn't take it well. That's when I accidentally knocked Max's drink out of his hand because I talk with my hands when I'm angry. The drink sloshed everywhere and it ruined my dress."

I freeze. This is important new information. "Wait a minute. You spilled *Max's drink*, not yours?"

She nods. "I gave him my drink as a replacement. I didn't want any more of it anyway, it was too tart for me. That's when we went down to the main level to try and clean the stain."

My mind flashes to Tess tapping her nails on the bottle of seltzer water. I vividly recall the delicate sound of her nails drumming, the fuchsia-colored stain on her dress and the wet napkin she was clutching. All of my observations seem to be lining up with her version of events.

If Tess spilled *Max's* drink, that means that the killer's poisoning plot failed. So he or she needed to use another, alternative method. I think of the needle cap I found in the elevator. Perhaps the killer brought a needle filled with poison to Mysa as a backup murder weapon.

"So what happened after you went down to the main level?"

"He went to have another drink and cool off. I went to get seltzer water for my dress."

I think of Marty's contributions to the cocktail timeline. Shortly after this Max would have been drinking the *Bananavit* by the elevator, talking on his phone about the Hyperion deal. He was emotional and flustered, which makes sense now.

He'd just been dumped by Tess again, and his deal with Peristyle Capital wasn't coming together how he'd hoped.

"Do you remember what you were doing during the next drink? The creamy banana one?" I ask.

She frowns in concentration. "I remember Edith almost crashing into me in the hallway. I thought it was intentional at first, and I nearly spilled that drink, too. I was annoyed, but she apologized."

"You said 'almost crashing' into you. Was she running?"

"She was, yes. I'd heard her scream a minute before. I figured she saw a mouse or something."

I nod. This is consistent with Edith's recollections. She saw Orson in the aquavit library and screamed, then ran down the hall.

"So you then went back up to the rooftop?"

"Yes. I asked a server where Max was, and they said he had gone back up there. So I took the elevator up to tell him goodbye."

"Were you alone in the elevator?"

"Yes." She dabs at her eyes with a tissue. "And that's when I found him."

I let a silence pass between us as she cries a little more and blows her nose.

"Did you know the other keyholders? Daniel, Claes, or Rosetta?" I say, watching her face to see if there's a reaction to Rosetta's name. There isn't. She probably has no clue the woman is dead.

"Not really, only Claes." She shakes her head in disgust. "I can't stand him. He's a schemer. Always asking Max to fund his wacky business ideas. *Deathsmith* is the only venture that ever seemed to make any money. Claes had this way of making Max feel like he *owed* him just because Max was the successful one. He was always very jealous of Max and saw himself as a failure in comparison." She gives a derisive laugh. "Then again, I mean, how could you not?"

"Do you think Claes could have killed Max?"

She shakes her head. "That I don't know. I told you, I think Max *did* kill himself, so nothing like that has crossed my mind."

I nod. "Is there anything else you remember from that night?"

"Only that Max and Daniel were desperately trying to close some business deal. Both of them spent half the night on their phones. It was rude, I thought. Daniel, especially. Max gave him a key and made that nice speech, and he didn't even stay for the whole party."

"You saw Daniel leave early?"

"Yes. I wanted my jacket because it was cold. When I went to the cloakroom, I saw Daniel and his wife getting their coats. They told me they were leaving."

"Can you remember what cocktail you were having when you got your coat?"

She considers the question, then nods slowly. "Yes. I remember they were serving that ombre purple drink around then because I declined it. I needed a break from all the cocktails. I don't drink very much."

Despite her initial defensiveness, Tess has helped us quite a bit. Her recollections match Daniel's account, that he left with his wife during the *Carmel Sunset* around 7:00 p.m., which eliminates him as the killer. Although I remind myself that I can't lose sight of the fact that Tess is still a suspect. Something about her steadfast belief that Max killed himself doesn't sit right.

She straightens her shoulders. "Look, I need to go. I have another tour that starts in a few minutes, and I don't want to be late."

36

It's 10:03 p.m. by the time we arrive at The Artichoke Inn, a quaint Victorian house with a wraparound porch. Noodles keeps his sniffer to the ground as we follow the narrow path that winds its way up to the entrance. The scent of burning fireplace mingled with aromas of baking bread greets us as we walk in the door. It's charming, filled with potted plants and polished antique furniture. Artichoke-themed knick-knacks throughout provide a playful reminder of the place's namesake.

I ring a bell on the desk, and a plump man with a face like a bulldog comes lumbering out of the back room. His surly demeanor is an amusing contrast to the homey surroundings.

"Welcome to The Artichoke Inn. I'm Bill," he says gruffly. "Sorry, I was in the kitchen preparing our welcome cocktail for you." His large, ruddy hands grasp a tray of delicate-looking drinks. He passes each of us a coupe with an artichoke-leaf garnish bobbing placidly in amber liquid. "Don't eat the garnish," he warns. "It's just for looks."

I smile politely and thank him.

As Marty checks us in, Paul gives me a smile and a wink. "Thanks for including me. It's helped take my mind off all the stress of the past few days."

I nod and give him a gentle pat on the back. It's the only moment we've had to ourselves since our conversation in the Drinks Cabinet, which is a relief. I'm still unsure how to process everything that he said, and I'm not sure I'm ready to.

"Drink up, folks. You're gonna need a free hand to climb all the stairs," says Bill.

We chug our drinks and set the empty glasses back on the tray.

"Well, that was relaxing," says Marty.

We pick up our bags and Bill leads us down a long hallway and up a narrow, creaky staircase. He opens the doors to two rooms across from one another and hands us each a key. "I hope you enjoy your stay," he says flatly, in a rote recitation.

I look to Paul, who gives me a knowing smile and mouths the words *I don't believe him*. Bill turns to leave and Marty hauls our bags into our room.

"Goodnight," I say to Paul.

"Get some sleep, you two. Big day tomorrow." He holds my gaze before going into his room.

I flip on the lights and look around. The place is everything I expect it to be. Snug and welcoming, with comfy furnishings and a wood-burning stove. A restorative sojourn for weary travelers. I can sense the happy memories of couples

A MURDER IN EIGHT COCKTAILS

and families who have stayed here on their way to some other destination.

"We should do more road trips. You have to admit this has been fun." I look over at Marty. He doesn't respond and continues unpacking his bag in silence. "Remember Joshua Tree? We could go back this summer when Zack is home and do one of those healing sound baths at the Integratron? He'd think it was a hoot." I'm sure this mention of Zack will prompt a response, but it doesn't. "You're awfully quiet."

"I'm exhausted, that's all. Your long-winded ex-husband made the car ride rather tiresome."

I flop down on the bed in a frustrated huff. "Don't be such a grump. I agree he's talkative, but don't you find his positivity just a little bit infectious? Paul is glass half-full."

"Oh yeah? And what am I?"

I shrug. "You're too busy studying the glass."

He looks down at me. "Don't get too comfortable. We're going for a walk."

"At ten-thirty at night? Why?"

"Come on."

We leave the inn and make our way down an illuminated walkway leading to the beach. I observe Marty as we walk. I can tell he is someplace else, hiding in his own head as always. As much as I want to say something, I stay quiet.

We arrive at the beach, and he turns to me. "What more can you want, Willa? Our lives are great, and you've found success with your ASMR channel."

I haven't seen Marty this agitated in a long time. It's jarring. "You don't get it. The YouTube thing is a band-aid."

"How can you possibly see it that way? I mean, look at you!" he says, gesturing to me wildly. "You're thriving!"

I cross my arms. "Marty, you're the first person who made me believe in myself. I'm grateful for that. You were always very supportive, but you were also . . . fun. We used to be spontaneous, remember? That's the Marty I fell in love with. It just feels like you're not open to new experiences, new foods, new . . . anything!"

He looks at me. There's a madness in his eyes I've never seen before. He starts marching toward the water. "You want spontaneity? Fine."

"Marty!" I shout after him. "What are you doing?"

He ignores me, ripping off his shirt and throwing it in the sand. Slack-jawed, I watch as he feverishly unbuckles his belt and takes off his trousers. He runs toward the ocean in his boxer shorts until he's waist deep in the water, then he dives in. From his whooping and hollering, I know the water is ice cold, yet he seems triumphant about this "brave" act.

"Come on in! Hurry! My 'personal business' is getting freezer burn."

Feeling a mix of emotions, I kick off my shoes. Fully clothed, I walk to the edge of the water. It swirls and foams around my ankles. I want to feel the same bracing exhilaration that Marty is experiencing, but the icy wet sand squishing between my toes only makes me cold and numb.

"I don't know what's going on with you," he calls out, his head bobbing in the water several feet away from me, "but I'm not going to let you take it out on me."

I wade in a bit farther until the water reaches my knees and begins to slow me down. The waves are getting higher. I stare out at the endless ocean, my mind churning. The pent-up emotions from the last few days are bubbling up in me. As cold as I am, I feel my cheeks flush with heat at the thought of the unknowable future of our marriage. Tears fill my eyes. Emotions have a way of doing this to me. Staying measured and controlled for a long time, then ambushing me when I least expect them to come to the surface.

I plunge into the water and squeeze my eyes shut, listening to the deep, swirling sounds of the ocean. For a moment, I relax underwater and allow myself to consider what my life might be like if I hadn't retired from interior design. If I'd built up my own business and still felt like I was *doing* something.

I pop my head back up and flip my wet hair backward. I look at Marty. "Happy now?"

He smiles. For several minutes, we splash around. My body acclimates to the cold as we alternate between floating on the surface and diving down into the water. I swim a bit closer to him until we're both treading water, facing one another.

"It just doesn't feel like you're 'in this' with me anymore. It feels like you're holding me down."

Marty gives me a gut-punched look. "So you're saying I'm a literal albatross around your neck."

"Not everything is about fucking birds, Marty!" I take a deep breath and dunk my head underwater again. When I come back up for air, he's staring at me.

"Do you know how many men my age are out having affairs? Or at least, trying to have affairs in quiet desperation? I'm sorry that my biggest offense is taking up a birdwatching hobby and not being exciting enough for you."

I close my eyes. They sting with guilt. I feel selfish for making him feel this way. We return to the shore, and Marty struggles to pull on his clothes and shoes over his wet body. He starts walking back toward the hotel, his shoes squishing.

I follow along behind him, shivering in the chilly night air. "Why do you love me so damn much, Marty?"

"Because I'm always chasing you, but I never catch you, and I guess I like that."

His answer surprises me. Although I don't know if I totally understand it. We keep walking. "I think a psychologist would say that means you have an 'anxious attachment style.'"

He shrugs. "Or maybe it's just who I am. It's why I like birds. Because they fly away."

I sigh. "Let's walk faster. I'm freezing."

We're both lying in the dark together in stillness. After we returned to the room, we each took a hot shower and got ready for bed in silence. We haven't had a fight like this in a very long time. It's unsettling. Staring up at the ceiling, I slow my breathing. I can feel it syncing with the rhythm of Marty's breaths.

He clears his throat. "There's something we need to talk about."

Suddenly, I feel nervous. His tone has changed. *Is he going to say The D Word?* Do to me what I did to Paul and end things right here, on the spot? My heart begins to pound in my chest.

"Okay. What is it?"

"The lemon cake."

I turn to him, confused. "What about it?"

"You think it's my favorite. I was so in love with you when we were first dating that of course I gobbled it up and told you how delicious it was. But honestly, it's too syrupy sweet for me. Lemon cakes should be a little tart, you know?"

My jaw falls open.

"Sometimes I can barely choke it down."

I sit up in bed and look down at him. "Why didn't you say something before? Are you kidding me? You've been forcing that cake down your gullet for over twenty-five years?"

"I've just never had the heart to tell you. You always seem so proud when you make it. I wolf it down because I love you."

My hands go up to my cheeks. I'm completely stunned.

"Let's get some sleep. We have a big day with Nina Hernandez tomorrow."

The Artichoke Inn

Ingredients:

1 part wood-aged rum
1 part Cynar
1 part simple syrup
1 part lime juice

Method:

Chill a coupe
Add all the ingredients to a shaker filled with ice and shake vigorously for 15 seconds
Double strain into the chilled coupe

Cynar is an amaro made from artichokes, which thrive in Central California's climate of mild winters and cool summers. Artichokes are the official state vegetable of California, and Castroville, a small town in northern Monterey County, has been deemed the "Artichoke Center of the World." Dining in Monterey is a sensorial experience, and many restaurants take great pride in serving only locally sourced ingredients bursting with freshness and flavor. The area's Artichoke Trail features over twenty culinary stops, where visitors can sample local delicacies, such as wood-grilled whole artichokes, fried artichoke heart po' boys, and artichoke cupcakes.

Thursday

37

A sharp rap on the door makes me sit up in bed. I look at the clock: 6:47 a.m. I step onto the chilly floor, wrap myself in an Artichoke Inn terry cloth robe and peer through the peephole.

"Who is it?" asks Marty, still in a fog.

"Paul," I reply.

"Of course it is," he grumps, throwing off the blankets. He ambles into the bathroom and slams the door.

I run my hand through my hair and pull my robe tighter around me, then open the door. "Good morning."

"Sorry for the early wake-up call, Wil. But I had to tell you right away." He raises his phone to show me the screen. It's a text from Daniel. "He sent it late last night."

I spoke to Max's estate planner in Sweden because I needed to get everything in order to probate his estate in California. It turns out the beneficiary of all his European assets, which are significant, was changed to Tess Hitcham about a month ago.

I gasp and lean against the doorframe. "Do you think this could be a motive? Tess broke up with him around that time.

She said he was struggling with their breakup, in denial. If she knew she was going to inherit some of his wealth, she probably figured he wouldn't change his will right away in the hopes they'd get back together."

"Yes. But why break up with him in the first place? If her motive was money, she could have just stayed with him until she killed him."

I sigh. "You're right."

Quickly, we gather up our things, check out of the B&B, and load up the car. On the drive to Nina's vineyard, Hernandez Estates, we discuss the various clues and what this new development about Tess's inheritance could mean.

As we get close to Jolon, a bucolic part of southern Monterey County, we turn off the two-lane highway, and a romantic chateau comes into view. Acres of vineyard spill out behind it and an orchard lines one side of the hill. We drive up the long, cypress-lined driveway and round a curve to the back. I can see a petite woman standing on the expansive veranda overlooking the vineyard, waving to us.

"Anyone who is anyone in the California liquor business knows Nina Hernandez," Marty explains as he puts the car in park. "Listen, you two, just like the others, we can ask our questions. But we are *not* telling her about finding Rosetta's body. She's an important business colleague, and I don't want to alarm her . . . or have her think we're all nuts."

Paul and I nod in agreement. We get out of the car and

begin walking toward the chateau. I take in the serene landscape, and the gentle scent of wildflowers tickles my nostrils.

"So, Nina was your client?" asks Paul.

"Yes," Marty responds. "Her company primarily does artisanal spirits, but she's also a great technical innovator in sparkling wine. She contacted me when she was having trouble diagnosing some problems with the vines here. They were making do and adapting to the changes, but they weren't addressing the root problem."

Sounds familiar, I think to myself.

"I determined it was an issue with their soil. So I developed a soil-amendment plan, and it worked out well for them."

"Do you miss that line of work?"

Marty shakes his head. "I don't. I was worried I would, but I've found joy in other things."

As we approach the entrance, Paul turns to Marty. "What is it that you love about them? Birds, I mean?"

"It's something in the majesty of being untethered. I love watching them soar in the breeze. It's pure freedom."

Hearing Marty's heartfelt words, I feel rocked. I realize I've never given him an opening to talk about birding. I used to accuse Paul of being self-centered and not wanting to engage in my interests, but I know that I can have those tendencies, too. It dawns on me that our reasons for retiring were dramatically different. Marty had accomplished what he wanted in his work life and that freed him to pursue another passion. I, on the other hand, had a strong intuition that I was quitting too early. It had been challenging to balance motherhood with a career. Marty was the breadwinner, so the housework and childcare often fell on my shoulders. I wasn't resentful about it, but it did prevent me from giving real energy and focus to interior design. And all the "retirement talk" had given me a false sense that a new adventure was waiting around the corner.

A staff member greets us at the entrance of the chateau and shows us in. The ground level boasts marble floors, enormous chandeliers, and intricate woodwork. A small tour group is sampling varietals in an impressive tasting room.

Nina Hernandez strides confidently toward us, hand outstretched. She's wearing black leggings that hug her tiny frame and a crisp white button-down shirt that contrasts with her bronze skin and matches her perfectly white teeth.

"Nice to meet you," she says, giving a firm handshake to Paul and me, then hugging Marty hello.

She leads us into a beautifully appointed office with soaring ceilings. Enormous pairs of French doors frame the long rows of grapevines outside. We all take a seat, and a staff person pours us each a glass of sparkling wine.

I raise the flute to my lips and take a sip. It's dry, full-flavored and earthy. The bubbles rise and burst in my mouth.

"So, I hear you're a cocktail influencer," says Nina, crossing her slim legs. "Tell me about your YouTube channel."

"Oh, well, I'm not some avant-garde mixologist or anything. It's more about the ASMR. Most of my followers are simply there to unwind after a long day and fall asleep. But I do like to add little touches. Unique barware. Funky garnishes. Relaxing cocktail-related stories." I pause, suddenly feeling self-conscious talking to such an accomplished entrepreneur about my niche little corner of the internet. Although, her energy is warm and curious, and she seems to be showing genuine interest.

I get up and walk over to a small bar cart in the corner of the room. I lift a mixing glass. "See this?" I take a coiled strainer and set it on top, gently clicking it into place. "That's an ASMR sound. One time I did a whole video using only that sound. I called it *Gentle Clicks*. It got over a million views."

Nina smiles brightly. "I think you'll need to create some sparkling wine cocktails for Hernandez Estates. Do you do brand partnerships?"

"I do," I say, smiling at the thought of Nina as a future client.

She sits back in her chair and looks at each of us. "So, tell me. What brings the three of you all the way out here?"

"We want to ask you about Max Magnussen," says Paul.

She sighs. "Yes, I was sorry to hear about his death."

"Did you know him well?"

She nods. "He was difficult, but a brilliant businessman. I was closer with his wife than I was with him."

"Bronwen, right?" I chime in, trying not to sound overeager.

She nods. "Yes. She was wonderful. We used to go paragliding together."

"Really? Do you have any photos of her?"

"Of course," she says, walking over to the fireplace mantel. "I'm a licensed paraglider pilot. Bronwen loved anything adventurous. That's why it's so sad that she passed how she did." She pauses. I can see she's getting emotional.

"It was a skiing accident, right?" I ask, realizing it's important to confirm this, given my only source of information on Bronwen's death thus far has been Claes.

"Yes," she responds. "In the Alps, when they were on holiday. Bronwen was such a bright light. I miss her. She taught me to always enjoy life to the fullest and never hold back."

Nina gestures for me to come over and look at a photo she is pointing to on the mantel. I get up and walk over to it. She hands me the frame. Bronwen is standing next to Nina in front of a large yacht. They have their arms over each other's shoulders, and they're both about the same height. I can immediately tell that there is no chance the woman I saw with Claes at the farmers' market was Bronwen. That woman was about five foot eight or nine, maybe taller. They don't look alike, either. How could Rosetta have mistaken that woman for Bronwen?

I feel a surge of surprise, followed by a sinking feeling in my stomach. Somehow it's disappointing that *Maybe-Bronwen* is definitively *Not-Bronwen*. Perhaps it's because Claes has always been the lead suspect in my mind. If Bronwen is out of the equation, it makes his motive less clear. The artwork that Edith caught him snooping through could still have something to do with it, though.

I take out my phone and show her the photo of the woman from the farmers' market. "Do you happen to know who this is?"

She studies it. "I don't know her, sorry."

We sip our bubbles together, and an attractive, well-built young man appears to top up our glasses. He exchanges a flirty look with Nina, and I suppress a smile, recalling Marty's mention of her preference for younger men.

I nod to a large oil painting of two men hanging above the doorway. "Is that Napoleon?" I ask, gesturing to the man wearing a bicorn hat.

"Yes," she points to the man next to him, "and that's Jean-Rémy Moët. Both great marketers. Napoleon, of himself, and Moët, of champagne. He promoted it among the nobles at Versailles. I suppose you could say he was one of the world's first influencers." She nods to Marty. "I do believe Moët would have been impressed with your wife's channel."

He smiles at me. "I knew you two would hit it off."

I turn to Nina. "You've accomplished so much, what do you want to do next?"

"This place is my main focus for now. I've got big ambitions for our sparkling wine. The champagne industry was defined by women: Louise Pommery, Lily Bollinger, Barbe-Nicole Clicquot. I want to do the same for California's bubbles. Women run businesses differently because we're wired differently," she gives me a wink, "aren't we?"

38

"Why are we slowing down?" I ask from the backseat.

It's been just under an hour since we left Nina's vineyard, and I've let Paul take shotgun next to Marty. It's amusing to watch the backs of their heads as we ride along, the two of them seated next to each other.

"Because I'm hungry," says Marty. "There's a great little wine bar around here where we can stop for a bite."

Paul shrugs agreeably. "Sounds good to me."

We turn onto a narrow road. A cell phone rings. It's Marty's. He answers, and the voice of Tim Kluver comes over the car's Bluetooth speaker.

"Marty, hey. My buddy ran the plate for you. Are you ready for this?"

I hold my breath.

"Your mystery farmers' market woman is a well-known fence in the art world, Lily Theisen. She's been in and out of prison several times. Looks like she's kept it pretty clean in the last few years, though."

"Thank you, Tim. We appreciate this," says Marty.

"You got it. Listen, please don't tell anyone I did this for you. Of a feather."

"Of a feather," responds Marty before hanging up.

I frown. "Is that some kind of Cluster Flock omertà signoff?"

"Hey, I don't need any mockery from you. I just did you a solid."

"You're right," I say, smiling appreciatively. "Thank you, babe."

Marty's been noticeably warmer and more easygoing today. Perhaps our argument last night, as intense as it was, provided a much-needed tension release for both of us. There's something about the way he's been helping with the mystery, whether it's coercing Daniel into opening up to us, or getting his contacts like Tim and Nina to help give us information. It's been . . . well . . . *hot!* I reach for his hand and give it an affectionate squeeze.

We pull up to a rustic establishment with a wooden sign, *Sediments*. Lights are strung across a brick patio, forming a twinkling canopy over white-cloth-covered tables. It's the late afternoon lull before the dinnertime rush so the place is quiet. A server guides us to a cozy spot near a fountain. We settle into our seats and study the menu. I smile as I look around the table at the three of us together.

"The flight of macaroni and cheeses paired with local wines is catching my eye," says Paul. "Maybe we could get the fried chicken bites, too?"

A MURDER IN EIGHT COCKTAILS

"I don't eat birds," says Marty, adjusting his glasses.

The server returns and takes our orders.

Paul Googles Lily Theisen and shows us a few YouTube videos on his phone. One is an interview from an episode of "20/20" about the world of art theft.

"Are you sure this is the same woman?" says Paul, frowning. "Her hair looks completely different."

"Oh, that's definitely her," I say, listening intently to the video. "I remember the sound of her voice from the hotel. She has a breathy vocal fry that's ASMR ecstasy."

I take out my notebook and pen, preparing to jot down further notes. "There has to be some kind of connection to the art I saw in storage at Mysa that Edith caught Claes snooping through. I looked up the photographer, Helga Riis. She was really famous in the nineties and died a few years ago. If the photos were valuable enough, was Claes partnering with Lily to steal them and kill his brother as part of the cover-up?"

"It's possible," says Paul. "But of all the valuable things Max owned, his brother was willing to kill him for just a few works of art? It doesn't feel like enough of a motive."

A server arrives with a tray of bubbling macaroni and cheeses in little ramekins, along with garlic toast points. She sets down another plate, piled high with breaded mac and cheese triangles and ranch dip.

"I'm going to use the restroom," says Marty, getting up from the table. "You two go ahead and start."

I reach for one of the bites, a golden wedge of fried dough

bursting with gooey cheese. Dunking it in the tangy, garlicky ranch complements the flavor perfectly.

Paul looks at me from across the table. "You know, I've been thinking about what you said the other day. How you might not be built for marriage. I think you're being too hard on yourself. You and Marty have something special."

I pause, a mac and cheese bite halfway to my mouth. "You really think so?"

"I do. You two balance each other out. He's your ballast. And you liven him up. He's *your north, your south, your east, your west.*"

"Faulkner?"

"Auden."

We eat together in comfortable silence for a few minutes. Over the past few days, I've noticed a mellowing of my existential anxiety about post-retirement life. Maybe it's been the sheer drama of it all. Max's death. Seeing Paul again. Kathleen's divorce. Discovering Rosetta. The marine layer that had settled over my brain for so long is finally starting to lift. Colors are more vivid, and the blurry edges of my life are starting to sharpen into focus.

I pinch the cool stem of my wine glass and take a sip. The acidity of the Sancerre cuts beautifully through the thick cheese. "So, how did your date with Kathleen go?" I ask. "You haven't said anything."

He nods, and I notice he blushes a little. "It was great. I like her."

"Wait a minute. What about Noodles? Will he get along with Benedict Cummerbund and Nosfuratu?"

"We've already introduced them, and it went well."

"You always did move fast," I say with a wink.

Marty returns to the table, and the rest of the meal is filled with discussion, theories and debates about the information we've gathered on our two-day journey. The ride back home is quiet. I can tell we're all tired.

As we pull up to Paul's home, he turns to us. "Why don't you both come inside for a few minutes? I can show you the house."

I look at Marty. To my surprise, he gives a pleasant *Sure why not?* shrug. I give his arm an appreciative touch.

As we enter the house, I note that it's quaint and mostly tidy. Paul leads us farther inside, and the three of us stand around together, wedged into the kitchen. Marty asks about the logistics of moving the tiny house from one place to another, and Paul gives him a detailed answer. It's nice to see them together, talking as friends.

My eyes scan the living area, where I note a black pullover sweater, covered in cat fur, draped across the chair. "Looks like someone forgot to put her sweater back on," I say with a wink.

Ears turning red, Paul smiles. "Kathleen stayed over." He stops. "Now I'm wondering what she had on when she left!"

We all share a laugh. It surprises me a little, but I realize that I'm happy for Paul. Kathleen could be a good fit for him. They're both a little chaotic and free-spirited. Neither of them has kids. The idea of Kathleen and Paul as our future couple friends is a pleasant thought.

It's hitting me that the universe has brought Paul back into my life after thirty years to remind me that my natural inclinations, to seek excitement and change, aren't always healthy or right. Especially when it comes to relationships. I feel a rush of clarity. As much as Paul appreciated me when we were together, and perhaps appreciates me even more now, he never truly *saw* me. He desired a version of me that wasn't really me. I was too neurotic to be the bohemian woman he wanted, even though I admit a small part of me wanted to be that woman, too. And that's why we never lasted. Our relationship was a funhouse mirror, reflecting a distorted, grumpy version of myself back to me that I didn't like.

Paul reaches for a pitcher of lemonade in the fridge. He pours each of us a glass, and we all sit down at the kitchen table. While he and Marty discuss the pros and cons of Paul's "tiny" lifestyle, my mind drifts. I run through all the clues in my mind again. The answer to who killed Max Magnussen is still eluding me.

I pull out my phone and scroll to the photo I took of Max standing next to his four "dear friends": Rosetta, Claes, Daniel, and Tess. Edith stands off to one side, holding the key box in her hands. For a moment, I'm transfixed by the photo, staring into each person's eyes. I look at Max. He seems entirely at ease, with an air of total assurance about the life ahead of him. Rosetta looks deeply sad. Claes' expression is neutral, unreadable. Daniel looks frustrated. Tess looks like she can't wait to leave. Edith looks angry.

Why had I so quickly assumed that one of these five people was the killer? There were nearly fifty people at Mysa that night. Maybe the killer was an intruder who stole one of the elevator keys, or a professional hitman who accessed the stairwell somehow. Did I make a rookie error in narrowing it down to this group so quickly?

I take a sip of lemonade, and the tang of the citrus helps to clarify my muddled thoughts. No. My instincts tell me that the killer is someone close to Max. Everything about the manner in which he died, from the drama of it to the suicide text and the discarded watch, feels deeply personal.

My eyes wander back over to Claes. I always suspected that he had something to do with Max's murder. Their different stations in life made for a toxic mix of jealousy and resentment. Not to mention Claes' criminal past. Paul had a point that Max probably owned all kinds of valuable artwork. So how could stealing those particular Helga Riis works justify murder? Then again, it would explain why Lily was mailing something to that collector, Millie Hagerty, in Wisconsin. She was probably conspiring with Claes on how to sell them, presumably for a massive sum.

I focus in on Claes' face in the photo. Lying to me about

drinking the *Aquavit Negroni* is the one thing that's really not sitting right. It's such a small lie, but it feels significant. Max wasn't killed until later in the evening, well after that drink was served. So Claes must have found it critical to lie about that particular window of time. What could that reason be, other than a cover up? His face was unreadable a moment ago, but something about his expression now seems almost smug. He looks like he's thinking he's clever. Clever enough to get away with murder.

A realization is finally beginning to crystallize in my mind: Claes is the killer. We've already ruled out Daniel after careful consideration. Both Tess and Edith moved to the front of the pack for a while, but both of their stories seem to line up with the facts of what happened. Edith has a motive, yes, but she didn't have much of an opportunity to kill Max, and she also doesn't strike me as the type of person to kill anyone. Conversely, Tess discovered Max's body, which of course makes her suspicious. But she doesn't have a motive.

It appears to me now that my initial gut instinct was right, and in this horse race of suspects, Edith and Tess have been overtaken by Claes. I still can't understand why he would want to kill Rosetta, though. Figuring out the motive to kill both her *and* Max is going to be an added challenge. Unless Rosetta's murder wasn't premeditated and just a case of wrong place, wrong time. Perhaps she walked in on Claes trying to steal something from Max's rental house? What am I missing?

"Alright, you two," says Marty. "We need to hit the road and get home. What's the plan for tomorrow?"

"Not so fast," I say. "I've been going over everything in my mind, and I'm pretty sure that Claes did it."

Together, the three of us review the cocktail timeline again, ruling out each suspect one by one and theorizing how Claes could have pulled it off.

"A lot of this is still circumstantial," says Marty. "How do we *prove* that Claes killed Max?"

I take in a breath. "What if we distract Claes somehow, while I do a search of his house? There's got to be some kind of clue he's left behind."

"I can keep him occupied," says Paul. "Claes has a small ownership stake in Mysa. He's been wanting to talk to me about its future. I could ask him to meet me for a coffee tomorrow. That'll buy you an hour or so?"

I glance over at Marty, waiting for him to say "no way." But he doesn't. It seems he's finally accepted that I'm determined to solve this and nothing is going to stop me.

Friday

39

While constructing a tomato and cheese sandwich for Marty's lunch, I receive a text from Paul confirming he's meeting up with Claes at a local coffee shop, which gives me at least an hour to do what I need to do. The plan is in motion.

Earlier in the day, I selected a gorgeous clay pot of succulents at *Petal Pushers*. On the card, I wrote:

> Claes, our sympathies are with you.
> Willa and Marty Keane

Now, I have my cover in case I get caught. I put the plant on the passenger-side floor of my SUV and head to Claes' house. I have no idea how I am going to get in. Maybe I can force open a window. I've tucked a screwdriver into my purse, just in case. (We don't own a crowbar.) I park the car on a side street, grab the potted succulent and walk around the corner to Claes' carefully maintained home.

Casually striding up to the front door, I ring the doorbell.

I'm no burglar. See, people! I'm out here ringing the doorbell. I know he isn't home, but I want to look legit in case some Gladys Kravitz neighbor is peeking out her window. My heart rate increases as I wait. It's mindboggling that this is the second time in a week I've found myself breaking into a house.

I try the doorknob. It's locked. Damn. I set the potted plant on a nearby bench and glance around. Nobody is in sight. Quickly, I walk around to the side of the house. There are two windows on the ground level, both firmly shut. I try one, but it won't budge. I could try jamming it open with the screwdriver, but the paint looks pristine and fresh. If I ruin the paint job, I'll be leaving obvious evidence that I broke in. I look up to the second floor. One of the windows is open halfway.

I need a ladder. My eyes move over to a sturdy-looking tree close to the house. I grew up climbing trees. Haven't done it in about forty years, but no time like the present. I walk over to the tree and slip off my shoes. I place them in my purse and sling it over my shoulder.

Slowly and carefully, I find a firm foothold a couple of feet off the ground. I make my way up the trunk, using knotholes and branches for grips as I go. As I feel the bark between my fingers, suddenly I'm a kid again. I reach a thick branch and look down, the ground swimming beneath me. Hoisting myself up onto the branch, I'm finally high enough. All those *Stretch Your Way to Strength* resistance band sessions have paid off! I balance myself on the branch and scooch out onto it.

Pausing to catch my breath, I edge my way closer to the window. Reaching toward it, I put my hand under the sash and push hard to raise the pane upward. I lean forward and place my foot on the sill. Carefully, I step onto it with my other foot and maneuver myself into the opening. It's an ungraceful movement to say the least, but I manage to land with a gentle thud on the wood floor of the bedroom.

After a short rest, I stand up and brush myself off. I take stock of the room. Neat and sparse, it's devoid of much stuff or any real character. Probably a guest room. I make my way downstairs to the main level. I go to the front door and unlock it. Quickly, I take the potted plant inside just in case I get caught. *Oh, hello there, Claes! The front door was unlocked so I came in to set this plant on your kitchen counter. You know, just being a friendly neighbor. That's how we do things in Carmel!*

As I get my bearings, my heart begins to race. I'm riding a dopamine high. This is the "new me" – a ballsy woman boldly creeping into an unsuspecting art thief's home to do some bona fide investigative work, baby! Am I effing nuts or what?! Nina Hernandez should see me now. This must be what paragliding feels like. Pure exhilaration.

I clutch the potted plant as I explore the home's interior. It's modern but classic, and the wide entry hall showcases some magnificent photography. I note a Robert Frank, a Man Ray, a Cindy Sherman, and a Weegee. There is no way Max's miscreant brother can afford all this. Some or all of it must surely be stolen. As I walk down the hallway, I peer into each room. Whatever I'm seeking, I hope I recognize it when I see it. Some kind of clue that provides an insight into Claes' motive, or physical evidence that proves he killed Max. I turn left into an intersecting hallway.

I hold back a scream. What am I looking at? Hanging from the ceiling is a huge chandelier made of human skulls and bones. It's grotesque. Terrified, I take in a few breaths. Is Claes some kind of serial killer? I flip on the nearest light switch. Bright light floods the space. Now I can see that I'm in Claes' *Deathsmith* office. It's a large, open room with various death-themed artworks lining the walls. Various metal and wooden sculptures are dotted around the room. I shudder at the thought of how many of these objects must be made from "lost loved ones."

I spy a curved black vase sitting on a shelf. Embedded in the ceramic is a mosaic design that encircles both the top and bottom. Upon closer inspection, I realize that the mosaic design is made from rows of shiny white human teeth. *Seriously? Ugh.* I spot a black velvet pillow, with a woman's face painted on it, resting on a chair. I pick it up for a closer look and wince. Coming out of the back side of the pillow is a long human-hair ponytail, tied with a ribbon.

I head toward a desk brimming with papers and pick up a glossy brochure titled *Deathsmith: Life is fleeting. Memorials are eternal.* I skim through it:

A MURDER IN EIGHT COCKTAILS

Death has sparked human creativity since prehistoric times. From The Divine Comedy to the Danse Macabre and Dia De Los Muertos, death is a global cultural obsession. At Deathsmith, we believe that the physical, artistic expression of a lost loved one can be something to treasure forever. Bring us their (c)remains and we'll give you a lasting objet d'art.

Ick. This guy is a weirdo, that's for sure. But he isn't Buffalo Bill. I relax a bit and look around some more. I notice that the walls on both sides feature an array of family photos, hung gallery-style. Max is everywhere.

I walk over to the photos. It appears that Claes and Max had become quite close over the years. Closer than Claes indicated when I interviewed him at Mysa. Each of the photos is framed in an identical style and signed. I note the signature: *H. Riis*. Helga Riis, the famed photographer behind the photos that Edith caught Claes snooping through at Mysa! I wonder what the significance of this could be.

One picture looks more recent. Arms draped over each other's shoulders, Max and Claes look healthy, happy and bronzed as they wave from the deck of a luxe sailboat. It's beginning to hit me that my identification of Claes as the killer no longer seems right. They look happy. Their poses in some of the other photos are silly, light-hearted, filled with laughter and smiles.

I take a step back and look around his home with renewed

perspective. It's clear that Claes truly loves art. Whether it's the creepy skull chandelier, the Riis photos, or the Man Ray, they're all presented with painstaking care. Not unlike the way Marty lovingly catalogs his record collection. A part of me wants to like Claes. He appreciates human creativity in all its forms, and it appears he loved his brother very much, despite their differences. I keep looking and come across a photo of Rosetta. She's part of a larger group, wearing her usual caked-on makeup and carefully fluffed bouffant. I can almost smell the Shalimar perfume just from looking at her.

The photo appears to have been taken during a celebration of the Hyperion purchase of *Strange Tinctures*. They're toasting with champagne, and a cake in the background features one of her bitters-bottle designs. Many emotions seem to be written on Rosetta's face as she stares into the camera. Boredom. Resentment. And yes, her namesake bitterness.

Her face is in profile, but another woman in the picture who is standing nearby is unmistakably Lola, Rosetta's sister.

A thought that I've never had before comes to me. It pops into my head like an inspiration for a new cocktail. Moments before, it wasn't there, and now, *Poof!* The solution is right in front of me. I'm finally having that elusive, Sherlockian *aha* moment!

How I can prove my theory to the police is another matter. But at least I finally know what I need to prove. I shuffle through all the clues in my mind, as if flipping through a deck of cards. I take out my phone, open my text chain with Marty and begin typing to him. He is the first person . . . the only person . . . I want to share this realization with.

I begin with who the killer is and how they did it. Letting out a slow breath, I hit send and begin typing a second, shorter message, asking him what he thinks we should do next to convince Officer Landry that Max was, in fact, murdered. I hit send and reread the texts I've just written. Barely believing it's all there, right in front of me.

As I slip my phone back into my pocket, I feel a sudden wave of homesickness for Marty. Why have I been so self-centered? We can figure out this third act together. Marty gives me support and breathing space to be my own person, and that's exactly what I need to feel whole. My ASMR journey would have never developed if I had still been with Paul, that's for sure. I would have been too caught up in "Paul World" to do something like this on my own. Marty isn't a showman or a charmer. But he loves me and reflects my whole, true self back to me. Marty makes me feel radiant and alive.

Suddenly, something strikes me on the back of the head. I gasp and fall to the floor. The potted plant smashes on the ground. Stunned, it takes me a moment to process what has just happened. I clutch my head in my hands and try to get up and run, but as I get to my knees, THWUMP! I feel another sharp pain. The world goes black.

40

My eyes open in musty darkness. The world is airless, stuffy, pitch-black. I try to move my arms, but they're bound tightly together in front of me. My mouth is taped shut and I'm blindfolded. A splitting headache suddenly switches on inside my brain like a halogen bulb. My heart pounds in my chest and my breathing is raspy. Then, somewhere in the dark recesses of my brain, I remember that someone hit me on the back of the head while I was in Claes' home, studying a photo of Rosetta's sister, Lola.

Yes! That's it! The realization of who killed Max Magnussen comes crashing back into my consciousness like a tidal wave.

But the cold reality of the situation I now find myself in pierces through the miasma of pain and confusion. Oh God. Someone is trying to kill me. How am I going to get out of this? I need to see Marty again and tell him I love him before I'm murdered. Some fresh air would be nice, too. And a slice of chocolate cake for my last meal. I feel woozy. Where's my phone? I also need to pee. Luckily, I've always done my Kegels, so I'm like a camel. I can hold water for hours. Good thing, because these linen trousers were expensive.

Get a grip, Willa! These cannot be your final thoughts on this earth.

I sense fast, forward motion as I bump around, realizing I must be inside the trunk of a speeding car. I'm scrunched up on my side. I want to feel around for that safety release thingy they always talk about in self-defense videos, but it's hard to move. Then I try to kick the lid but it's no use. Tears of frustration mixed with sweat roll down my face.

My body pitches forward and back again as I feel the car make a sharp turn. It accelerates and then abruptly screeches to a stop. The car door opens and shuts. I begin to shake. The trunk lid pops open.

Someone drags me out of the trunk, and I drop onto the ground with a dull thud like a sack of flour. *Ow. That hurt.* I lay there unmoving, not knowing what to do. My captor grasps my arm and yanks me to my feet.

We walk together in silence. My senses are working overtime. I can tell we're at Mysa because I smell the familiar, cedar-like scent of the perennial bushes planted around the entrance. I remember asking Marty if he knew anything about them as we walked up the stairs together the night of the party, and of course he did. *Those are woolly blue curls. They've been planted to attract bees and butterflies.* Sweet Marty. Always caring about nature and seeking to learn more about the world around him. Why have I been taking him for granted? How can I have been so shortsighted?

I hear some fumbling to get the door open, and soon we're inside. They pull on my arm and steer me to the left. We're heading to the elevator . . . oh God . . . to the roof! I think about making a break for it, but with the blindfold over my eyes and my hands bound, how far can I realistically run? And they might have a gun.

I hear the elevator doors slide open and feel a shove from behind. My mind races for the short ride up. Willa, calm down. Use your brain! Think! The elevator doors open, and with a few more purposeful shoves, my unwanted companion escorts me through what I sense to be the large seating area arranged around the firepits. We pause briefly and another surge of fear rises from the pit of my stomach. This cannot be how it ends. I have a good life. I don't want to go out like this.

The kidnapper forces me to sit down on what feels like a cushioned ottoman. I can hear the ocean in the distance and smell the salty breeze. My neck hairs prickle, sensing that the person is standing directly over me. Eerily silent.

I have to do something. I could be living the last minutes of my life. I think of Zack and Marty. My two sweet guys. I need to see them both again. *Do something, NOW!*

"Hello, Rosetta," I say, summoning my last reserves of adrenaline.

A stony silence hovers in the air.

"Would you take off this blindfold?" I continue, keeping

my voice level. "I know it's you. Can we at least have a final conversation before you kill me?"

I feel a hard yank on my head, and gasp as the designer-scarf blindfold that was wrapped around my eyes flies off. The late afternoon sun is bearing down, blinding me, but I can just make out the silhouette of the person hovering over me. I blink, waiting for my vision to adjust. Standing above me is Rosetta Rawling. The Bitter Woman. Alive and well, and as mauve-alicious as ever.

"Hello, Butter Biscuit," she says.

I stare up at her fluttering false eyelashes and smeared-mauve-lipstick grimace. Then I look past her and realize that we are situated dangerously close to the ledge where Max had fallen to his death. My stomach flip-flops.

"Stay there," she orders, as she goes back into the lounge area and lugs a barstool out to a spot beside me. "God, my feet are killing me." She kicks her legs in the air and her red-soled Louboutins fly off in different directions. "Damn things! All those years of Jimmy Choos and Manolos. My bunions are as big as melon balls." She hoists herself up onto the stool. "So, Rainbow Sprinkles, how did your inquisitive, ASMR-addled brain figure out that I did it?"

"Well, it took longer than I would have liked," I admit. "I should have figured it out from the moment I realized you were lying to me about Bronwen."

A smile creeps across her face. I can see lipstick on her teeth.

"You told me the woman at the farmers' market with Claes was Bronwen so convincingly that the idea of Max's dead wife not really being dead occupied my thoughts for days. An invented, back-from-the-dead ghost story was the perfect red herring. It was a distraction to throw me off the scent of the real clues, wasn't it?"

Rosetta's cheeks flush a deep pink. "Of course it was. So, go on then. Tell me how I did it."

Relieved to have a moment to stall, I begin. "You killed Lola at Max's rental house. Because you two look enough alike, you planned to assume her identity. You're a recluse and you live alone, so it would have been weeks, perhaps even months, before anyone reported you missing. You wanted to start life over again as Lola. Because your sister, in death, could give you the one thing you desired – a fresh start at a happy life without the shackles of bitterness."

She nods. "Yes, yes. That's the easy part. What I want is for you to tell me how I killed Max."

"Okay," I say. "You paid Nick Coates so that he'd unwittingly poison Max's *Haunted Lingonberry*. That little brown bottle with the smiley face contained some kind of toxic substance that would make the cause of death look natural, or mimic the effects of having too much alcohol."

She smiles and reaches into her pocket. Producing the brown bottle, which she stole from my purse, she holds it up in the air between her thumb and forefinger. "You're right about that. It's methanol."

A MURDER IN EIGHT COCKTAILS

"If it came out later that Nick had received an anonymous payment to poison Max, so what? An investigation didn't concern you. You were going to be living life as Lola by then. But your poisoning plot failed because Tess spilled Max's drink when they were on the rooftop. You quickly realized this once Max and Tess came downstairs and you saw her ruined dress, along with the fact that he was holding a drink with the correct garnish. But this wasn't a problem because you came to Mysa armed with a needle, your backup plan. The needle was loaded with some kind of fast-metabolizing poison that you probably got from the hospital where you volunteer. I know this because I found a needle cap in the elevator." From her nodding, I can tell I'm off to a strong start.

"It wasn't poison, it was a paralytic. But other than that, you're pretty spot on, girlfriend. It's kind of freaking me out. Alright, tell me *why* I killed Max then."

"That's easy. First, Max upset you decades ago when he loved Lola and not you. You felt he toyed with your emotions. Then, years later, when he acquired *Strange Tinctures*, he betrayed you when he didn't deliver on his promises. But his third act of duplicity, selling the company off to Peristyle Capital at a fire sale price, after all you'd been through and done for him, was the last straw. You were fuming. But because you were in love with him, the sense of betrayal mixed with unrequited love formed a potent *cocktail* of rage."

"Damn, honey, you're good."

"You were determined to kill him at Mysa because you realized it might be your only opportunity. If the sale of *Strange Tinctures* went through, it was very likely you wouldn't be able to see much of Max at all, or ever again."

She folds her arms. "How did I do it then?"

"You watched Max all night. After your poisoning plot failed, he went back up to the rooftop alone to take some calls about closing the Peristyle deal. Because you were one of the few guests who had a key, you knew this was your chance for a rare, private audience with Max. This was during the *Bananavit*, which you were halfway through finishing when you saw him take the elevator. I know this because I have a photo of you drinking it. You lied to me about dumping the *Bananavit* down the sink because you realized it was the critical time window in which Max was killed, and you were unaccounted for. So, you painted a little picture for me about freshening your makeup in the bathroom and hearing someone crying in the stall to convince me you were elsewhere when Max was murdered."

Her face flushes a deep pink.

"While you hid in the aquavit library, waiting for your chance to go up in the elevator unseen, Edith came in to gather the take-home aquavit gift baskets for the guests. You didn't want her to see you in there, so you sent Orson running toward her as a distraction. This caused Edith to shriek and run away." I pause to take a breath. "I know because I heard the scream myself. You realized this was your moment, so you

A MURDER IN EIGHT COCKTAILS

slipped into the elevator using your key. During the ride up, you uncapped the needle . . ."

Her eyes twinkle as I speak. I can tell she is thoroughly enjoying this little summary of her murderous actions.

". . . and you stabbed Max in the neck, taking him by surprise. He probably assumed you were coming up there to talk to him about the Peristyle Capital sale, or complain that he wasn't using your bitters in his drinks, or maybe even cry to him about his loving Tess and not you. You aimed for his neck tattoo, knowing it would obscure any marks in an autopsy. Fortunately for you, he was in the process of having it removed, so the redness and bumps from the laser further concealed the puncture wound. This was all done during the preparation for the *Fikatini*, so the loud grinding of the espresso machine would have covered up any screams, if he even had time to scream. You unlocked his phone using his frozen face and sent the fake suicide text at 7:46 p.m. But in your frenzied and emotional state, before rolling him off the rooftop, you decided you would keep the Minifon watch because of its sentimental value to you. The special watch you gave to the man you loved who never loved you back."

She gasps. "Okay, this is getting spooky. How did you know about that? I think you have more than ASMR, you have ESP."

"Educated guess," I explain. "I've spent my whole life reading clients and picking up on subtle clues that hint at their underlying motivations and preferences. The Minifon is a rare and special watch, but it isn't extremely expensive like the others in Max's collection. You mentioned that you and Max exchanged thoughtful gifts over the years and that you always liked to get him something no one else would think of. That made me start to think it might have been a gift from you, especially after learning more about him. Max liked to manipulate people and mess with their heads, to know he could still control them. Like giving Tess's Verdura pineapple watch to Edith. Or flaunting his own expensive watch collection in front of his father. Or making the servers go out of their way to tempt Daniel with alcohol. Wearing the Minifon that night was just another cruel way of reminding you that he still held the puppet strings."

Her eyes become glassy as she blinks back tears. "So then what happened?"

"Just before you shoved Max off the edge of the roof to his death, you removed the Minifon from his wrist. You went down the fire-escape stairs and re-entered Mysa through the sliding glass doors on the lower level. They had been left unlocked after Claes went out to the secret beach to smoke a cigarette. Lucky break for you. Otherwise, you might have had to come back in through the main entrance, or tried to come back down via the elevator and risk being seen. But then again, you weren't thinking very clearly, were you? This was a premeditated murder, yes, but you were so overwhelmed by your emotions and feelings for Max that you made some critical errors that night. Like taking the watch."

A MURDER IN EIGHT COCKTAILS

"No need to be judgmental."

"You came back up to the main room just in time for the eighth and final cocktail, the *Fikatini*. That was the only drink that wasn't presented formally, so it was easy for you to grab one off the bar counter and pretend like you had been there the whole time. But that's when you had a small panic, realizing you'd made a critical error. You couldn't keep the watch. Having it in your possession would directly point to you as the killer. It was a foolish, sentimental move on your part to try and keep it. So, you waited for us to discover the body and gather on the roof. When we finally did, you crept away to the other side and tossed the watch over the railing. It smashed against the rocks below, freezing the time at 7:53 p.m."

Rosetta's mouth becomes a straight line. "Okay. Go on."

"Taking the watch was your biggest mistake. If there hadn't been the discrepancy between the text message time stamp and the smashed watch face, I probably never would have pursued this murder investigation as seriously as I did. It seems that, even in death, time was on Max's side."

"I'm impressed," she says, reaching inside her bag. I watch her pull out a needle. A very large, very scary-looking hypodermic needle. "You and your asinine ASMR. Do you think anyone believes that cringey stuff? You should join *OnlyFans*, you'd make more money." She uncaps the needle and holds it up, her thumb positioned expertly on the plunger. "Tell me. Are you tingling now?"

The sun goes behind a cloud, and the sky is now leaden

and ominous. My body begins to tremble. It feels like time has slowed to a crawl. I needed to think clearly, and fast. "Please, Rosetta. We're members of the same community. I care about you. I can help you come back from this."

Rosetta smirks. "What a load of crap." She holds up the needle. "This is succinylcholine, it's a paralytic, my *caring* friend. It metabolizes within minutes and never leaves a trace. One jab of this and it's goodnight for you. Then I'll untie you and use your frozen face to unlock your phone before I send you on the same trip down to the rocks that Max took."

I gasp in horror.

"It's really too bad you had to pursue this whole murder mystery thing. You became a liability for me." She holds up my phone, which she must have taken from my purse after she knocked me out. "Once I paralyze you, I'll text Marty. He'll get a message explaining that you've been having an affair with Paul, and you're overwhelmed with regret. You can't live with yourself anymore. Another unfortunate suicide. And you did it at Mysa, the very place where you reconnected with Paul, the love of your life. That's poignant, don't you think?" She smiles. "After I get rid of you, I'm moving far away from civilization for a while. I bought a nice remote cabin up in the Yukon Territory."

"The Yukon Territory? Doesn't it get bitter cold there in winter?"

"Honey, I'm bitter all year round."

My heart is pounding. This mauve maniac is really going

to kill me. She steps down from the barstool. I can tell there is no reasoning with her. My only option is to continue to stall.

"Rosetta, listen. I need to hear it from you. Please. Before you kill me, tell me why you killed Lola. It's the only part of this story that I still don't understand. Why kill your sister? Jealousy over Max?"

"No." She pauses and looks down, her expression unreadable. "Lola heard about Max's death and told me she was coming into town right away to see me. I didn't want anything to do with her, but she insisted. She kept calling and texting me, asking about the business and the Peristyle Capital sale. I guess she was having money troubles. She was always bad with money." She shakes her head in disgust at the memory of her irritating sister. "So, she showed up at my house, and I gave her the key to Max's rental. I'd taken it because I wanted to look through any *Strange Tinctures* documents he might have had. I told her she could stay there for a while. I knew he had it rented for the summer, and I didn't want her staying with me. I told her we could sit down and talk the next day."

"That's when you went over to Max's rental house, on Sunday. The night we were there watching it," I say.

"Yes. We got to talking about everything. The sale of the business, Max . . . She used that sneering tone she always took with me. Started hassling me about Orson. Asking why I allowed a disgusting, scaly reptile to slither around my life. Then she accused me of killing Max and said if I didn't give her the family home, she'd go to the police." Rosetta's whole body tenses. "That house is mine. She wanted to sell it."

"And that's when you lost it. You killed her. But Marty and I showed up at the front door, interrupting your plan. That's when you got the inspiration to switch identities. You set Orson aside, ripped off your wig and quickly traded your clothes with Lola's. You propped her body up on a chair, hooked Orson onto the brooch and planted your wig on her head."

"Yes. I hid in the garage. When you finally left, I went back in the house and wrapped the body in a blanket. I dragged it across the hall and into the garage. It was only a few feet. You were gone for a while, at least fifteen minutes. That gave me enough time to hoist the body into the back of her rental car." Rosetta puts her hand to her forehead. "I didn't think I would have the strength, but the car was a Jeep, so the rear door made the whole thing easier than I would have thought. The adrenaline probably helped too."

"So you drove off in Lola's rental car while we were at a gas station calling the police. What did you do with the body?"

"I drove to SFO airport and parked in the long-term parking lot. Just another traveler's vehicle left behind for a few days. I knew the body would get discovered eventually, but it bought me some time. I took a cab to a small apartment I own in the city and stayed there for a bit. That's when I started getting voicemail messages about a 'welfare check' from the Carmel Police Department. I knew you had to be behind all that. So I came back into town to deal with you once and for all." She takes a step toward me. "Listen, if it makes you feel any better, I didn't want to kill you at first."

I nod. "That's why you were following me. Posting threatening messages online and breaking into my house. You were trying to scare me off."

"Yep. But you were relentless. Part of me admires that about you. I have to say, I'm going to miss your ASMR channel. Maybe I'll ask Claes to make me one of those horrible *Deathsmith* keepsakes to honor your memory."

I feel dizzy as I glance down at the rocky cliffs below. I'm really panicking now. "Rosetta! Please don't do this!"

She takes another step closer. "It's time to say goodnight, Bumblebee."

A last-ditch idea hits me. "Listen, I have Orson! I found him on the front porch of Max's rental house that night."

Rosetta freezes.

"I've been taking care of him for you!"

I can see that I've struck a chord.

"Orson is alive?"

"Yes! He's such a sweet boy! We've been pampering him just the way you would have. Giving him nightly sprays, building him a little log cabin, and feeding him the finest mealworms money can buy."

Rosetta's tortured face crumbles. "Really? Oh, that's such a relief." She walks toward me and places her hand on my shoulder. "Have you been letting him bask in natural sunlight?"

"We absolutely have," I say, realizing how strangled my voice sounds. "He's basking all the time! Basking up a storm! His vivarium is located in our bedroom. I open the curtains every day for him." My heart pounds as I tried to anticipate what this unhinged woman might do next.

Rosetta stares into my eyes for a moment and then bursts into tears. "I looked for him, but I thought he'd run away. I want him back! Where is he?"

"He's right here."

We both turn sharply to see Marty standing on the other side of the railing, holding Orson. For a minute, I think I'm hallucinating, either from sheer terror or from the crazy impossibility of seeing terrified-of-heights Marty standing near a ledge holding a pygmy chameleon. But either way, it's the best thing I've ever seen – this Marty Mirage.

"How the hell did you get up here?" Rosetta yells. "Orson, come to Mama!" She starts moving toward him, the hypodermic needle still in her hand.

Marty grasps Orson's leash tightly. He's holding his Swiss Army Knife up to Orson's little neck. "Freeze, or the lizard dies!"

She screams. Her eyes are riveted on Orson. Then she remembers the task at hand and reaches down to yank me upright from the ottoman. She holds the needle to my neck.

I shriek. So does Marty.

Orson, spooked by the struggle, leaps from Marty's hands and scurries under the railing toward Rosetta.

Then we all hear a click.

Officer Landry steps out from the shadows with her gun aimed directly at Rosetta. "Drop the needle, Rawling."

For a moment, everything comes to a standstill. No one moves or even breathes. Then Orson, looking frightened, suddenly darts toward the ledge.

"No, Orson, don't!" Rosetta cries out.

Throwing me and the needle to the ground, she charges after him, but he scurries over the ledge, out of sight. In her rush to save him, Rosetta trips and stumbles over one of her Louboutins lying near the ledge. Toppling forward, she falls.

I gasp as her figure disappears over the edge.

Her screams echo as she plummets through the evening air. Finally, she's silenced by the rocks below.

Horrified, I stand there, my battered head spinning. Everything has happened so fast, it feels impossible to make any sense of it. Rosetta had just come back from the dead only moments ago, and now here she is, dead. Again.

Landry catches her breath and looks to me and Marty. "Are you two okay?"

We both nod silently.

"I'm going down there. I've already called for backup. There'll be more officers here to help in a minute." She exits through the fire escape door.

Marty bolts over to me and unties my wrists. He holds my face in his hands.

"I've never been so happy to see someone in my whole life!" I squeeze him tightly. "Are you sure you're my husband?"

He smiles. "Well, I wasn't exactly swashbuckling, but I did my best."

"I can't believe you said 'Freeze, or the lizard dies!'"

"I can't believe we're still alive!"

"Wait a minute," I say. "Where's Orson?"

"I'll find him. I have some dried silkworms in my pocket."

Marty belly-crawls along the ledge, feeling around the underside as he does so. He finally pauses and scatters some dried silkworms around. Orson's little head pops up and his long tongue protrudes from his head to gobble up the treats. Marty places his palm out and, after finishing his snack, Orson crawls onto it.

I tear up at the sweet image. "Can we keep him?"

"Yes, we can keep him," Marty says, placing Orson in the shoebox he had used to transport him to Mysa.

"How did you find me?"

Marty comes back over to me. "The GPS tracker. You still had one on you." He hugs me tightly, then pulls back and looks into my eyes. This time he's really looking at me.

After a few moments of silence, he puts his hand under my chin and tilts my face toward him. He kisses me deeply, with an intensity neither of us has felt in a long time. My stomach flutters. It's a kiss that tells me he loves me, and we are both going to be okay.

41

"The lemon cake thing was awfully harsh," I say to Marty, as I take a seat at the kitchen table. "But I also realize that I've been quite a handful this week. So, I forgive you."

Marty squeezes my hand. "You know I love all your amazing cooking and baking. I never take it for granted."

We've been home for a few hours and have ordered in a pizza and are about to crack open our usual Friday night bottle of Caymus. After everything that's happened, it's a welcome relief to get back to our routine.

"Well, don't ever lie to me again. Okay? I always want to know where I stand with you. Cake-wise, emotion-wise, life-wise."

"Okay. If you want me to bare my soul then here goes: my real favorite is your pecan pie. It's gooey, comforting deliciousness, and I love the flaky crust."

I look at him across the table and give him a wink. "Okay. I'll make it next weekend when Zack comes home. Landry's asked me to come to her office at nine tomorrow morning to go over everything." I pause to laugh. "You know, it's funny . . . her tone has totally changed. She almost likes me now . . . I think."

I take a bite of pizza and Marty tops up my wine glass. Behind him, I notice his laptop is open and there's a news article onscreen. I can barely make out the headline from here, but I see it's an old one, and the accompanying photo, of a young woman, looks dated.

"What's the article you're reading over there?" I ask.

"Oh, it's nothing," he says wryly.

I raise an eyebrow. "Come on. Tell me, what is it?"

He finishes a mouthful of pizza and reaches for his glass. "Well, remember when Tim was telling us how the last murder that occurred here was twenty years ago? It just sort of piqued my curiosity. So I've been reading up on it. It's an interesting one. A cold case about a local news anchor who was found dead right before she was supposed to go on air. It happened about a year before we moved here. When you were pregnant with Zack."

"Right. I remember hearing about that story."

"Maybe it needs fresh eyes? I could ask Tim if he can help us access the case files."

I slowly meet his eyes. Is he toying with me? Or does he really like the idea of solving another mystery? "Are you being serious?"

He shrugs. "It could be fun. I'm finding that the key to a healthy marriage is having shared interests."

The doorbell rings.

"To be continued," I say, giving him a kiss on the forehead. "That's Paul. He's leaving in the morning so he just wants to say goodbye." I wipe my hands on a napkin and go into the foyer to open the door.

Paul is standing on the front porch with Noodles at his feet, wagging his tail. "God, I'm so glad you're okay, Wil."

We hug, and I give him a pat on the back.

"That really could have gone very wrong . . . I feel guilty that I wasn't there to protect you."

"It's okay. Marty had it covered. He practically swung in on a chandelier. You would have been impressed. So, what did Claes say?"

"Well, it turns out he was planning to donate the majority of Max's art collection to a new museum that Millie Hagerty, the Wisconsin philanthropist, is bankrolling."

"Did you ask him why he lied about drinking the *Aquavit Negroni*?"

"He said he knew that people would suspect him of killing Max or trying to steal his art, given his criminal past, so he got nervous when you started asking questions. He went into defensive mode. His farmers' market companion, Lily Theisen, reformed her fencing ways and is now a respected art consultant. She was sending some documents and photographs of Max's collection to Millie so she could help Claes decide which items to donate and which to keep."

"Wow. Okay. I guess that all makes sense."

"The Riis photographs you saw in the basement of Mysa were a few of the works he was looking to keep for himself. She was a close friend and had taken many of their family portraits over the years."

I draw in a breath. "Claes Magnussen is a changed man, I guess. Good for him."

Paul's eyes meet mine. "Do you think I'm a changed man, too?"

I see pure, unguarded emotion behind his eyes. Suddenly, I feel a surge of affection for him. Something finally feels settled between us. "Yes, I do."

"Maybe I'm rushing things, but I really like Kathleen. I've invited her to come down and visit me in San Diego next weekend." He shrugs. "I spent so many years playing games. Why is it always so difficult for men and women to simply tell each other how they feel?"

"That's wonderful, Paul. I'm happy for you two."

"If you'll allow me this one indulgence before I go," he says, "I want to say something a bit sappy to you."

I laugh. "Let me guess, some more poetry? Go for it."

"No, no, these words are all mine." He places a hand over his heart. "You are, and always will be, the most beautiful woman I've ever met. And I'm a total idiot for ever fucking things up with you."

I swallow. For a moment, I'm overwhelmed. Then I feel a

wave of relief. Relief knowing that it wasn't just me who had been wounded after our marriage ended. I take a deep inhale and sigh it out. "You know, I've been thinking . . . Divorce doesn't have to be the end of a relationship, does it?"

He breaks into a smile. "No, I don't think it does." He extends a hand. "Friends?"

I give it a firm shake. "Yeah. Or something like that."

"So, what are you going to do now?"

"Well, I'm going to make some changes with *Sips and Whispers*. I was thinking I could redesign the Drinks Cabinet and make some ASMR videos about that process, then use the videos as a way to launch my own design business again. Maybe I could start by helping people create cozy cocktail corners in their homes. My audience might go for that."

"Using ASMR to market a design business is a genius idea. You're a brilliant woman, Wil."

As we hug goodbye, Marty comes up beside me and shakes Paul's hand. We wave to him together and I blow a kiss to Noodles.

I check my watch. Last Friday at this time, Marty and I were at the Mysa party, sipping on cocktails with absolutely no clue of the weeklong adventure that lay ahead of us. I turn and look at him, taking in his supportive, good-natured face. He puts my hand up to his cheek, then gives it a gentle kiss. I feel a swell of something inside. It's not the heat of infatuation, it's the solid dependability of knowing someone deeply and knowing they understand me in return.

He looks into my eyes. "And you said middle age wasn't going to be interesting."

"You're right about that. Middle age is not for the faint of heart."

42

"Happy Anniversary, babe!" I shout.

Marty and I are standing side by side on the plateau of a steep cliff in Big Sur, which is the launch site for our twenty-fifth anniversary paragliding adventure. I'd booked it after solving Max's murder had given me the "go-for-its." Nina Hernandez's paragliding photos had sparked the perfect anniversary gift idea. Marty had already given me my "gift" – the couples massage interrogation with Edith – so I wanted to give him something equally bonkers in return.

After some research, I learned that paragliding is one of the best ways for humans to partake in the thrill of flying like a bird, and it would be possible for Marty to soar up to his feathered friends and see them eyeball to eyeball.

It's a clear, cloudless day, and the ocean is bright and sparkly. Each of us is strapped to a paraglider pilot, wearing goggles over our eyes. Outfitted in hooded tech-fabric jackets, life vests, helmets with chin straps, goggles, and sturdy leather hiking boots for those bumpy landings, we both look ridiculous. We completed a brief training session the week before, and today we would each be riding in tandem, strapped to a licensed pilot.

Marty is okay with my "go-for-its," but likes to know the facts in order to be prepared for the "what ifs." So I've assured him that paragliding is, statistically speaking, as safe as hiking or running, and fifteen times safer than driving.

I call out to Marty. "Do you think a murder mystery is the only thing that could have drawn us out of our slump?"

"Our swamp?" Marty yells back. "What do you mean?"

"OUR SLUMP!" I repeat.

He shakes his head. "I can't hear you!"

We laugh as his pilot inches their paraglider a bit closer so that we can hear each other better.

"I hope I've earned another pecan pie after this!" shouts Marty. I laugh as he leans over to me. "So, is this the beginning of the rest of our lives?"

I shake my head. "Nope! It's the second half of an already great life."

"You guys ready?" asks Marty's pilot.

"Hang on a minute, please," I say. "Marty, I need to know something: if you met me today, knowing all my quirks and annoying tendencies, would you still want to marry me? You know, even though I'm a cuckoo bird?"

"What, and have a normal, quiet life?" He reaches for my

hand and gives it a squeeze. "I'd marry you all over again in a heartbeat."

He blows a kiss to me, and I send one back.

"You two ready to jump now?" asks my pilot.

I look over at Marty and realize I love him more in this moment than I ever have before. He gives me a smile that makes me want to cry, laugh, and kiss him all at the same time.

"Okay," I say. "Let's jump."

Willa's Pecan Pie

Ingredients:

3 eggs, beaten
2/3 cup sugar
½ tsp salt
¾ cup light corn syrup
1 tsp vanilla
1/3 cup melted butter
1 cup coarsely broken pecans
2 cups whole pecans
1 x 9-inch unbaked pie shell (preferably homemade, see Easy Homemade Pie Crust recipe on next page)
Whipped cream

Method:

Beat the first 6 ingredients. Spread the broken pecans in the bottom of the unbaked shell. Pour the egg mixture over the pecans. Arrange the whole pecans in concentric circles on the top, taking care not to press too hard, so the nuts don't sink into the filling. Bake at 160° C fan oven (350° F) for 50–60 minutes, until the filling is firm. Use a pie crust shield (or foil) until the final 10 minutes of the bake, then remove. Serve with whipped cream.*

*Option to make bourbon-vanilla whipped cream by adding a tablespoon each of vanilla extract and bourbon (1 tablespoon at a time, to taste) as you whip the cream.

Easy Homemade (no rolling pin needed) Pie Crust

Ingredients:

1¾ cups flour
½ tsp salt
2 tbsp sugar
½ cup vegetable oil
2–3 tbsp milk

Method:

Mix all the ingredients together and press into a 9-inch pie pan. Flute the edge with thumb and index finger.

Acknowledgments

I will always thank my mom first in any book because she is the only reason that I am an author. Mom, thanks for teaching me to love stories, reading everything I write, and making me laugh harder than anyone.

I am forever indebted to my editor, Emily Griffin. Thank you, dear Emily, for your vision and thoughtful partnership. You always see things that I can't, and you provide the perfect alchemy of inspiration, support, and challenge. Collaborating with you is a dream.

Thank you to the whole team at Century: Venetia Butterfield, Selina Walker, Rebecca Ikin, Olivia Thomas, Camila Ilardia Jimenez, Amelia Evans, Lucas Lockyer, Sophie Shaw, Claire Simmonds, Monique Corless, Anna Tuck, and Rachel Malig. I truly cannot imagine a better team to have behind me.

Carmel and Big Sur have always been two of my favorite places in the world. But it's important to note that I've taken a lot of creative liberties, so this story is not meant to be an accurate depiction of the Monterey area, nor should it serve as a travel guide because many places are invented.

ACKNOWLEDGMENTS

To all the booksellers who have supported me from day one, thank you. In particular, I'd like to thank The Poisoned Pen Bookstore, The West Kirby Bookshop, Criminally Good Books, Barnes & Noble Jordan Creek, Storyhouse Bookpub, The Curious Cat Bookshop, The Book Elephant, Annabelle's Book Club LA, Waterstones Piccadilly, Foyle's Charing Cross, Waterstones Leamington Spa, Waterstones Brentwood, Barnes & Noble Fifth Avenue, and Goldsboro Books. Also a big thank you to Janice at Waterstones Gower Street for inspiring one of the cocktail-related clues!

To my brilliant agent Judith Murray and the whole team at Greene & Heaton, thank you for all your support and kindness. Thanks also to my wonderful agents at WME, Nicole Weinroth and Carolina Beltran.

Thanks to my ride or dies Jordan Smith and Rebecca Rienks for helping me with the cocktails. Their wonderful company, Bevlebrity, provides beverage consulting services. You can visit bevlebrity.com for more information.

A special shoutout to the amazing authors who so generously supported my first book: Rob Rinder, Jeremy Vine, Chris Chibnall, Lucy Clarke, Jennie Godfrey, Steve Jones, Elizabeth Day, Jeneva Rose, Clare Mackintosh, Heather Gudenkauf, Ellery Adams, Lindsay Jill Roth, Carinn Jade, Amanda Reynolds, Ragnar Jónasson, Judy Greer, Nia Vardalos, Vaseem Khan, Jo Callaghan, Kia Abdullah, Lola Jaye, Kristen Perrin, Stacey Halls, and Liza Tully.

The list of friends I need to thank has grown significantly since my first book was published. It's going to be impossible to thank every single person in the limited space I have here, so instead I will say one big thank you to all of you who helped

ACKNOWLEDGMENTS

me along the way. You know who you are, and I appreciate you very much.

To my family and my wonderful in-laws, thank you so much for all your support, inspiration, and advice as I grappled with the challenge of writing my second book in one year while working full time!

Thank you, Philip. You and "the fur" are my life.

Finally, a big thank you to any reader who has ever taken the time to review or recommend my books to others.